"WE GOT THE BASTARD!" SCREAMED CAPTAIN JONES, DANCING UP AND DOWN.

As the explosion subsided, Captain Jones flicked on the ship's public address system and spoke into the microphone. "Officers, men, this is the Captain speaking. This is an historic moment, eh? We have just become the first naval vessel since World War Two to sink an enemy submarine in action." There was a cheer from the men on the bridge.

The XO tapped Jones on the shoulder. "There, there," the XO shouted, "see it? There's something in the water."

Jones and the XO leaned over the railing to watch the sailors on the main deck retrieve pieces of wreckage with long boat hooks. Jones turned to Lustig. "Ask the talker down there what they've picked up, eh?"

Lustig said a few words into his headset, listened, then looked up at the Captain. A sickening odor wafted up from the sea around the *Ebersole*.

"It's whales, Captain," Lustig said. "We sank a bunch of whales!"

SWEET REASON
by
Robert Littell
author of
**THE SISTERS
THE AMATEUR
THE DEFECTION OF A. J. LEWINTER
THE DEBRIEFING
THE OCTOBER CIRCLE
MOTHER RUSSIA**

SWEET REASON

Robert Littell

BANTAM BOOKS
TORONTO · NEW YORK · LONDON · SYDNEY · AUCKLAND

SWEET REASON

A Bantam Book / published by arrangement with
the author

Bantam edition / April 1986

ISBN 0-553-25547-9

Published simultaneously in the United States and Canada

Bantam Books are published by Bantam Books, Inc. Its trademark,
consisting of the words "Bantam Books" and the portrayal of a
rooster, is Registered in U.S. Patent and Trademark Office and in
other countries. Marca Registrada. Bantam Books, Inc., 666 Fifth
Avenue, New York, New York 10103.

PRINTED IN THE UNITED STATES OF AMERICA

O   0 9 8 7 6 5 4 3 2 1

For Richard Stone

Any penetration, however slight, is sufficient to complete the offense.

from the *Uniform Code of Military Justice*

Contents

YANKEE STATION

The First Day

Lieutenant Lustig Puts His Money Where His Mouth Is

It rained during the midwatch—thick sheets of monsoon rain that slanted in at a ridiculous angle and chipped away at the flaking gray paint on the superstructure. Just before the four-to-eight watch came on deck it stopped, leaving behind the smell of wet wool hanging in the air and the sounds of a ship at sea. One was continuous: the river of ocean water brushing past the thin skin of the destroyer like a felt-tipped pen underlining never-ending sentences. The rest was punctuation: creaking joints, the dull throb of the main propulsion shafts, engines, reduction gears, fans, condensers, generators, exhausts, intakes, pistons, pumps, boilers, bilges, banging doors and banging plumbing, a tin cup clattering around the scullery, a muffled curse from somewhere below deck when nobody picked it up, a hundred thousand bubbles of air bursting as the two huge propellers pushed off into the sea, creating the river that brushed the hull. Astern the churning, phosphorescent wake played out, as if from a giant reel, into a starless, pitch-black night.

On the open bridge the messenger of the watch, a squirrelish seaman deuce with dirt under his fingernails and blackheads sprinkled across his forehead like freckles, squatted on his haunches polishing brass plaques with navy-issue rags, elbow grease and Kool Aid granules left over from the ban on cyclamates. He had already finished one plaque

> EUGENE F. EBERSOLE DD722
> SWIFT AND SURE
> BETHLEHEM STEEL COMPANY
> STATEN ISLAND 20 DEC 1944

and was halfway through a second, which the Captain had had the shipfitters weld up the day the *Ebersole* headed for the war zone—a stretch of ocean known as Yankee Station.

> FIGHT HARD WHEN WE F
> WORK HARD WHEN WE
> PLAY HARD WHEN
> AN
> AVOID UNN
> DURING

"What he say then, Calvin?" the starboard lookout asked. He was standing with his back flat against the pilot house, his elbows locked into his chest to steady the binoculars through which he studied the night, sector by sector, the way he had been taught at boot camp. All the binoculars did was make the blackness seem closer and thicker and more oppressive. But he studied it all the same.

"Your father, I mean," the starboard lookout said again, trying to do what nobody else was able to do, which was keep a conversation with Calvin Tevepaugh going for more than three minutes. Anything to make the watch pass more quickly. "What he say after that?"

Tevepaugh dabbed the damp rag into the pail of Kool Aid powder and rubbed away at the plaque in small concentric circles. "She-it," he said, grudgingly holding up his end of the conversation, "he wanted me to be sumptin else than I am, but he couldn't figure out what he wanted me to be. Neither could I. So here I am, what I am."

The plaque was clean now and Tevepaugh buffed it with a dry rag, digging the caked Kool Aid granules out of the etched letters with his thumbnail.

FIGHT HARD WHEN WE FIGHT
WORK HARD WHEN WE WORK
PLAY HARD WHEN WE PLAY
AND
AVOID UNNECESSARY MOLESTATION
DURING PERIODS OF RELAXATION

The starboard lookout let the binoculars dangle from the strap around his neck. Tevepaugh started polishing the brass acceleration plaque.

0—15 knots	1 min
15—18 knots	½ min
18—22 knots	1 min

"So here you are, but what *are* you, Calvin?" the starboard lookout asked after a while. He could hear the pilot house clock ticking away inside the door.

"What am I? What I am is the only single solitary member of the one-man orchestra on the oldest mother in the whole goddamn You-nited States of America Navy, that's what I fuckin' well am."

Tevepaugh's description of himself was as accurate as any supplied by the computers in the navy's Bureau of Personnel. On watch he was a messenger of the watch, polishing brass, carrying coffee, waking reliefs, doing whatever anyone who was senior to him (which was everyone on watch) told him to do. Off watch he was a seaman deuce deck ape whose job in life was to keep every square inch of brass and woodwork forward of the midship's passageway gleaming or get his ass reamed by Chief McTigue, who ran the deck gang and Mount 51 with an iron hand. But when the *Ebersole* plowed through the seas alongside an aircraft carrier for under-way refueling operations, Tevepaugh came into his own. As the two ships steamed on parallel courses fifty feet apart, the destroyer sucking in vast gulps of fuel from the carrier's cavernous tanks, he would hold court on the deck that used to house the torpedo tubes which were taken off in the early 1960s, ten full years after they had been declared obsolete. Sitting on a folding canvas captain's chair, cradling a small, red electric guitar plugged into two enormous speakers, Tevepaugh would produce overlapping waves of hard rock that drowned out the thirty-man polished-brass bands on the carrier's hangar deck which stuck doggedly to "Anchors Aweigh" and "When the Saints Go Marching In."

Tevepaugh's peculiar brand of one-upmanship was already an *Ebersole* institution when J. P. Horatio Jones took over as captain. Even so, the new skipper thought seriously about phasing out the act. "It's not navy," he complained to his executive officer. "Besides, you can hardly hear anything on the sound-powered phones for the noise." But any idea the Captain had of sidelining Tevepaugh was shelved during a refueling operation off Norfolk when Jones focused his binoculars on the flag bridge high up on the carrier's superstructure and spotted a smile on the thin lips of the Rear Admiral who nested in that rarefied atmosphere.

"XO," the Captain said, motioning toward Tevepaugh strumming away on the torpedo deck, "what's that sailor's name?"

"Tevepaugh, Skipper. Seaman deuce Tevepaugh," the Executive Officer answered.

"Tevepaugh," mused Captain Jones. "All right, let's see if we can't get him a folding canvas chair to sit on instead of that fuel drum, eh?"

"Aye, aye, Skipper," snapped the Executive Officer, who dispatched a chit to the supply officer, who walked the chit through to the destroyer tender in Norfolk and came back with a spanking new folding canvas captain's chair.

"Goddamn right that's what I am," Tevepaugh was saying to the starboard lookout. "A one-man orchestra." He rubbed the sleeve of his foul-weather jacket across his blackheads.

"Me," offered the lookout, trying to eke out another drop of conversation, "I'm a shorttimer, that's what *I* fucking am."

"Shorttimer, my ass," sneered Tevepaugh. "She-it, you're career bait, man. You got career writ all over you. You'll re-up the minute you smell the money."

"Won't we all," the starboard lookout said, and he and the messenger of the watch laughed at the barefaced truth.

Suddenly the blackness that the lookout had been staring at shattered into shards of strobe-bright light, and it flashed through his brain that, improbable as it seemed, there was a barnfire raging on the horizon. What it was was only Tevepaugh leaning against the open bridge railing an arm's length away, lighting a cigarette with one of the ship's store's flame-thrower lighters.

"WHO LIT THAT FUCKING LIGHT?" screamed the Officer of the Deck, a balding, chubby, round-faced, wide-eyed lieutenant junior grade named Lawrence Lustig. His voice was shrill with tension. "Don't you know about darken ship? Next time that happens I'm going to put somebody on report." ("Why don't you signal them with a flare pistol," Lustig imagined himself saying icily. He always went over his conversations, word for word, afterward. In these mini-daydreams there was never any need for threats or temper tantrums, for he invariably came up with a razzle-dazzle rejoinder that permitted him to bury his adversary under an avalanche of irony and logic and dignity. "Better still," Lustig would have added if he could have run the reel through again, "why don't you put up a neon sign that says 'Here comes the *Ebersole*!'")

"She-it," Tevepaugh muttered under his breath, crunching out the cigarette in the ashtray next to the captain's chair.

Taking his cue from the Officer of the Deck, the bos'n mate of the watch, gunner's mate third class Melvin Ohm, a squat Californian with a receding chin and a grating voice that sounded as if it originated in a cement mixer, popped his head out the pilot house door. "Jesus, Calvin, the lookout here couldn't see the enemy with his prick dangling if he was right under his nose," he said loudly enough for Lustig, who was the *Ebersole*'s gunnery officer as well as Ohm's division officer, to know that he was cracking down on the offender. Too often petty officers tended to let this kind of thing slide. But not Ohm, who knew which side his bread was buttered on. "Don't you know nothing about night vision, Calvin?"

"I know a lot," Tevepaugh said sullenly. "The navy pays me for what I know."

(Lustig thought of "No wonder you're always broke," but as usual it was too late to get it into the conversation, for by then the talk in the pilot house had moved on to other things.)

"I knowed a girl once who shaved it off because she thought men went for women who looked like little girls," said the helmsman, a hairy deck ape named Carr who looked like King Kong from the back. He watched the compass card under the lubber's line slide past 310 and put on three degrees left rudder to ease her back.

"You're kidding," said Tevepaugh, straddling the pilot house doorway, his polishing chores over. "I mean, she-it, I never seen no such thing. You're kidding, ain't you?"

"If I was telling a joke," the helmsman said with exaggerated dignity, "it'd have a punch line. I wasn't telling no joke. I was telling a social phenomenon." He kept his eyes glued to the dimly lit compass card. It held on 310 for a second, then slid past in the other direction and Carr shifted the rudder to bring it back again. "She shaved her snatch to look like a kid. That's what I said she done'n that's what she done."

"Was it someone you knew?" Tevepaugh asked, trying not to appear overeager.

"More'r less," allowed Carr.

"I'll be fucked," said Tevepaugh and he poked Ohm, who was absent-mindedly inventing games he could play on the radar repeater. "You never seen nothin' like that, have you, Melvin?"

Ohm swiveled the range bug around so rapidly it left an electric wake on the radar scope. By varying the range with his left hand as he swiveled the bug with his right, he could create sinuous designs, something like waving a burning ember in a dark room.

"I heard of a girl once," Ohm said, fiddling with the radar as if it were a pinball machine. "Her old man was due back from a Med cruise, so she knotted red ribbons in her pussy to surprise him. Halfway to the ship she jumped a light and whammed into the back of a truck, and when they stripped her at the hospital . . ."

"She-it," giggled Tevepaugh.

"The way I heard it, her husband, who was a boilerman third on the Manley, finally found her—in the loony bin at Norfolk General. And he had one hell of a time convincing them she wasn't no nut." Ohm couldn't keep from laughing at his own story.

"She-it," groaned Tevepaugh.

"Red ribbons!" moaned Carr. "Whoosh, that there must have been a sight for sore eyes."

Lustig stuck his cherubic face through one of the open portholes. The roundness of the porthole provided a perfect frame for his head. "You running one of your pools today, Ohm?" he asked.

Hardly a day went by on the *Ebersole* when Ohm didn't have some sort of pool going: the anchor pool, the maximum roll pool, the fuel consumption pool, the freshwater production pool. You name it, Ohm had a pool on it.

"Naturally, Mister Lustig," Ohm rasped. "I'm running a sixty-bet sheet on which minute of the hour we take our first shot at the enemy. You want to buy in? Buck a throw. Winner takes fifty-five bucks."

"Put me down for a buck," Lustig said, and he handed a dollar bill through the porthole to Carr, who passed it over to Ohm. "What numbers you got open?"

Ohm consulted his sheet, which was divided into sixty squares, most of them with names of bettors already written in. "You can have, let's see, seven, twenty-seven; ah, I skipped thirteen. Also forty-one, forty-three. That's it. No, here's another. Fifty-nine."

Lustig thought a moment. "I'll take lucky thirteen,"

he said finally, and Ohm wrote his name in the square with the number thirteen in the upper-right-hand corner.

"Lucky thirteen it is, Mister Lustig," he said.

Combat Information Smells a Skunk

Nighttime watches on the bridge of a destroyer have a distinctive rhythm. For the first hour or so there is a considerable amount of physical movement and the constant chatter of sea stories, some true, some half-true and some that have been told so many times nobody can remember whether they are true or not. An hour into the watch come the doldrums, when everybody is bored with himself and everyone else and realizes that bored or not, the watch still has three long hours to go. At this point the men on watch tend to stand or sit in one place, without moving a muscle, for long periods of time, letting their minds or the conversation meander. Their sole aim in life is to forget the clock ticking away on the bulkhead, on the theory that when you forget it time passes more rapidly. But they concentrate so hard on forgetting the clock they can't get their minds off it.

Lustig's watch had reached the doldrums. Except for an occasional report from the talker with the headphones ("Combat Information has a skunk bearing zero one seven at twelve miles and tracking on a parallel course"), the officers and men whose job it was to run the ship from 0345 until 0745 were subdued, moodily withdrawn into their private selves. Ohm had given up toying with the pilot house radar and was sitting on it, staring at the pit log, which told how fast the ship moved through the water, thinking about the second-class exam he would take the following week. He had flunked it twice already but Lustig had agreed to give him another shot at it. Carr, the helmsman, played a game that he often used to while away the time on watch. The idea was to see how long he could keep the lubber's line on a given heading. "One one-hundredth, two one-hundredth, three one-hundredth, four," he counted to himself. The lubber's line moved off and he brought it back. Then he put on enough opposite rudder to hold it and began counting again. "One one-hundredth, two . . ." Tevepaugh retreated to the flag bag aft of the pilot house, fetched up an armful of signal flags and nestled in the bag using the flags as a cushion. He sat there trying to conjure up the image of the girl tying red ribbons in her pubic hair.

Nearby two Negro signalmen—who like most blacks on board kept pretty much to themselves since the fight on the mess deck back in Norfolk—sat on the wooden deck with their backs to the Captain's sea cabin, their knees drawn up to their chests. Both of them were smoking pot, passing the cigarette back and forth and cupping the burning end with their palms. If any of the officers or petty officers saw them, they never said a word—darken ship or no.

"I want out, man," Angry Pettis Foreman was saying. Angry Pettis was a tall, rail-thin black who always had one toothpick jutting from between his teeth and three or four spares stuck into his Afro. He went to great pains to look like what he thought a street blood ought to look like—menacing, angry, sexy, above all cool. "Trouble is," he added, barely moving his lips, "don't nobody know how to get out."

There was a long silence as the two men sucked in

turn on the cigarette and held the smoke in for as long as they could.

"What would you do if you were out, Angry?" asked Jefferson Waterman, a southern black who had been drafted into the navy by an all-white draft board midway through his senior year at a southern Negro college. "I'll tell you what you'd do. You'd be so shit-scared you'd duck right back in—especially when they lay that thick wad of re-up money on the table."

"Fuck the bread, this time I gonna keep my black ass out, you see." Angry Pettis dragged on the cigarette, held his breath and exhaled. When Waterman didn't say anything, he started to get belligerent. "You don't believe me, man? I want oh-you-tee out. I'm not sure I wanna even live in the U.S. of A. when I get outa this navy, man. When I say out, I mean *far* out. Maybe I'll even try me another country."

Waterman thought about that for a moment. "Somebody once told me there are only two countries no matter which country you're in. There is city country and there is country country."

"If'n that's so," laughed Angry Pettis, "the *po*-litical pricks put them borders in all the wrong places, man."

A V-wedge of Phantom jets, their twin tail pipes spouting orange flames, roared low overhead. The sound hammered against the bridge like a thunder clap. The planes were headed for a predawn strike on the mainland, flying at masthead level to keep under the enemy radar screen.

"MOTHERFUCKERS," screamed Angry Pettis—but his voice was lost in the storm of sound.

"Sons of bitches," yelled Jefferson Waterman.

"Bastards," muttered Ensign Joyce, the *Ebersole's* tall, thin, hollow-eyed communications officer. Joyce had earned a degree in English Literature at Princeton and had set his sights on graduate school. Then, to everyone's amazement, he had joined the navy (going through Officer Candidate School at Newport) to get off what he called "the academic treadmill." In his spare time he wrote poems that he kept pressed, like forgotten flowers, between the pages of *The Complete Works of William Blake*. Aboard the *Ebersole*, Joyce was universally known as the Poet. It was a nickname that gave him more pleasure than pain.

"Why bastards?" Lustig asked his junior officer of the deck. "They're doing what they're ordered, same as us."

"Jesus, Larry," Joyce said, "that's almost a political remark. You really want to open that bag?"

Lustig laughed. "You know the drill, kid—an officer can talk about anything on a man-o'-war except religion, sex or politics."

"Which is why the only thing anybody talks about anymore is how True Love clogs the XO's urinal all the time."

"Which is why," agreed Lustig. "What time does reveille go today?"

The Poet took a folded plan of the day out of his pocket. "Reveille's at o-six-thirty, star time is o-seven-o-one, sunup is o-seven-sixteen. I heard all the shore fire assignments out here are at sunup. Is that true?"

"Most of 'em, yeah. It puts the sun behind us shining right into their eyes that way," Lustig explained. "Makes it hard on their gunners if they want to counter fire."

"That's the way the Japs used to attack during World War Two—out of the rising sun," Joyce said, remembering the comic books with the Japanese Zeros silhouetted against a yellow ball. "Funny how we're brought up to think it's treacherous to attack out of the rising sun when all the time it's just good tactics."

"I guess," Lustig said noncommittally. The longer he was on the *Ebersole* the more noncommittal he seemed to become. It was his protective coloring. A graduate of the Kings Point Merchant Marine Academy, Lustig had only recently decided to make a career out of the regular navy rather than switch to the merchant navy when his three-year hitch was up. He could make more money on merchantmen, true. But money wasn't everything. The regular navy had glamour and status. (During the *Ebersole's* last few weeks in Norfolk, Lustig had taken to wearing his dress blues, with their tarnished gold lieutenant junior grade stripes, on dates instead of civilian clothes.) The ticket to a successful career in the navy, as far as Lustig was concerned, was to offend as few people as possible. Which was why he turned a noncommittal face to the world and kept his quips, including the few he could think of in time to get them into a conversation, locked up in afterthoughts.

Switching on his flashlight with the red filter, Lustig glanced at his wristwatch. "Half-hour to reveille. Shit, the minutes really drag. What else's on the plan of the day?"

"The usual note from our erstwhile executive officer about taking coffee cups off the mess deck. He's escalating. This one says quote personnel failing to comply with the above and who are caught will be held accountable unquote. Then he has a parenthetical note quote this means turned over to the supply officer for two hours' extra duty unquote. Did you ever notice how every other sentence out of the XO's mouth is enclosed in parens. With him, parens are almost a life-style."

Lustig didn't have the slightest idea what Joyce was

talking about, but he nodded agreeably. "Any other goodies on the plan of the day?" he asked.

"The second-class exam is scheduled for next Wednesday. And here come the parens again. Note colon the careers officer will hold a career information seminar in the after wardroom for all interested hands at sixteen-thirty. Jesus H. Christ, *I'm* the Careers Officer, and I go on watch again at fifteen-forty-five. Doesn't the XO read the watch bill before he schedules—"

A burst of static came from the squawk box and the red light next to "CIC" winked on and off. Lustig flipped down the lever and yelled: "I can't make out a word you say on this contraption. Use the voice tube."

An instant later a voice, metallic and surprisingly clear, came floating up the tube. "Mister Lustig, sir, I think we got land on radar bearing three one zero, range about thirty miles or so."

Lustig flicked his radar repeater over to a longer scale. On the next sweep the outline of a land mass—thousands of electronic pinpricks that brightened and then faded as the antenna swept past—appeared in the upper-left-hand corner of the scope.

"I guess that's the enemy," Lustig said.

The voice tube spoke again. "Mister Lustig, sir, you know the skunk we been tracking on a parallel course all night? Well, it's changed course now."

"Changed course? In what direction?"

"As a matter of fact, it seems to be heading straight for us."

Tevepaugh Wakes the Captain

Tevepaugh took the steps two at a time and knocked softly at the Captain's cabin, one deck below the bridge.

"Enter."

Tevepaugh opened the door, stepped inside and spoke into the darkness. "The Officer of the Deck sends his respects, Captain, sir. He got the Commie coast on radar at thirty miles."

"Thirty miles, eh? What bearing?"

"What bearing?" Tevepaugh repeated.

"That is correct. On what bearing, which is to say in what direction, has the enemy coastline appeared at thirty miles?"

"Mister Lustig didn't tell me nothin' 'bout bearing, Captain."

"Mister Lustig didn't tell you, eh?"

"No sir, Mister Lustig didn't say no word 'bout bearing. He jus' told me to tell you the Officer of the Deck sends his respects 'n' says he got the Commie coast at thirty miles."

Captain Jones switched on his night reading lamp and propped himself up on an elbow. Directly over his head was a framed motto on the bulkhead that read: "Give me a fast ship for I intend to go in harm's way." Under the motto was the signature: "John Paul Jones." "That's all he said—the Commie coastline on radar at thirty miles?"

"Also that there was a skunk on a parallel course which ain't on a parallel course no more but's heading straight for us."

17

"How far away is this skunk?"

"Mister Lustig didn't tell me that either, Captain," Tevepaugh said in a low voice.

"Very well, son. Now hightail it back to the bridge and tell Mister Lustig that the Captain sends *his* respects. Tell him to call the ship to General Quarters if the skunk is less than ten miles from us. You got that?"

"Yes sir, GQ if the skunk is under ten miles."

As Tevepaugh turned to go, the Captain added: "I know you—you're Taylor, the guitarist."

"No sir, Captain, I'm Tevepaugh the guitarist."

"Ah yes. Tevepaugh. Well, on your horse Tevepaugh the guitarist."

The Ebersole *Sounds General Quarters*

Ten minutes later Lustig strode across the pilot house to the three color-coded alarms on the bulkhead (red for general, yellow for chemical, green for collision) and pushed down the red handle. Instantly an electrifyingly persistent DONG DONG DONG DONG DONG DONG DONG DONG reverberated through the *Ebersole*. As it faded Ohm put his mouth so close to the microphone of the public address system it looked as if he intended to bite into it, and yelled: "This is not a drill. This is not a drill. Now all hands, man your battle stations. Now set condition one Able throughout the ship."

The *Eugene F. Ebersole*, a relic of another era and another war, emerged from its stupor. Men grabbed their shoes and dungarees and raced off toward their battle stations. Doors, some of them presumably still watertight after more than two decades of sea duty, clanged shut, their teeth biting into the bulkhead like some medieval portcullis. In the wardroom, Doc Shapley, a hospital corpsman second class who tended to become faint at the sight of blood, laid out packets of surgical instruments and tapes on the green felt dining table, then stretched out on the couch and dozed. Chaplain Rodgers came into the wardroom, pushed aside the surgical instruments and began playing solitaire. At each of the five-inch mounts sailors in battle dress—helmet on, dungarees tucked into socks, shirt collar buttoned—depressed the guns and took out the tampions that were screwed, like corks, into the tips of the barrels to keep out seawater. On the bridge Lustig passed the watch over to the ship's engineering officer, a thin-lipped, nasal Naval Academy graduate named Moore. "We're on course two nine zero, speed ten knots, all four boilers with superheats on the line, but since you put them on the line you know more about that than I do." Lustig smiled at his own joke. "You got it, John?"

"Got it, Larry," said Lieutenant junior grade Moore, who didn't like bridge watches and wasn't supposed to be up there during general quarters except the *Ebersole* was so shorthanded there was nobody else free to do the job. In a loud, formal voice, Moore went through the ritual of taking over the watch. "Very well, sir, I relieve you," he intoned.

Helmsman Carr and Bo's'n Mate Ohm raced off down the port ladder as soon as they saw their reliefs coming. Angry Pettis, the signalman, waited around long enough to soul-slap the palm of his black relief as if he were passing the baton in a relay race. Then he started down the ladder—just as a white sailor started up. The two stopped short and glared wordlessly at each other; then the white had second thoughts and backed slowly down. Angry Pettis coyly cocked his head and continued on his merry way.

Four minutes after GQ sounded Captain Jones stepped onto the bridge. His nonregulation Adler elevators were spit-shined to a mirror finish. His khaki trousers and khaki shirt were creased in all the authorized places. The silver oak leaves on his collar and the gold braid on his blue baseball cap (with the "Swift and Sure" emblem on it) gleamed. Even his double chins, freshly shaven and pink, glistened. Except for a small patch of toilet paper clotting the blood on a shaving nick, J. P. Horatio Jones looked like a figment of his own military imagination.

"Now the Captain is on the bridge," Tevepaugh yelled into the ship's loud speaker system.

For an instant Jones stood on the threshold of the pilot house savoring the moment. For thirty years he had dreamed of commanding a ship. Now the dream had come true. Jones pressed his eyes shut and saw himself standing next to the helm of a full-rigged fifty-gun ship-o'-the-line, saw himself casting an experienced eye on the trim of the sails, saw himself demanding a slight alteration in the mizzen topgallant staysail from the XO, who barked at Lustig, who put a megaphone to his lips and sent the half-naked seaman scurrying up the halyards.

It was the XO who snapped the Captain out of his reverie. "Six minutes twenty seconds," he said, punching a stopwatch when the Officer of the Deck slammed the inboard door to the pilot house and drove home the teeth with a whirl of the wheel. "Not bad, Skipper." Holding his stopwatch and smiling broadly, the XO could have passed for an astronaut—clean-cut, crew-cut and crisp. He was wearing work khakis now, but in his starched white uniform he looked like a sail waiting to see which way the wind would blow.

"Not bad," the Captain agreed.

"Not bad at all," Lustig chimed in from the other side of the open bridge where he had taken up his general quarters post as gunnery officer. ("You could have timed this with a calendar," he came up with later.)

Suddenly there was a loud knock on the bulkhead door leading from the inboard ladder to the pilot house.

"My god, what in Christ's name is that?" asked the XO.

"It would appear, XO, that the ship is not cleared for action after all," the Captain said dryly. "I suggest that somebody open it."

Tevepaugh, who was the messenger of the watch during general quarters also, sprang to the door and spun the wheel, disengaging the teeth from the bulkhead. Then he pulled open the heavy door.

In stumbled Wally (The Shrink) Wallowitch. He was dressed in cowboy boots, skivvy shorts and a tennis sweater and wore a sword strapped to his waist. Mumbling about how it was "impossible to get any sleep in this hotel," Wallowitch made his way past the Captain and climbed up to his battle station in the main director.

Wallowitch's Curriculum Vitae

"I swear to God I thought she said 'pecker,'" exclaimed the Shrink, whose nickname came, albeit illogically, from the fact that almost anytime he wasn't on watch he could be found stretched out on the wardroom couch.

"Bullshit," said the Poet.

"No, no, I swear, really. Listen, it was a natural

mistake. There we were on the back porch of the sorority house. Sort of cuddling together to keep warm, right? And she, being a political science major, is holding forth on the single most important thing that Capitalism and Communism have in common. 'They both have a *pecker* order,' says she. Well, I naturally thought it was one of those newfangled sexual theories, but just to make sure I says 'pecker as in prick?' 'Not pecker,' she says, red in the face, 'p-e-c-k-i-n-g order.' Like I said, it was a natural mistake. And anyhow, it broke the ice."

The Poet laughed appreciatively. "Shrink, you are a man without a conscience."

Wallowitch flailed his arms over his head. "Conscience is crap," he said excitedly. "You know what Mencken said about conscience. Conscience is that little old inner voice that warns you somebody is looking. Only me, I give 'em something to look at." Here Wallowitch went into the spastic routine that he swore almost got him out of NROTC—bending his wrists back as far as they would go to make it look as if his hands were deformed, craning his neck, twitching one ear, letting his lower lip hang slack until saliva ran down his chin.

Stretched out on the wardroom couch, his cowboy boots propped up on some books to keep the blood rushing to his head (one of his medical theories was that this increased potency), Wallowitch cut a ridiculous figure. He had a large, bulbous nose, a prominent Adam's apple that bobbed when he talked, body odor, shaggy hair and a loose fitting uniform that looked like a hand-me-down from another war. Only much later, when the Poet pointed it out, did everyone become aware that the constant flow of jokes formed a moat around Wallowitch, keeping everyone at arm's length. Nobody could say for sure what the Shrink thought about anything or anyone; he was the wardroom clown who lived in terror of being caught in the act of holding a serious conversation.

From the moment he reported aboard the *Ebersole* (at which time, according to legend, he took one turn around the rusting deck and put in a formal request for transfer to a "ship"), the Shrink kept dipping into a seemingly inexhaustible well of humor. Very early on he started making up the names of knots; "take a turn on that bollard," he'd order some seaman, "with a double crossover sheepshank half-hitch double-bitch, okay?" In one of his milder escapades, egged on by a klatch of junior officers, he honed his ceremonial sword to a razor's edge and shaved with it on the fantail in full view of half the Atlantic destroyer force. Another time he suckered Chaplain Rodgers into a theological discussion.

"Does God have sperm?" the Shrink asked innocently.

"I'd imagine so," the Chaplain said thoughtfully.

"And if he has sperm, do you think he jerks off?" Wallowitch pursued.

"Now come off it, Shrink, that's not one single bit funny."

"But Chaplain, the question has serious implications. If he has sperm and a sex drive and jerks off, we have nothing to worry about. But if he doesn't relieve the tension somehow, it'll build up until we have another immaculate conception. And we all know how much trouble the last one caused."

Then there was the time Keys Quinn lost the tip of his middle finger at Iskenderun; it was sliced cleanly off when a mooring line whipped taut while the *Ebersole* was tying up alongside the burning tanker. With everyone around staring in wide-eyed horror, Quinn casually strolled away to find the Doc. At which point Wallowitch scooped up the digit and went racing down the deck after him. "Hey, Keys," he yelled, "let's not leave personal belongings lying around the deck."

Now and then one of the Shrink's sallies got him into hot water with the Captain. The first time that happened was when Otto Rummler was riding the *Ebersole* on an anti-submarine exercise in the Caribbean. Rummler, a former German U-boat skipper who was about to become captain of a destroyer that the Americans had donated to the West German Navy, was extremely well liked by J. P. Jones, who considered him a thoroughgoing professional, "the kind of man a country can count on when the chips are down."

One night in the wardroom Rummler was politely discoursing on "ze great American poze—zat you dislike vaws und fight zem mit reluctance." "On ze ozzer hand," Rummler went on, "vee Chermans come across az eager beafers, a reputation vee hardly dezerve conzidering ze reluctance of ze Cherman Staff to follow Hitler into Czechoslovakia in zirty-nine. Ach, mein friends, ze world it haz a miztaken notion of uz Chermans; vee are not vaw criminals but careerists, pure und zimple careerists. Zat is ze joke."

Rummler exhaled a cloud of cigarette smoke, which wafted into Wallowitch's face and made him cough. Wallowitch screwed up his face as if he were wearing a monocle and, enunciating each word precisely, said: "Az all ze world knowz, ze Cherman joke iz not a laughing matter!"

Captain Jones sensed instantly that the Shrink had insulted his guest and insisted that Wallowitch apologize then and there, which Wallowitch did.

"No offenze intended," he muttered.

"None taken," Rummler said quickly.

Frantic that Rummler would report the incident

anyhow Jones apologized again later, and Rummler, charming as always, told him that as far as he was concerned the affair was closed, besides which Germans had to put up with that sort of thing all the time and he, Rummler, was used to it.

The skipper's anger had just about worn off when Wallowitch did it again. The *Ebersole* had raced up to Iskenderun from Rhodes when an Italian-built Panamanian-licensed, British-insured, German-owned, American-leased tanker full of jet fuel for the U.S. Air Force base at Adana, Turkey, caught fire. The Greek-Spanish-Turkish crew had long since abandoned the burning ship when the *Ebersole* arrived on the scene. It was late at night and the flames from the tanker provided a beacon to Iskenderun that could be seen for thirty nautical miles.

Soon after the *Ebersole* anchored in the bay the Captain assembled the officers in the wardroom to discuss the situation. Lieutenant j.g. Moore, the engineering officer, back from a longboat tour around the burning tanker, reported that the decks were red-hot in places and that she might blow up at any moment.

Jones shivered in a spasm of indecisiveness. Chewing away at the inside of his cheek, he pored over the text of the message ordering the *Ebersole* to the scene, explicating it like a poem, poking in and under and around the words for some nuance that would let him know whether his superiors in Washington actually expected him to put the *Ebersole* alongside and fight the blaze or stand off a few miles and report on its progress. (As was usual in cases like this, the orders had been carefully worded so that the admirals could claim they meant either one.) The Captain even polled the officers, something he had never done before. Only Ensign de Bovenkamp voted for going alongside. Everyone else (except the XO, who seemed to be voting "yes" and "no" at the same time, and Lustig, who was noncommittal) came out against doing anything rash.

"But what about this phrase 'will render all possible assistance,'" the Captain said. In agony he read the message again, and then again; sometimes the emphasis seemed to fall on "all," sometimes on "possible." Finally he slapped his palm down on the back of his other hand as if he were tossing an invisible coin and said: "Well, hell, what've we got to lose, eh?"

The decision stunned everyone except de Bovenkamp, who jumped up from the wardroom huddle with a "hot damn," and Wallowitch, who piped up with his remark heard 'round the ship.

"Thank God," he mumbled, "I have but one life to give for my captain's career!"

Jones's eyebrows shot up. "I heard that, Mister Wallowitch," he shouted, wagging his finger at the Shrink. "I heard that and I won't forget it either."

Wallowitch Puts a Shot Across the Skunk's Bow

"This is not my idea of a joke," Captain Jones yelled after Wallowitch as he made his way, sword clanking against stanchions and bulkheads, to his main director battle station. There, his hairy legs and sword dangling from the tractor seat, Wallowitch put his eye to the director optics. Squinting into the hazy, predawn dimness, the Shrink reported that he could make out the target fairly clearly.

"Looks like a junk to me, Larry," he told Lustig over the sound-powered headset.

"Wallowitch says it looks like a junk, Captain," Lustig told Jones on the open bridge.

"It's kind of long for a junk," said the Captain, peering intently at the skunk through binoculars. "And you don't see any sails, do you? I think it might be . . . I bet the sonovabitch is a Commie patrol boat. What do you think, XO?"

"Sonovabitch looks like a patrol boat to me, Captain. I think we're in for a piece of the action, that's what I think."

"Damn if you're not right," agreed the skipper, biting his cuticles. "She's probably moving slow like that so we'll think she's some sort of junk or something. But she doesn't fool me for an instant. Mister Lustig, put a shot across her bow, eh? If she heaves to it'll be a junk and we'll inspect her for contraband; if she turns tail and runs for it that'll mean she's a patrol boat and we'll blow her out of the water."

"Good thinking, Captain," said the XO.

"Hey, Shrink, the Captain thinks it may be a patrol boat. He wants you to put a shot across its bow."

"One shot across the bow coming up," said Wallowitch. He drew his sword and pointed it at the target as if he were about to charge.

"Mount Fifty-one, stand by on the port barrel, I repeat, on the port barrel," ordered Lustig.

"Mount Fifty-one *starboard* barrel loaded and ready," reported McTigue over the sound-powered phone system.

"I SAID PORT BARREL, CHIEF."

"Jesus shit, Mister Lustig, the port hoist is making grinding noises, so I switched to the starboard. It don't make no difference, does it?"

Lustig shrugged.

A voice came up the voice tube: "Bridge, this is Combat, target tracks dead in the water."

"Hey, Larry," Wallowitch called, "I just thought of something—I don't know how to put a shot across somebody's bow. They don't teach that kind of thing at gunnery school any more."

"Listen, Shrink, it's a snap," Lustig said. "The target is dead in the water, see. So all you have to do is take a range and bearing to her bow, crank in a small lead angle and shoot, got it?"

"You mean the shot should go in front of her bow, not actually over it?" Wallowitch asked.

"Yeah, right, in front of the bow," Lustig said.

"Then how come they always tell you to put a shot *across* her bow?"

"Come on, Shrink, it's only a figure of speech. Just do it, will you, before the skipper blows a gasket."

"Can I shoot now?" Wallowitch asked.

"You can shoot anytime you want to," Lustig said.

Wallowitch put his sword down, double-checked the range and bearing to the target's bow, cranked in a small lead angle and picked up the remote control trigger.

On the open bridge the voice from Combat floated up the voice tube. "Bridge, it's me again. Belay that last, huh. Someone forgot to plug in the DR bug. The target appears to be moving at, oh, say eight knots."

"Eight—Jesus. Hey Shrink, hold off—"

The starboard gun in Mount 51 fired and recoiled. The brass powder case, hot enough to singe the skin off a man's hand, kicked out onto the deck and rolled against the railing. Looking like an ad for cigarettes, a perfect sphere of orange smoke emerged from the tip of the barrel. Three thousand yards away the target sailed into the round of VT frag, flared up as if someone had ignited a book of matches and disintegrated.

The time was exactly 0713.

For the space of a long breath there was no sound on the *Ebersole* except the bow wave lapping softly against the sides of the hull. Then, as if a punch line had clicked in his brain, the Executive Officer burst into long rolls of cackling laughter. And Tevepaugh poked his head out of the pilot house to ask Lustig: "D'you think we can say we seen action now?"

Lustig Strikes It Rich

"That was fine shooting, my boy," Jones said, pounding Wallowitch on the back of his tennis sweater when he emerged from the main director hatch. "Fine shooting. Think I'll have all my officers wear sidearms to GQ from now on, eh? Creates the right kind of atmosphere, isn't that so, XO?"

"Good going, Wally," the XO said, reaching down and pumping the Shrink's hand.

"Just call me 'One Shot,'" Wallowitch said shakily.

As the sun edged over the horizon the *Ebersole* took a turn around the area looking for survivors. The only thing it found was some chunks of splintered wood, a cork life jacket wrapped around an armless, headless, legless torso, and an empty cardboard box marked "U.S. Government Issue Prophylactics."

Jones dispatched an "action report" to Vice Admiral Haydens, the commander of the task force of which DD722 was a part, announcing that the *Ebersole* had been attacked by an enemy patrol boat, which was sunk in the subsequent exchange of gunfire. By breakfast time a sailor who had been a tattoo artist in civilian life was putting the notch in the pistol grip—painting the silhouette of a sinking patrol boat on the side of Mount 51. And Jones was hunched over a portable typewriter recommending himself for the silver star, the nation's third highest military decoration. (In the war zone the medal was handed out on a quota basis; shortly after the *Ebersole* arrived on Yankee Station it received a routine dispatch from Admiral Haydens soliciting recommendations from the destroyer force. Haydens was bucking to become Chief of Naval Operations and he was only too happy to give out the medals, since that made *him* look good.) The final version, which the XO and Lustig signed and submitted later that day, contained such phrases as "setting a resolute example of gallantry" and "conspicuous disregard for his personal safety."

Lustig carried the recommendation to the radio shack for transmission to the aircraft carrier. As he left Ohm buttonholed him in the passageway.

"Congratulations," he said, handing Lustig fifty-five one-dollar bills. "Lucky thirteen won the pool."

Angry Pettis Spots a White Radish in the Water

Moments before the bo's'n's mate piped lunch, while the ship's yeoman was running off a special edition of the *Ebersole Eagle* with the text of Admiral Haydens' congratulatory telegram in it, Angry Pettis spotted a huge white radish floating past the ship.

"Hey Mista Moore," he yelled to the Officer of the Deck, "lookee here—there's a white radish in the water. Let's pick it up and put it on the menu."

It wasn't a radish but a dead body floating face down, bloated and chalk white from being in the water.

"Put the longboat in and see if it's Oriental or Caucasian," Jones ordered when Moore called down with word of what they had found. "If it's Oriental, log it and leave it; if it's Caucasian, retrieve it."

"Longboat away," Ohm growled into the public address system. Wallowitch, who was the longboat officer, took his place in the bow and directed the helmsman toward the body.

"We'll have to turn it face up," Wallowitch said when they got there. "Pass me the boat hook."

The Shrink reached down with the boat hook and tried to flip the body over, but the dull brass point of the hook punctured the carcass and tore it open like soggy tissue paper. Wallowitch turned his head away and vomited. The sailors in the longboat finally managed to wedge the body against the side and turn it over, but they couldn't tell if it was Caucasian or Oriental because it had no face.

Stumbling back on board the *Ebersole*, Wallowitch was shivering and shaken. "I didn't mean to hurt it," he said softly. "I swear to God I didn't mean to hurt it." And he vomited again and again and again until there was nothing left inside him to throw up.

The Shrink's well of humor had run dry.

The Captain Convenes a War Council

"We all hate violence, me as much as any man in this wardroom," Captain Jones began. Gripping the back of the chair at the head of the table with his thick fingers, rocking rhythmically on the balls of his spit-shined Adlers, the commanding officer of the *Ebersole* warmed to his subject. He was a good public speaker, casual and forceful at the same time, careful to let his normally monotone voice roam back and forth across half an octave, generous in his use of pauses.

"Reread your history books, gentlemen," Captain Jones went on, nodding his head and raising an eyebrow to indicate he was making an important point. "Irregardless of what these effete journalists would have us believe, the essence of the American tradition is a healthy distaste for violence. But somewhere along the way somebody has got to stand fast, somebody has got to draw a line in the dust with his big toe and say: 'This far but no further.'"

Jones sucked in his stomach, which had a tendency to spill over his web belt. "Well, gentlemen, we're at that line, that frontier of freedom"—he nodded his head again; another important point!—"right out here on this Godforsaken stretch of ocean. And *they've* stepped over the line. Ergo, they've got to deal with the fightingest man-o'-war in the U.S. Navy, the *Eugene F. Ebersole,* eh?"

The war council (as the skipper liked to call it) had been convened in the forward wardroom immediately after lunch. Only Wallowitch, who had retreated to his bunk after the business with the body in the water, and Moore, who had the bridge watch, were absent. The rest of the officers, self-conscious about the .45 caliber pistols dangling at their waists, had filled in, quipping but curious.

"Is the artillery going to be uniform of the day from here on out?" asked Ralph Richardson, the Harvard Business School graduate putting in two years as supply officer.

"The artillery, as you call it, is required for war councils and the bridge watch during general quarters," the Captain had explained. "I want to create a reasonably warlike atmosphere on this ship."

Not knowing quite where to tuck the guns as they sat, the officers had taken their places around the long, felt-covered table. To emphasize the seriousness of the occasion, Angry Pettis had been posted outside the door armed with a loaded M-1 rifle.

"Ain't no motherfucker, black or white, goes in till the Captain he comes out," he told True Love, the wardroom's junior steward, an incredibly dumb but immensely innocent black whose real name was Truman Love.

Inside the wardroom the civilian luxuries—an eighteen-inch color television, a plastic philodendron, a tape deck—had all been stored away. The décor had been stripped down to what the Captain considered the bare essentials: the gold basketball de Bovenkamp had picked up from Commander Destroyers Atlantic; a photograph of the late and posthumously decorated Lieutenant Commander Eugene F. Ebersole, the chubby skipper of an American submarine sunk, under heroic circumstances, by Japanese depth charges during World War Two; the annual Christmas card from Ebersole's widow (long since remarried) Scotch-taped to the bulkhead; a framed, embossed edition of John Paul Jones's code of conduct for naval officers; a model of the *Eugene Ebersole* in a bottle.

"I want to commend you," the Captain was saying, "on the good start we made this morning. Especially Mister Wallowitch, who unfortunately has taken ill." The Captain cleared his throat. "That was heads-up shooting, I can tell you. And I'm not the only one who thinks so. As we say in the navy, now hear this."

Jones took a pasted-up message from his pocket and read it. "'Well done, *Ebersole*. Your performance in the face of the enemy this ayem was in the finest traditions of the naval service. Happy to have a can-do tin can like the *Ebersole* aboard on Yankee Station. Endit.' And it's signed: 'Rear Admiral Winthrop G. Haydens.'"

The Poet and Richardson exchanged glances. The Chaplain and Lustig kept their eyes glued to the table. The junior officers around the wardroom table stared back at the Captain in embarrassed silence. Only the Executive Officer (who was beginning to catch the cues) and Ensign de Bovenkamp (an ex-college basketball star who instinctively responded to the pep-talk atmosphere) reacted the way the Captain expected his officers to react—modestly pleased at the praise, proud to be a member of the *Ebersole* team, smilingly anxious to get back into the thick of things.

Captain Jones looked around the room uncertainly. "I've no doubt some of you are uneasy"—again he cleared his throat—"uneasy because Oriental human beings were killed in this morning's action." The Captain pulled out his chair and sat down. He started to speak in what he thought was a fatherly tone—low-pitched, confidential—to indicate that he could understand weaknesses and forgive them. "I respect that. I respect the fact that you feel this way. It's what I was talking about before—about how we all hate violence. But let's face it, gentlemen, trite as it sounds, war is, eh, hell." Jones said this slowly as if it were a quotable phrase. "Isn't that right, Mister Lustig?"

Lustig's eyes were fixed on the Captain, but his mind was wandering. "Could you repeat the question, sir?"

"I asked you, 'Isn't war hell?'" Jones was clearly annoyed.

"Yes sir, it definitely is," Lustig responded gamely. "Anybody who's ever been in one knows that much."

("War isn't hell, at least not for us it isn't, Skipper,"

Lustig heard himself say when he went over the scene later that day. "If war isn't hell, then what the hell is it?" bullied the Captain, furious at being crossed in public. To which Lustig replied with supreme confidence: "War isn't hell—it's a career opportunity.")

"Most of you young men in this wardroom," the Captain was saying, "most of the men on this ship are too young to know much about World War Two, or even the Korean War. I didn't hate the Japs. I didn't hate the North Koreans. I don't hate the Slopes or the Chinks, or even the Ruskies for that matter. But I fight the enemies of my country."

"In other words, my country right or wrong," interrupted the Poet, trying hard to keep the irony out of his voice.

"That's it!" exclaimed the XO, nodding vigorously. "That's it exactly. Corny as it sounds, that's the heart of the matter, isn't it, Captain? My country, right *or* wrong."

"Somebody has to be my country right or wrong," the skipper said. He wasn't quite certain whose side the Poet was on.

A Word from Sweet Reason

Jones paused to collect his thoughts. "About these leaflets," he said finally. Every officer around the table leaned forward.

Using both palms the Captain flattened the paper (which had been rolled up in his napkin ring and served with breakfast by True Love that morning) on the table. Every time he took his palm off the leaflet it snapped back like a window shade. He weighted the ends with a salt and pepper shaker, a sugar bowl and a "Swift and Sure" ashtray.

Four copies of the leaflet had turned up so far. Besides the one served up to the Captain at breakfast, a second had been found tacked to the mess deck bulletin board, a third was discovered taped to the wardroom photograph of Eugene F. Ebersole ("Sacrilege," fumed the XO as he ripped it off) and a fourth was located (by then the hunt was on) taped to the pay telephone in the midship's passageway.

The leaflet, single-spaced and indented, began:

Comrades in arms

("We used to use 'comrades in arms' all the time during the war," Jones had mused when he and the XO first discussed the leaflet that morning. "I guess the boys in the Kremlin ruined that.")

Today the officers and enlisted men on the *Ebersole,* which for all practical purposes is a segregated ship, will be ordered, by our racist Pig captain whose hobby is collecting coxod concentration camp barbed wire, to kill innocent men, women and children, kill them just as surely as if some Pig sadist Nazi put a rifle to their heads and spattered their brains in the mud. DON'T LET THEM MAKE KILLERS OUT OF US!!!! Don't make war on ioox innocent men, women and children.

For 20 years Amerika has been acting as if peace is a Communist plot. Let peace start today on the *Ebersole* when the guns go silent. You can do your part by letting the equipment

break down. If the *Ebersole* can't get there, if
the guns won't work, they can't make us KILL.

Remember: Nobody can force you to pull
a trigger!

The Voice of Sweet Reason

"About these leaflets," the Captain was saying. He
changed pace now, speaking quietly and quickly, using
the earnest tones of a man who has been wronged,
squeezing all the sincerity he could into the space
between words. "I want to make one thing perfectly
clear. I strongly resent the suggestion that I personally
harbor any racist feelings, or that I preside over a
segregated ship. I've been in this man's navy since
before some of you were born, serving both as an
enlisted man and an officer, and I have never treated a
colored sailor any differently than I treat white sailors,
never, absolutely never. As for the *Ebersole* being a
segregated ship; since that fuss on the mess deck in
Norfolk, a few of our colored crewmen have chosen—*of
their own free will and volition, mind you*—to congre-
gate on one side of the mess deck. But to suggest that
this constitutes segregation, well—"

Jones flung his arms wide in the air, as if to say that
the charge was so ridiculous it needed no further
rebuttal.

More about the "Fuss" on the Mess Deck

The "fuss" on the mess deck had taken place while the ship was tied up to a pier at the Norfolk destroyer base. After the evening meal, with Jones and the XO and most of the officers off drinking at the Officers' Club, Ohm had flipped on the mess deck's black and white television set to *The Beverly Hillbillies*. Angry Pettis had insisted on watching a special starring James Brown, Soul Brother Number One. There was some preliminary name calling. In an instant the disagreement had erupted into a rip-roaring bar brawl, with sailors pouring into the mess deck from surrounding compartments and fists and coffee mugs flying in all directions.

Despite a considerable amount of screaming, Lustig (who was in charge while the Captain was off the ship) had been unable to bring the battle to a standstill. It was de Bovenkamp who solved the immediate problem by commandeering the color television from the first-class lounge and installing it on the other side of the mess deck. With that the two camps, glancing over their shoulders sullenly, had settled down to watch their respective programs. The next morning at breakfast the blacks on board all took seats on the James Brown side of the mess deck, while the whites filed in on *The Beverly Hillbillies'* side.

The Captain had laughed off reports of a race riot. "If you ask me, it was a clear case of high spirits."

On the mess deck the separate but equal arrangement quickly froze into the status quo.

More about the Barbed Wire

"As for the business about the barbed [he pronounced it 'bob'] wire," the Captain was saying. "This is a perfect example of how something can be distorted all out of proportion. Some of you may have noticed the bob-wire display in my cabin. I was born and raised in La Crosse, Kansas, which happens to be the bob-wire capital of the world. You probably aren't aware of it, there's no reason why you should be, but it so happens there are hundreds of types of bob wire, not any one all-purpose bob wire. When I was a youngster"—the Captain's eyes glistened with a faraway look—"my God, I used to enter the splicing contests every year. Once I turned in an eleven-second effort and walked off with a second prize against contestants from all over the state."

Jones shook the memory out of his head. "But that's neither here nor there. The point is that I collect bob wire the way some people collect stamps. The display on my bulkhead is part of my collection. The strand in the center, the one surrounded by gold braid, happens to be a collector's item. It's worth five hundred dollars if it's worth a penny. It's an actual strand of wire made in La Crosse in eighteen sixty-two and used to fence in the Indian reservations. The bobs are on the inside so as not to hurt cattle on the outside. Now to make out that there is some connection between this and concentration camps, well, it's downright offensive. There's nothing wrong with bob wire per se. In the hands of Americans, it was used to open the West to civilization and create a

39

lucrative cattle industry. In the hands of the Nazis, of course, it's something else again."

"Captain," the XO piped up after a moment's hesitation. "I think I speak for all the officers in this wardroom and for all the men on this ship when I say that there is no question that the insinuations made against you personally are slander, pure and simple."

"It never occurred to me you would see it any other way, gentlemen," Jones said generously. "I don't mind telling you that without your marvelous support, this kind of thing could give a commanding officer a complex."

(Later Lustig thought of: "You already have one—a military industrial complex.")

"Nevertheless," Jones plunged on, "I wanted to set the record straight, so to speak. Which brings us to the main order of business." Jones nodded again to underscore the question that followed. "Who, gentlemen, who is Sweet Reason?"

The Captain allowed the question to sink in. Then, letting his eyes traverse the table, he added: "Let's face facts. We are dealing with a lousy, stinking fifth-column rotten apple. And we've got to stamp out this rotten apple before it infects the other weak apples in the barrel. But we've got to do it delicately—we mustn't bruise any of the good apples going after the bad."

"It's got to be a surgical strike," said the XO.

"Precisely," agreed the Captain. His facial muscles quivered and he brought a hand up to his cheek to restore order.

"Captain, sir, with all respect, have you considered the other possibilities?" asked the Poet. "There's always a chance it's a joke, isn't there?"

"Mister Joyce, the person who signs himself Sweet Reason has invited the officers and men on board this ship to commit sabotage and mutiny. That's no joke.

We're dealing with a rotten apple, and I mean to crucify him. Before we can do that, however, we have to find him. I'm open to suggestions, eh?"

Ensign de Bovenkamp raised his hand.

"There's no need to raise your hand here, Mister de Bovenkamp," the Captain said in a kindly voice. "Just speak up, my boy."

"Proper," de Bovenkamp said, his jaw working on a wad of chewing gum. "How about putting Proper on it, Captain?"

Proper's Curriculum Vitae

Sonarman Third Dwight Proper was obviously the man for the job. A short, wiry sailor with beetle eyebrows and an abnormally low hairline, he had been a member of the Chicago Police Force for two years before enlisting in the navy. (No matter that he had been a uniformed patrolman on the traffic detail.) Proper quit the force and went to sea for a breath of fresh, pollen-free air; he had hay fever, rose fever, and was allergic to dust, fresh fruit, corn, mayonnaise, cats, dogs and wool. Unfortunately, he turned out to be allergic to navy-issue pillows and mattresses too, a fact of life that forced him to go around armed with a Benzedrex Inhaler at all times.

Proper's experience as a Chicago cop had already been put to good use in Cartagena when Chaplain Rodgers discovered that there were 753 men ashore from various U.S. Navy ships in the port—but only fourteen of them could be seen, sipping soda through honest-to-goodness Spanish straw, on the main drag.

"Can't account for the whereabouts of seven hundred thirty-nine sailors," the Chaplain frantically radioed Captain Jones, who had the day's shore patrol command duty.

"Find those seven hundred thirty-nine men, Proper," the skipper had ordered, and in no time at all the ex-Chicago cop had solved the case. All 739 of them, it turned out, were on The Hill, a labyrinthine quarter on the edge of town with narrow, muddy, urine-soaked streets and hundreds of half-naked urchins running around barefooted soliciting for the whorehouses.

"Look at all those fucking sailors!" exclaimed Proper when he arrived on the scene.

"Well I'll be damned!" muttered the Chaplain when Proper returned to The Hill with him in tow.

Proper Picks Up the Scent

"Several things are readily apparent," intoned Proper in his preliminary report to Captain Jones an hour after the war council.

"Point A: True Love is definitely not your Sweet Reason. I questioned him very carefully. He swears that the leaflet was already rolled up in your napkin ring when he picked up the breakfast tray in the galley and brought it topside. He thought it was a plan of the day. The other stewards said the same thing. And I believe them." Proper said it as if the fact that *he* believed them left no room for anybody else to doubt them. "If they were guilty, Captain, they wouldn't have left the incriminating leaflet somewhere that cast suspicion on them, you get my point? Which means that someone slipped in during the night and put that leaflet in your napkin ring."

"But I thought the galley was locked during the night?"

"It is, Captain, but the key is left under the rubber mat in front of the door because the steward who locks up at night is not the one who opens it in the morning and there's only one key."

"I see," nodded the Captain. He was impressed with Proper's thoroughness. "Go on, go on." Jones chewed away on the inside of his cheek as Proper continued.

"Point B: Sweet Reason is a poor speller."

"A poor speller, eh?"

"Yes sir, a poor speller. You'll notice he spells 'Amerika' with a K. It's not a typing error, because the K is nowheres near the C on a typewriter. You get my point?"

"Yes, I think I do. What about fingerprints?"

"That's my point C, Captain. Point C: It would be useless to dust the evidence for fingerprints because too many people have already handled the merchandise, if you know what I mean. And the chances are pretty good that the culprit was careful to keep his prints off in the first place."

The Captain was beginning to get edgy. "You don't sound very hopeful, Proper."

"On the contrary, Captain, I have every reason to believe I can identify your Sweet Reason by tonight."

"Well, that *is* good news. How?"

"Captain, do you notice anything about these four leaflets?" Proper spread them out on the desk, putting weights on the corners of the window-shade one to keep it flat.

Jones studied the leaflets intently for a few moments. "Only that they're the work of a goddamn rotten apple," he said finally.

"With all respect, Captain, you have to look at this with a detached eye, if you get my point. Now the first thing I notice when I look at these four leaflets is that they were typed on the same typewriter. The one in your napkin ring is the original; the other three are carbon copies. See how they get less distinct as you go along?"

"By Jesus Christ Almighty, you're right!"

"I tried typing with the same grade of paper—it's sold in the ship's store, by the way—and I discovered that I could make an original and five readable copies if I used new carbons, and four readable copies if the carbons were old ones. Get my point?"

"Go on, Proper, go on, my boy," the Captain said impatiently.

"There are probably one or two copies of this seditious leaflet still in circulation on the ship, if my guess is right."

"All this is very interesting, my boy, but how will it help you find Sweet Reason?"

"Oh, that's simple. I'll just check the type on every typewriter on the ship until I find the one that typed this leaflet. The sailor who owns that typewriter or has access to it is your Sweet Reason."

Captain Jones Takes the Conn

Lustig, who was the Officer of the Deck, and the XO, who was trying to improve his sun tan, were chatting on the wing of the bridge. The *Ebersole* was plane-guarding for an aircraft carrier, steaming on the port beam of the giant ship as it raced into the wind and recovered its jets from a strike against the mainland.

"That's the thing about people like that," the Executive Officer was saying. "Sweet Reason, my ass. They only know the bad side, never the good side. A country as big as ours is bound to have faults. But it's a place where a man can start with nothing and pull himself up by his own bootstraps. My God, it's a place where anybody can become President."

(*"Anybody* has," Lustig thought of saying—too late to fit it gracefully into the conversation.)

"Sweet Reason," the XO went on, shaking his head mournfully. "What a misnomer that is."

Noncommittal as always, Lustig took a bearing on the carrier's superstructure jutting like a high-rise apartment from one side of the flight deck and discovered that the *Ebersole* was slightly off station. "Helmsman, steer three one seven," he called into the pilot house.

Ohm appeared at the pilot house door waving a scrap of paper that the messenger had just brought up from the Captain's cabin. "Permission to pass the word?" he said.

"Granted, Ohm."

Ohm clicked on the public-address system. "Now all hands with"—he studied the next word for a moment as if he didn't believe it—"typewriters, lay aft to the after wardroom with same."

Ohm's voice was still echoing through the ship when the jet fighter crashed three quarters of a mile from the *Ebersole*, bounced twice like a flat stone skidding off a lake and sank back into the sea.

As a great arc of sea spray with a rainbow through it settled gently around the plane, all hell broke loose on the *Ebersole*.

"Left full rudder, all engines ahead flank," boomed Lustig, his pulse racing wildly. "Get the Captain up here."

"Captain to the bridge," Ohm yelled into the public-address system and listened to the words echo from speaker to speaker below deck: "Captain to the bridge, to the bridge, the bridge."

Jones came bounding up the ladder as the *Ebersole* heeled hard over to port.

The voice of someone who fancied himself a radio announcer, supremely calm and dulcet-toned, clicked onto the primary tactical circuit from the carrier: "Elbow Room, Elbow Room, this is Isolated Camera. One of our pigeons is down, over."

"Roger, Elbow Room on the way, out," Lustig told the carrier.

"I have the conn," cried the Captain. He lined up the downed plane in the cross hairs of the telescopic alidade. "Come back, Jesus, come back to two four seven," he screamed at Carr, the helmsman.

"Nobody gave me no course to come to," Carr muttered to anyone within earshot, and added: "Loony bin, goddamn loony bin." He shifted the rudder and steadied on 247.

"Steady on two four seven," he called out.

The Captain ignored him. "Tell main control to

stand by to back down fast and give me all stop," he yelled to Lustig.

"But Captain, we have superheats on," Lustig said. It took ten or twelve minutes to lower the superheats to the point where main control could safely stop the engines without permanently damaging the boilers.

"What are the goddamn superheats doing on?" screamed Jones. He was dancing up and down now and pounding the railing with the flat of his hand.

"You ordered them on," said Lustig.

"Well, get them off!"

The *Ebersole's* bow knifed through the water toward the downed jet, 400 yards away.

"All back full," yelled the Captain.

The gap closed rapidly.

"All back emergency," Jones shrieked. "Give me everything you've got."

The lee helmsman jiggled the bells to indicate emergency astern. The *Ebersole* began to lose way rapidly.

"You'd better alternate between ahead and astern bells, Skipper, or we'll back away from her," the XO whispered over the Captain's shoulder.

"You think so, eh?" Jones said without turning around. "All engines ahead one third," he called to the lee helmsman.

The *Ebersole's* bow, with a rescue team poised on it ready to dive in and save the pilot, cut toward the plane. It looked as if the destroyer had come to a dead stop about twenty yards away when the one-third-ahead bell began to take effect.

"Back, back, Christ Almighty, all back full," screamed the Captain—too late.

The bow lifted on the crest of a swell and sliced down like a cleaver, gashing the jet behind the cockpit.

The swimmers from the *Ebersole*, long safety lines tied
to their waists, leaped into the sea on top of the plane.
With water pouring in through the gash in the fuselage
the jet began to sink. One of the swimmers, Signalman
Third Jefferson Waterman, yanked at the canopy, but it
had been jammed shut in the crash with the *Ebersole*.
The plane plunged under now and the swimmers
standing on it were in seawater up to their shoulders.
Waterman made a last try, diving down and hammering
on the cockpit with his bare fists, hammering and pulling
and clawing at it until blood poured from his hands.
Then he shot up gasping for air and crying like a baby.

The men on the bridge could still see the sinking
jet, magnified and shimmering under twenty feet of clear
blue water. The yellow flight helmet of the pilot, with a
screaming eagle decalcomania on it, lay twisted at an odd
angle from the body, bobbing gently up and down in the
water-filled cockpit.

"He was probably dead anyhow," the Captain said.
"Chances are he was dead, eh?"

Jones Holds a Post-Mortem

"There's no question he was dead when the plane
hit, Captain," the XO assured Jones later that afternoon.
The two were sitting in the Captain's cabin waiting for
the department heads to assemble. "Admiral Haydens
must have come to the same conclusion. Look at the way
he phrased this cable. My God, there's nothing ironic
about it. 'Good try Ebersole. We mightily impressed
with the leadership qualities necessary bring veteran

destroyer like Isolated Camera up to this level of performance Endit.'"

"It's true, there's not a word about us coming too close, to the jet I mean, eh?" the Captain said thoughtfully.

"Not a word, Skipper," the XO agreed. "Anyhow, what is *too* close? According to the book, you're supposed to deposit your swimmers as close as possible in the shortest time possible. As far as I can see, that's precisely what you did. It was hard luck that the jet sank before they could get the pilot out, that's all."

"I'd give anything to know who the sonovabitch was who advised me to ring up that one-third-ahead bell." Jones licked his lips absent-mindedly, trying to identify the voice that had come floating over his shoulder in the midst of the excitement. "You're sure it wasn't Lustig, eh? Maybe it was Sweet Reason?"

"I doubt very much whether it was Sweet Reason, Captain."

"Who else was on the bridge besides Lustig?"

"Wallowitch and Joyce were up there. So were de Bovenkamp and Richardson. Moore was too, I think. Just about everybody came up when the shit hit the fan. Want me to nose around, Skipper—discreetly, of course?"

Jones weighed the offer for a moment. "Negative," he said finally, still trying to recreate the scene. "Negative. Since everything turned out for the best, let's let it drop, eh? But I want you to keep the goddamn sightseers off the bridge, XO. Put a memo to that effect in the plan of the day, eh?"

Jones Meets the Department Heads

"That was tough luck, hitting the plane at the last second, Captain," Richardson said solicitously as the department heads—Lustig for gunnery, Moore for engineering, the XO for operations and Richardson for supply—pulled up seats around the Captain's desk.

"I wasn't aware we hit the plane, Mister Richardson," the Captain shot back coldly. "The object in an exercise like that is to get to the downed plane as quickly as possible. And that's what we did. You do a fine job in supply, Mister Richardson, but it seems to me that you could safely leave judgments about seamanship to those of us who have some considerable experience in such matters, eh?" And Jones nodded once to underscore the point that his tone of voice had already underscored.

"No offense intended, Captain," Richardson said lamely.

"None taken, my boy, none taken," the skipper responded.

Jones strung some long moments of silence together to create the right mood for what was to come. Lustig shifted uncomfortably in his chair. The others, afraid that their breathing would be the loudest in the room, held their breaths.

"I called this meeting," the Captain began—and the department heads exhaled. "I called it to discuss the operational readiness of this ship. I have yesterday's eight o'clock reports"—every day at twenty hundred hours the department heads complied a list of equipment that was "down" and sent it to the Captain—"and

50

it's just plain ridiculous. If word of this ever got out the *Ebersole* would be pulled off the firing line within the hour. And you gentlemen are aware, I'm sure, of what that would mean for your careers."

The list of "down" equipment was imposing, more so because there was a general tendency to omit items that were minor or were about to be repaired. The 21 MC, an internal communication system, was still too full of static to use from CIC or main control. The SPA-6 air search radar repeater in CIC had loose wiring. The SQS-40 sonar was overheating again; de Bovenkamp had tried channeling air to it from a nearby vent through a cutoff dungaree leg, but it hadn't helped. The Mark 5 Mod 5 sonar fire control system was not getting a ship's course input, which made problem solving impossible. Moore had shut down the number two boiler to inspect tubes after a possible low water incident; the striker who was supposed to watch the "glass" had fallen asleep on the job. The port turbine reduction gear shaft had been shut down when the Chief Petty Officer detected a slight thump-thump; "bearing problem," Moore had noted next to the item. Generator number one, an old workhorse that broke down regularly, was off the line. The main condenser seawater intake had clogged again, probably with fish. Two TED transmitters and a RED receiver had been shut down to replace tubes. The LORAN receiver was on the fritz. The Mark-25 director radar had been taken off the line for "routine preventive maintenance," which was Lustig's way of saying that it didn't work and he didn't know what was wrong. The entire MARK-56 director system, which controlled the two three-inch mounts aft, was inoperative; the fire control people thought the trouble had something to do with the parallax input, but they weren't sure. The winch for the starboard anchor had jammed. The remote control signal bridge lever for releasing depth charges was inoperative; it hadn't worked since before Captain Jones took command of the *Ebersole*, but nobody seemed to be able to track down the trouble. The port dredger hoist for Mount 51 worked—but with such a grinding noise that Chief McTigue had ordered it shut down for overhaul. Two of the three toilets in the after crew's quarters refused to flush; something to do with the water pressure aft dropping. "And I have it on good authority," the Captain added, "that the coin slot in the pay telephone amidships is stuffed with gum."

The Eugene F. Ebersole's *Curriculum Vitae*

The list in the Captain's hand was the tip of the iceberg—the visible part of the *Ebersole*'s age and infirmity. In cramped compartments and obscure corners, in crawl spaces between bulkheads and decks, in nooks and crannies that had not been inspected by anyone in years, *the ship leaked*—seawater, freshwater, steam, fuel oil, lube oil, hydraulic fluid, grease, compressed air, sewage, bilgewater, smoke.

Take the boilers. There were four of them on the *Ebersole*, four giant furnaces that converted freshwater into steam and then squeezed the steam through nozzles to spin the turbines that drove the main propulsion shaft that turned the two huge screws that pushed the ship through the water. It was supposed to be a closed system, one which converted the steam back into water at the end of the cycle and then started all over again. But there were so many water and steam leaks along the way that the *Ebersole* had to operate its condensers (which made freshwater out of seawater) overtime just to provide water for the boilers. And that left precious little for things like washing and laundry.

The *Ebersole* was an ancient mariner living on borrowed time and endless ingenuity. She was so old that Otto Rummler, the former German U-boat skipper who had sunk 200,000 tons of allied shipping in his day, was amazed she could still get from one place to another. "Mein gott," he told Captain Jones at dinner one night, "no offenze intended but I sink zere is more vasser inside ze *Ebersole* zen outzide, ya."

The *Ebersole*, DD722 in navy parlance, was named after Eugene F. Ebersole, an unremarkable ensign who graduated three hundred and forty-eighth in his class of 362 from the Naval Academy and went on to win the Congressional Medal of Honor by mistake. While commander of the U.S.S. *Snakefish* in waters off the Japanese mainland toward the end of the war, he fired a spread of torpedoes at a hulk on the horizon (which turned out to be smog) and then sent his famous transmission: "My fish frying fascists." The Japanese homed in on the radio transmission and blew the *Snakefish* to the surface with depth charges, at which point Ebersole radioed: "I shall surrender." In Washington, a bright PR-minded admiral inserted the word "never" and sent the message off to the newspapers. The submarine was lost with all hands, but its young commander became an overnight hero. When the government came to naming the next destroyer that slid down the Staten Island ways, it decided to honor the late Eugene F. Ebersole.

Originally the *Ebersole* had been one of fifty-eight Allen M. Sumner class destroyers completed at the high tide of the Second World War. By the mid-1960s, sixteen of the original fifty-eight were still operational—fifteen of them as reserve training ships that stuck close to home ports spoon-feeding weekend warriors who were accumulating pension credits. Only the *Ebersole* still sailed with the fleet, a nostalgic piece of gray flotsam chugging along beside the atomic destroyers and super-carriers.

The *Ebersole* would never have ended up in the combat zone except for the fortunes of war and the slip of a pen. When the President ordered the air force to bomb the enemy, the navy—anxious to get into the act—promptly dispatched a squadron of destroyers from the Mediterranean to beef up the fleet on Yankee Station. The *Ebersole*, finally about to be assigned to the reserve training program, was ordered to fill the breach in the Mediterranean. A few months later two destroyers patrolling Yankee Station collided in a thick fog, forcing one of them to limp back to the states for structural repairs. In the Pentagon, a senior admiral who had quietly been relieved of his command at sea when it was discovered he regularly entertained teenage whores on his flagship, scanned the list of available replacements. Spotting an "E" for "engineering excellence" next to the *Ebersole* (put there by a careless yeoman who thought he was writing in the DD732 column) the Admiral ordered DD722 to the war zone.

Captain J. P. Horatio Jones's Curriculum Vitae

For Captain Jones, the assignment to join the fleet off the enemy coast came with a small unspoken postcript that said: "This is your Golden Opportunity." At forty-seven Jones was an old skipper by destroyer standards, older than all but a handful of the other three stripers on the navy promotion lists, and precariously near the end of a plainly mediocre career. He had been passed over for promotion to the fourth stripe twice already; one more time and he would be on his way out of the service, headed for retirement in some colony of ex-sailors who cluttered their cottages with bottled ships and prints of British frigates under full sail.

Jones had started out in the navy as a seventeen-year-old seaman deuce, a wise-assed kid with a fair amount of drive and a flair for exaggeration. Putting both of these qualities to work, he had won a commission and threaded his way through the bureaucratic thicket of the postwar navy, not as rapidly as his contemporaries, but always in the nick of time. Jones was never what the selection boards thought of as a "comer"; he was more of a plodder, winning promotions and assignments by standing in line and waiting his turn. The navy carefully handed out a certain number of promotions to people like Jones so that the others like him would not lose heart and quit, leaving the navy with a plentiful supply of leaders but no followers.

Vietnam could change all that. A flashy performance, a stroke of luck, even a well-turned phrase (something alliterative like "Sighted Sub Sunk Same") that caught the eye of a headline writer could propel him to the front of the line. For J. P. Horatio Jones (the J.P. stood for Jerry Pierce, but Jones stuck to the initials on the outside chance someone would think it stood for John Paul; the Horatio was his father's idea of a joke), war could mean a fourth stripe or even the scrambled eggs of an admiral on his cap.

A great deal, of course, depended on the *Ebersole* and the way it performed. Jones had reported aboard the *Ebersole*, his first command at sea and his first destroyer assignment, with something of a romantic's notion of a destroyer as a swift, sure greyhound of the sea plunging recklessly into the waves at thirty-one knots toward harm's way. Long after he discovered that the *Ebersole* was neither swift nor sure, Jones had been careful to present himself to his superiors as a can-do, "E"-eager captain. To this end he never washed his dirty linen in public. Since he had taken command there had been no courts-martial (all punishment was meted out at captain's mast), no reports of racial friction on the ship, no indication that the sailors were smoking pot. (Once, during a fleet exercise off Norfolk, the Captain made a surprise visit to the Combat Information Center, a darkened compartment below the bridge level that houses the radar repeaters. As he crossed the threshold, Jones caught a whiff of the unmistakable odor of pot— and ignored it. But he was careful never to make surprise visits to any compartments after that. And since he never smelled pot again, he felt justified in assuming that there was none on board his ship.)

Above all Jones went to almost any lengths to make sure that the *Ebersole* met its operating obligations, even when the equipment necessary to meet those obligations wasn't working. The *Ebersole* "vectored" aircraft in search patterns while the air search radar was under repair (the Captain simply sent the planes out, counted to fifty and brought them back in again). In tandem with another destroyer, DD722 hunted target submarines off the Guantanamo, Cuba, naval base while the sonar was under repair (Jones took the other destroyer's sonar contact, offset it a hundred yards and attacked the spot). She even got Electronic Counter Measure fixes on "enemy" surface ships while the ECM equipment was under repair (for this one the Captain had sneaked a look at the target ship's operating orders and knew where it was supposed to be).

There were other little tricks of the trade that Jones had picked up from ambitious skippers during his naval career. The *Ebersole*, for instance, always underestimated the number and assortment of spare parts it had on board so it could get more *before* it had a need for them. At sea, Jones lied again when asked what he had on board so he wouldn't have to share his spares with other destroyers that hadn't laid in a stockpile.

From Captain Jones's point of view, all of these efforts had paid off in an assignment to Yankee Station. "Proceeding at thirty-one knots," he radioed his superiors—in an echo of Arleigh Burke's famous up-and-at-'em cable announcing that his outnumbered, outgunned destroyers were racing to engage the Japanese battle fleet. The *Ebersole* rounded the Cape of Good Hope on two boilers (the other two were "down" for repairs) and made its radarless way (the antenna bearings had burned out) through the Indian Ocean to join Task Force 77 on Yankee Station. On arrival, the *Ebersole* refueled underway from the U.S.S. *Taluga* (which had a sign on the hull saying "We give green stamps") and filled the munitions bins from the U.S.S. *Virgo* (which had a banner stretched across the superstructure proclaiming: "Welcome to the frontier of freedom"). Then

Jones locked himself in his cabin for two hours trying to compose a suitable message to Admiral Haydens announcing that the *Ebersole* stood ready to go to war. What he finally came up with was: "A hundred percent fuel, a hundred percent ammunition, a hundred percent eager to do what ship was built for and we were trained for—join battle and vanquish enemies of freedom and justice wherever they are. J. P. Horatio Jones, Commander, U.S.N."

The first day on Yankee Station had gone unexpectedly well. Patrolling off the coast in the predawn darkness, the *Ebersole* had—according to Jones's action report—been "attacked by a North Vietnamese patrol craft, which was sunk in the subsequent exchange of gunfire." Later the *Ebersole* made a good stab at saving the downed pilot. Now if Jones could chalk up a few more successes his career would be assured. But everything depended on keeping the *Ebersole* on the firing line.

Jones Lays Down the Law

"Our country is depending on us to keep the *Ebersole* on the firing line, gentlemen," Jones was saying to the department heads assembled in his cabin. "And that brings me right back to Sweet Reason again." The Captain sat with his legs spread wide, leaning forward with his forearms resting on his thighs. "It's one thing to have had equipment inoperative up to now; this is an old ship and on an old ship, no matter how many man-hours of preventive maintenance you put in, things break down. But from here on out, gentlemen"—Jones's eyebrows shot up—"we have to be alert to the possibility that one or two misguided sailors may respond to Sweet Reason's call to sabotage, eh? That's why I called you together this afternoon. Henceforth, I want a full report from the department heads, in writing, on every piece of equipment that breaks down. I want to know if the breakdown was suspicious, if anything had been tampered with, et cetera, et cetera. And I want the crew to know we're checking; that way anybody tempted to follow Sweet Reason's advice and tinker with a piece of equipment will think twice. Do I make myself clear, gentlemen?"

"Question, Captain?" said Lustig.

"Shoot." Jones was all business.

"When is this effective? I mean, if I have something out at noon today, do you want a report on it?"

"Let's say that anything not listed on last night's eight o'clock report falls under this new order. Okay?"

Lustig looked sheepish. "Well, sir, I guess I'd better let you know about Mount Fifty-two then."

"Mount Fifty-two? What's the matter with Mount Fifty-two, eh?"

"It's just out, sir," Lustig said.

"Out how?" the Captain wanted to know. "What's the matter with it?"

"The mount captain isn't sure, Captain."

"What are the symptoms, Mister Lustig?" Jones was trying to be patient.

"Well, actually, I'm not quite certain, Captain. At this stage all I can say for sure is that the mount is not working."

"Who's the mount captain?" asked Jones, exasperated.

"Keys Quinn, sir, Gunner's mate first. He's the one

that's been on the *Ebersole* since she was commissioned, so there's no question of sabotage."

"Get him up here, Mister Lustig. This is a good opportunity for me to show you gentlemen how I want these investigations conducted."

"Now?" asked Lustig, the eyes in his round face widening.

"Now."

Keys Quinn on the Carpet

"Gunner's Mate First Quinn reporting as directed, sir," Quinn snapped. He stood inside the door of the Captain's cabin, holding his hat in one hand, saluting with the other.

"How long have you been in the navy, Quinn?" the Captain asked quietly.

"Twenty-six years come next month, sir."

"Somewhere along the way, Quinn, didn't anyone tell you that sailors in the United States Navy don't salute when their heads are uncovered, eh?"

Quinn's hand whipped down to his side. "No offense intended," he said.

"Now what's this I hear about Mount Fifty-two, Quinn?"

Quinn stood at attention, shifting his weight from one foot to the other, painfully embarrassed. The keys on the ring hanging from his belt jingled musically. When he started to speak his voice was almost inaudible.

"Speak up, Quinn, I can't hear a word you're saying," the Captain snapped, raising his own voice.

"I said that Fifty-two's not working, Captain."

Jones leaned back in his chair and crossed his legs. "He says that Mount Fifty-two is not working, Mister Lustig," the Captain said quietly. Then he added in a hard voice: "I am well aware that Fifty-two is not working, Quinn. Why the hell do you think you're here?" Jones switched back to the calm register. "What—if I may make so bold as to ask—what is causing Mount Fifty-two not to work?"

"I don't know yet, sir." Quinn looked at Lustig for help. Lustig concentrated on his fingertips.

"You don't know." Still in the calm register. "You don't know." Then coldly, biting off each word, Jones repeated the phrase: "You-don't-know! Here we are, patrolling off an enemy coast, momentarily expecting to go into battle, and *you don't know*. What is the navy coming to when the mount captain of Fifty-two doesn't know why his mount is not working? You'll have to do better than that, Quinn."

"Aye aye, sir," Quinn said weakly.

"Perhaps I can help you, Quinn." Jones had once been assigned, by mistake, as gunnery officer on one of the new aircraft carriers that carried no guns and fancied himself something of an expert on the subject. "Have you checked the firing circuits to make sure they're getting four hundred and forty volts?"

"Yes, sir," Quinn said, "that was the first thing I thought of."

"Did you check the pressure in the hydraulic system rammer?"

"Naturally, Captain—no sweat there either."

"What about the, eh, electro servo coupler?"

"The electro servo coupler?" Quinn said, dumfounded. "Captain, there isn't no electro servo coupler in Mount Fifty-two."

There was absolute silence in the Captain's cabin.

Jones leaned forward again. "Are you calling me a liar, Quinn?" he asked in a low, husky voice.

"Sir?"

"I said, are you calling me a liar?"

"No, sir." Quinn shook his head vehemently.

"Then get back to your mount and check out the electro servo coupler."

Quinn stood rooted to the deck, an expression of agony on his face. Tears of frustration coated his eyes.

"What's the matter, Quinn? Don't you know an order when you hear one?"

"Captain, sir, I just don't know what to do," Quinn said. He looked around the room for help. There was none to be had.

"It's really very simple, Quinn. Turn around, open the door, walk to Gun Mount Fifty-two, and check out the electro servo coupler to see if it is contributing to the malfunction of your mount."

"But there is no electro servo coupler, Captain, there just isn't none."

Jones turned sharply to the XO: "Get this man out of here before I lose my temper," he said, biting his cuticles.

"That's all, Quinn," the XO said roughly. He didn't want the Captain to doubt whose side he was on.

Still Quinn was not bright enough to turn and flee. "Aye aye, sir," he said again. "But what do I do about the electro servo coupler?"

The Captain pounced jubilantly. "So there is an electro servo coupler after all, eh?"

"No sir, there is no such thing. I know every nut and bolt in them mounts. I'd know if there was. And I swear on the Bible I'd tell you, Captain, I swear to God I would."

It was Lustig who finally put Quinn out of his misery. "On your horse, Quinn. Out. That's all. Go."

Totally confused, wishing desperately there was an electro servo coupler he could check, Quinn backed out of the Captain's cabin, stumbled over the door frame and closed the door softly for fear the click of the latch would disturb the Captain's equilibrium and bring on the demons again.

Inside, Jones looked as if he had just produced a rabbit from a hat. "And that, gentlemen," he said, "that will be our answer to Sweet Reason, eh?"

Quinn's Curriculum Vitae

A short, heavy man with thick thighs and skin that looked like the hide of a bull elephant, Quinn rated as the senior man on board the *Ebersole* in point of service. He had reported aboard in 1944 two days after the ship was commissioned and had been with her ever since — through the kamikaze attacks at Okinawa during World War Two, through Korea, through the invasion of Beirut, through fifteen Med trips and ten shipyard overhauls, through a dozen skippers and a hundred chief petty officers. The day after he lost his finger at Iskenderun, Quinn had put in what for him was a routine request to extend his tour on board the *Ebersole*, which was almost up. He had long ago discovered that life was one long battle to *belong*. To walk into a place where he didn't belong was excruciatingly painful to Quinn. Once he had begun to feel at home in the *Ebersole*, once he had begun to relax in its womblike familiarity, he had made up his mind never to leave. He planned to stay forever if they'd let him.

The ultimate symbol of Quinn's *belonging* was the eighty-eight keys that jingled from a large iron ring hanging from his navy-issue web belt. There were skeleton keys and latchkeys, rusted keys and bright silver keys, keys of every shape and size. Somewhere among them was one that could open almost any door on the *Ebersole*. It was more or less an *Ebersole* custom, in fact, for the petty officer in charge of a space to give a spare key to Quinn, saying: "Hey, listen, Keys, will you do me a personal favor and hang on to this in case I lose the original?" And Quinn, strictly as a favor to the petty officer, mind you, would add the key to his huge ring.

Every once in a while someone would actually lose a key. Then the Quartermaster of the watch would pass the word on the ship's loudspeaker system, "Now Keys Quinn, lay up to the midship's passageway on the double." Feeling more than ever as if he belonged, Quinn would rush down the passageway, his keys jingling on the ring, his eyes shining with a brightness that comes from being needed.

Two hours after the confrontation in the Captain's cabin over the electro servo coupler, Quinn's application for another tour on the *Ebersole* came back. The first hint he had that something was wrong came when the XO passed him in the passageway and said, "The Captain feels it's a violation of navy regs for one man to have keys to all these compartments—you'll have to turn in your ring, Keys." And the XO held out his hand.

Keyless, the usual jingle missing from his walk, Quinn made his way back to the ship's office and forced the yeoman who everyone thought was a homosexual to dig the application out of the service files.

"Request for extension on board *Ebersole* denied,"

the Captain had written in an almost illegible scrawl, "pursuant to BuPers Bravo 3756 Romeo of 21 May 1953, which states that petty officers are to be rotated from sea duty every two years unless (a) such rotation would be detrimental to the war readiness of the ship or (b) except in unusual circumstances."

Quinn flew into a rage. "The motherfucker," he screamed. "I'll break his balls, I'll kill him."

"Jesus shit, take it easy," McTigue told Quinn. "Maybe he don't understand you been here since the ship was commissioned. I'll talk to the XO. He'll see things different."

The prospect that McTigue, the senior noncommissioned officer in the gunnery department, would intercede on his behalf calmed Quinn for the moment. "He better change that endorsement," he said. "He fuckin' well better."

Proper Comes Up with a Suspect

"But you distinctly said tonight, Proper," fumed Captain Jones. He was sitting on the bunk of his sea cabin aft of the pilot house, spit-shining his Adler elevators. The night reading lamp over his head filled the small, bare room with angular shadows. A flashlight and a worn Mickey Spillane paperback lay on the deck within arm's reach. "You've let me down, Proper, you've certainly let me down."

"I'm sorry, Captain, but the typewriter thing didn't work out the way I thought it would. I checked out every single one on board; two in engineering, three in operations, three in supply, two in gunnery, the XO's, that's eleven, plus thirteen private portables. That's twenty-four in all. Not-a-one fitted the type on the fatal leaflet, not-a-one."

"Sweet Reason must be hiding his typewriter then."

"That's always a possibility, of course, but I'm beginning to think that your Sweet Reason may have typed these seditious leaflets before we sailed from Norfolk."

"But we didn't know we were going to war when we left Norfolk." The Captain got a certain amount of satisfaction out of having caught Proper in a slipup.

"Good point, Captain," Proper conceded. "You're certainly right about that. Revise my last to read: he probably typed them up in some port before we arrived in the war zone. And if that's the case, this may be a one-shot affair."

Jones looked relieved—and disappointed. "I don't mind telling you, Proper, it galls me to think that Sweet Reason can get away with this, can get off scot-free. Not that I want any more of these things to turn up, you understand, but it galls the hell out of me."

"Captain, there's something I'd like to tell you but I'm not sure how to begin," Proper said. He stuck his hands in the pockets of his foul-weather jacket and drew his head, turtle-like, back into the neck.

"Well, speak up, Proper. Don't worry, my boy. Anything you say here is strictly between us."

"Well, Captain, sir, I have a person—that is, I have a suspect who—"

"A suspect? A sailor you suspect of being Sweet Reason? Why didn't you say so before?"

"Not a sailor, Captain."

"Not a sailor! What the hell are you talking about, Proper?"

"My suspect's an officer, Captain."

Jones stared at Proper. "An officer, you say." He toyed with the idea the way one toys with a loose tooth. "Jesus, I never thought of connecting an officer with Sweet Reason," he said more to himself. Jones turned on Proper and demanded: "Okay, out with it, my boy, who is it?"

"I want to stress that he's only a suspect, Captain. Innocent until proven guilty and all that sort of thing, you get my point?"

"Yes, yes, I understand. Now who is it?"

Proper lowered his voice to a whisper. "The Poet, Captain."

"The Poet?"

"That's Ensign Joyce, Captain. Everyone calls him the Poet, even to his face. He's the one."

"What makes you suspect him, Proper?"

"Well, sir, there are a couple of things. First off, I found out that Ensign Joyce is very friendly with Boeth—"

"What's suspicious about that?"

"Boeth is an *enlisted* man, Captain. The word is he and Boeth actually went to New York together last Christmas. And I know the two of them spend a lot of time down in Main Plot—"

"Just what is it you think they're doing down there?" Jones asked, visions of homosexuals dancing in his head.

"I know what they do, Captain. They sit around and listen to classical music!"

Jones looked dubious. "Friendship with an enlisted man certainly shows poor judgment, but I don't see—"

"There's one more thing," Proper said. "When I was checking the typewriters in the after wardroom I had occasion to pass by Ensign Joyce's bunk. Captain, sir, he has a bulkhead smack full of subversive pictures over his bed!"

The Poet Stands Corrected

"Do I understand you correctly, Captain? You want to know about the photographs I have over my bunk?"

Joyce sat stiffly in the straight-backed wooden chair next to the washbasin. His long, thin face looked longer and thinner because of the shadows in the room.

He and the Captain had already been through the business about Joyce's friendship with Boeth. "You know why I don't allow myself to become friendly with the enlisted men, or with anyone for that matter?" Jones had asked. "I'll tell you why. It's entirely possible we may come under atomic attack some day. You may remember that when a ship comes under atomic attack, everyone gets off the weather decks to protect against radioactive poisoning. Well, Mister Joyce, let me put it to you—what would happen if everyone was inside and the ship suddenly came under attack from enemy aircraft? What would happen is I'd send some men topside to man the antiaircraft guns aft, that's what would happen. I'd order these men to expose themselves to deadly doses of radioactivity, and I'd do it without batting an eyelash. Now this may sound callous to you, Mister Joyce, but I don't want to take the risk that I'd hesitate to send a man to certain death merely because he was my friend. *So I keep my distance*"—the Captain's eyebrows shot up to underscore the point—"and you'd do well to take your cue from me."

But quite obviously, Joyce's friendship with Boeth didn't interest the Captain as much as the pictures over the Poet's bunk.

"You understand me correctly, Mister Joyce," Jones was saying. He swung his legs onto the deck so he could face the Poet. "Among other things, I'm responsible for the morale of this ship—"

"Do you mind if I ask who told you about the photographs, Captain?"

"That's neither here nor there, Mister Joyce."

"It was Proper, wasn't it?"

"I said that's not important, Mister Joyce. What is important is those pictures. Now what about them?"

"It's really very simple, Captain. Some people collect stamps. Some people collect paperweights. Some people collect barbed wire. I collect photographs of people being killed. I have one showing a soldier getting shot during the Spanish Civil War. His body is being pushed backward by the force of the bullet passing through him. I have another of a South Vietnamese police chief putting a pistol to the head of a suspect and blowing his brains out in the streets of Saigon. I have a shot of the Nazis stringing up some partisans in Yugoslavia. There's a photograph of a beaming Cambodian soldier brandishing two severed heads. And another of two small children in a South Vietnamese village called My Lai taken just before they were gunned down by American soldiers. There is another I consider a collector's item—"

"I think I get the idea, Mister Joyce."

"Do you, Captain?"

"You're queer for dead people."

"No, sir, that's not it at all. I'm terrified of dead people. When my father died I didn't even go to the funeral because I couldn't stand to see him like that, laid out in a coffin with his hands folded and a plastic carnation in his lapel. You know something, Captain, I'd never even seen a dead body in my life until Wally tried to pull that one out of the sea today."

"Then I guess I don't understand, Mister Joyce. If you're trying to avoid the sight of dead people, I can see why you prefer the navy to the army. But then why all the pictures?"

"But that's precisely it, Captain." The Poet leaned forward, eager to explain. "Out here on a ship or in a bomber, ten miles from the target, it's easy to forget that there are people being killed when we shoot. It's all so mechanical, so impersonal. The computers shoot at coordinates on a map. It's easy to wage war this way because you never see the war. There's no morality involved. It's all a game. Everyone gets a certain amount of satisfaction out of playing well—coping with the mathematics and the mechanics involved and hitting a target you can't even see. But I want to remember all the time that there are people on the other end of this game—and that we're killing them. I want to feel sick to my stomach everytime I hear a gun go off."

"Will that help them any, or just make you feel better, eh?"

The two men looked at each other across a vast gulf. Jones reached down and hefted the flashlight, flicking it on with his thumb. He got a feeling of power from being able to touch something across the small room with the beam of light.

"Captain, I haven't expressed myself very well, I know. Maybe I can tell you a story that will explain how I feel."

Toying absently with the beam of light, Jones nodded. "Come ahead, my boy. I've heard a lot of things in my time. I suppose I can hear one of your, eh, stories."

"I remember," the Poet began, talking earnestly

and fast, "I remember once I was with some friends on a picnic. We were eating lunch when this little girl walked by with her mother. They were holding hands and the mother was very angry. I remember she said to the little girl—I suppose it was her daughter—she said: 'Now that's no way to treat a butterfly.' Something like that: 'That's no way to treat a butterfly.' I remember I spent all afternoon trying to guess what the little girl had done to the butterfly—whether she had torn its wings off or squashed it with her foot or swatted it in midair with her hand or pinned it to the ground with a bobby pin." Joyce lost some of his steam. "Does any of this make sense to you?"

"Frankly, I don't understand a goddamn word you're saying, Mister Joyce. I suggest you forget about these butterflies of yours and concentrate on what you were sent here to do."

"No questions asked, is that it, Captain?"

Jones nodded. "No questions asked. No conscience salved."

Joyce shrugged. "I won't argue with you, Captain. I stand corrected—maybe I am salving my conscience. But at least I don't pull the trigger. I have that going for me."

"But you communicate, don't you, Mister Joyce?" The Captain was suddenly very angry.

"Communicate?"

"You heard me. Communicate. As my communications officer, you communicate for this ship, don't you? And you do it efficiently too. You don't pull the trigger or give the order, I'll give you that. What you do is advertise you have a conscience by hanging photographs over your bunk. And when you go back to civilian life you'll boast that you didn't pull a trigger. You leave the dirty work to people like me who have always been there when the country needed them. Of course you're a fake, Mister Joyce. You receive and decode the messages that tell us what target to shoot at, and you make sure that I see those messages. You're part of the system and it's time you realized it. Do you know why I called you up here? Because for a moment there I actually thought you might be Sweet Reason. But you don't have the guts to be Sweet Reason, Mister Joyce. You're not worried about the people on the shore; all you're worried about is what people will think of you."

Jones waved a hand toward the door. "That'll be all, Mister Joyce. Just make sure you keep on communicating. And one more thing. Get those goddamn dead people off your bulkhead and put up some good, clean tit pictures, eh? You can consider that an order, Mister Joyce."

Boeth Peels Away a Shell or Two

"Tit pictures?"

"Tit pictures. He sat there playing with his phallus-flashlight and ordered me to put up tit pictures."

"Jesus, he's incredible," Boeth said, and he shook his head sympathetically and turned back to the hard-boiled eggs that the Poet had swiped from the officers' pantry. He rolled the first one against the side of the computer until the shell was completely cracked. Then he began picking at it with his thumbnail. The bits and pieces of shell that came away he laid out neatly on the deck—almost as if he intended to start in where all the king's horses and all the king's men had left off.

In the background the allegro from one of Bach's

Brandenburgs rippled softly through the small room from Boeth's tape deck.

"Maybe you should feel flattered," Boeth said, his mind more on the egg than the conversation.

"What do you mean flattered?" Joyce challenged. Obviously in a black mood, he sat with his back against a shore fire control console, his sloping shoulders hunched forward, his legs thrust out in front of him. "The neonautical John Paul Jones insults me and you think I should be flattered. Some logic."

"You don't understand." Boeth shrugged his heavy shoulders. The shrug was his way of giving ground during a conversation. It was something he did grudgingly, but his friendship with Joyce was what made life on the *Ebersole* bearable. "He's trying to track down the one man on this ship with a conscience and you're the first suspect he comes up with. So you should feel flattered. That's all I meant."

Joyce drew his knees up to his chin, exposing thin, hairless ankles. He reached over quickly and jerked up his socks, which were green. "Wallowitch says conscience is an inner voice that warns you when someone is looking. Out here"—the Poet waved his hand to take in all of Yankee Station—"nobody is looking, so there is no such thing as conscience."

Boeth finished peeling the first egg. He put it aside, took up the second and rolled it against the side of the computer. "You know something, Poet, the more I know you the more I realize how innocent you are."

Frown lines formed around Joyce's eye sockets. He remembered that Mariana had accused him of being innocent too—though she had been talking in a sexual context.

Boeth saw that the Poet was annoyed and shrugged again. "I'm not saying that innocence is anything to be ashamed of. I'm not saying that. It's only that the world equates innocence with profundity, and you do too. But innocence has no depth. It doesn't respond to the complexities of life with complexity of thought."

"But you haven't said why the shoe fits me. How am I innocent?"

Boeth looked up from the egg. "No offense intended—" he said with a smirk.

"—none taken," Joyce laughed. He had told Boeth about how the expression was bandied about in the wardroom and it was a joke between them. "No, listen, seriously, this is straight talk. Say what you think. How am I innocent?"

"Well, for one thing you have a very innocent idea about morality. You think morality consists of taking moral positions, when what it really involves is *defending* them. What I'm getting at is that you're basically a passive moralist. You wouldn't knowingly kill someone. But you wouldn't go out of your way to prevent someone from being killed either." Boeth bent his head toward the egg and began peeling again.

"You're a goddamn Jesuit," Joyce said lightly. "You're hairsplitting—"

"I'm not hairsplitting—"

"You're attacking me—" Joyce was agitated now.

"I'm not attacking," Boeth protested. "Don't be so fucking sensitive."

"Okay, criticizing. Is that better? You're criticizing me for renouncing the use of force as a means of persuasion—"

"As a means of defending morality—"

"Well, I admit it," Joyce said. "I admit it openly. I renounce the use of force because I can't be sure—nobody can ever be sure—to what end it should be applied."

"But don't you see, you're being innocent again,"
Boeth said excitedly. "That's not it, that's not it at all.
You renounce force because *you think the world is in
order*—" Now Boeth leaned forward. "Think back, Poet.
Do you remember the last contact we had with the big
wide world outside the *Eugene Ebersole*?"

"New York. Christmas in New York."

"And do you remember anything being out of order
in New York over Christmas?"

"I remember the sewer—the water gushed out of it
and flooded the street. I remember the neon sign
sizzling during the day and snapping off at dusk just as
the other signs flashed on. And the stoplight. I remember the stoplight frozen in go and everyone fighting to
cross the intersection at once."

Boeth shook his head. "That's not what I had in
mind when I said the world is out of order. What I had in
mind was Mariana." Boeth looked hard at Joyce. "You
remember Mariana, don't you?"

Joyce remembered her very well.

Ensign Joyce's Curriculum Vitae

She had a boyish face that looked handsome in
shadows but pale and puffy in bright light and short dark
hair that she kept fluffing with her fingers when she was
nervous. She was nervous now. "I was born on a Tuesday,
but I'm Wednesday's child," Mariana said.

"Wednesday's child?"

"Wednesday's child is full of woe. I'm full of woe.
That makes me Wednesday's child," she explained.

"Are you going to cry?" he asked.

"We've been through that," she said, annoyed.

"You looked like you were going to," he insisted.

She winced and put a palm flat against her chest and swallowed hard. "What's the matter?" Joyce asked.

"Something's stuck."

"What?"

"How the fuck should I know—maybe an emotion," she said.

They fell asleep for a while, or at least Mariana did; the Poet lay there staring at the high ceiling trying to remember what it had been like. Thinking about it gave him an erection. In her sleep she turned toward him and felt the erection and folded her hand over it.

They hadn't been able to find her until the night of their last day in New York. Boeth had been telephoning since they arrived, but there had been no answer. Once he got a busy signal, but when he dialed back there was no answer and he assumed someone else must have been calling at the same time. Then on the afternoon of their fourth day in New York she had picked up the phone. "It's me," Boeth had said, and she had quickly agreed to meet them for a concert that night. When they met, Boeth and Mariana did most of the talking; the Poet watched them, trying to figure out whether there was anything between them. In the end he wasn't sure.

At the concert she sat with Boeth, and Joyce had to settle for a seat two rows in front of them. When he turned around she looked at him without smiling, almost without recognition. Below them, standing alone in the middle of a large stage, his eye sockets wide open but his lids closed, an ear cocked, the violinist listened to his own music like a blind man. The only tenseness visible was around his mouth; his lips were pressed together as if there were no teeth behind them. Beads of sweat glistened on his sideburns during the saraband.

Afterward Boeth, Joyce and Mariana drank beer in a bar a few blocks from her apartment and she told them about the abortion. There was no transition; she just started to talk about it.

"The worst part was the cops. When I told them I'd been raped, they smirked and asked me if I'd put up a fight. How could I put up a fight with a switchblade pressed against my stomach the whole time? The cops were sicker than the guy who raped me. They asked all kinds of questions. They wanted every detail. Like did I spread my legs or did he force them open? Every time I answered they looked at each other and smirked. Later one of them asked me if I wanted to go out and have a drink with him—to unwind. That's what he said. To unwind."

Mariana sipped her beer. "I guess I didn't resist the raper enough to convince the pigs I was raped. And since it wasn't rape, I wasn't eligible for a legal free abortion. They were going to *make* me have the fucking baby. Well, fuck them. I heard about this doctor in Queens. Five hundred bucks for five minutes' work. You know what he did with the fetus. He flushed it down the toilet. That's what he did with it."

Mariana collected the moisture from the side of the beer glass on her fingertips and then rubbed them across her forehead. "I stained again this morning and ruined my last pair of underpants. Fuck!"

After a while Boeth asked: "Where'd you get the bread for the abortion?"

"I borrowed it from a bank—I told them it was for home repairs." That brought a laugh.

"How do you feel now?" Joyce asked.

"Empty," she said. "I feel empty. How do you think I feel?"

Joyce looked for the waiter and caught his eye and

ordered three more beers. Then he looked back. "You must have cried a lot," he said.

Mariana looked at him strangely. "What makes you say that?"

"I don't know. It's normal for people to cry after something like that, that's all." He studied the bubbles rising in his beer.

"Well, it's not normal for me. I don't cry."

"Why?" the Poet asked. When she didn't answer immediately, he said: "What do you have against crying?"

"I don't have a goddamn thing against crying," she said. "I don't cry for the same reason all people who don't cry don't cry; I'm afraid if I start I won't be able to stop."

They walked down Saint Marks Place through the slush, past a Salvation Army band surrounded by a group of hecklers, and turned right on Second Avenue. Two teenage girls, one carrying a sleeping baby propped on her shoulder, stood on the corner next to a snowbank panhandling, and Joyce gave the one with the baby a quarter. The traffic light on Second Avenue was frozen on green and cars and people were jammed into the intersection. They crossed in single file with Boeth leading the way and Mariana sandwiched between them. In the middle of the next block Mariana stopped to talk to two men shivering in a doorway. She handed one of them some bills and he handed her an envelope. When she came back to Joyce and Boeth, she was angry. "Fucking inflation," she said.

She lived in a fourth-floor walkup in an old brownstone just off Second Avenue. The front door to her apartment had three locks on it. Inside there was a living room with a kitchenette on one end, and a bedroom. The bathroom was off the bedroom. Boeth and Joyce sank into chairs in the living room; Mariana went to the bathroom and then came back and put on some Vivaldi.

They sat for a long time rolling joints and smoking, listening to records and talking. Boeth, fondling one of Mariana's two cats, described the race riot on the mess deck. He told about Ohm's daily betting pools and about how everyone smoked pot on board and about how Captain J. P. Horatio Jones made it his business not to find out about it. He described McTigue, who was his immediate boss, and Lustig, who was McTigue's boss, and told about the night baker, he didn't know his name, who played Nat King Cole cassettes all the time, and about Tevepaugh's single solitary one-man band. Joyce asked Boeth if he had heard the one about Wallowitch reporting aboard and demanding a transfer to a ship, and Boeth laughed and said no he hadn't heard it. Then Joyce told about True Love putting the sweepings in the XO's urinals.

Mariana asked if they liked the navy and they both said no, but Boeth said it was changing, said he had heard about a destroyer skipper who had sideburns and allowed his men to grow beards.

"It figures," said Mariana. "The strength of America is its ability to co-opt everything that's not in the mainstream. The kids wear long hair so the officers wear long hair and suddenly you think there's been a qualitative change. Are the guns on a ship more humanitarian because the men who shoot them have long hair?"

"The guns aren't," said Joyce, "but the bureaucracy is. Sideburns and long hair do something to the people who wear them."

"Bullshit," said Mariana. "A bureaucrat is a bureaucrat is a bureaucrat. The world is one big bureaucracy. If there were two men left in it one would ask the other for a government job."

Joyce said: "We wouldn't need governments if people loved each other—really loved each other."

"Oh we love each other all right," said Mariana, "but not at the same time. That's the trouble."

It was close to two A.M. and Mariana yawned. "It's late, and I'm stoned," she said. She looked at Joyce. "You want to get laid?"

Joyce looked at Boeth, who smirked and waved his hand toward the bedroom and said, "Be my guest."

"But I—" Joyce said. His face turned beet-red. "I mean I thought—" He was embarrassed at his embarrassment. "What I mean is I thought you just had an abortion."

Mariana laughed and told him he was innocent. "There are other openings in the female body," she said, and she led him by the hand into the bedroom. From behind them came the excruciating sound of a phonograph needle being scratched across the grooves of a record.

Afterward she disappeared into the bathroom for a while and Joyce heard her brushing her teeth. When she came back she propped herself up on some pillows. That was when she told him about being Wednesday's child.

A little after four in the morning she went to the bathroom again, and the sound of the toilet flushing woke Joyce and so they talked for a while. At one point she cupped her breasts, which sagged more than they should have for a girl her age. "Do you like my body?" she asked.

He said yes he did, yes he liked it very much.

"Shit you do," she said. "Well, *I* like my body. I like everything that's biodegradable."

Joyce laughed. "Everybody likes his body," he said, "and not because it's biodegradable."

"You *are* innocent," Mariana said. "*He* doesn't like

his body." And she motioned to the next room where Boeth lay stretched out on the couch. Suddenly Mariana saw that Joyce didn't know what she was talking about. "I thought you knew—about him, I mean. I thought, you being friends and all, he would have told you. Shit, that was pretty stupid of me—"

"You thought he would have told me what?"

"About *it*." Again she jerked her head toward the living room.

"What is *it*? What are you talking about?"

"Shit, why do you think you're in here and not him? Because *he can't*, that's why. You understand? He can't. He was born with a deformed penis. He was in and out of hospitals for grafting operations until he stopped growing. He's perfectly normal now physically, but he's convinced it's not normal, he's convinced it's ugly and deformed. He's been going to psychiatrists off and on for ten years, but he's never had a hard-on in his life."

"My God, he never told me—I didn't know—"

"Maybe I shouldn't have either. I found out by accident. I met him at school. He was getting a master's in physics and I was in comparative history. We hung around together for a while, you know how it is. I was pretty active politically and he sort of became active too, more or less to keep me company. One day at a sit-in in front of the dean's office—we were protesting against the university accepting government research grants—I asked him if he wanted to go to bed with me. It wasn't something we'd talked about, but it never occurred to me anything was wrong. Anyhow, I asked him if he wanted to make it with me. All of a sudden he got furious and told me to fuck off. Then he jumped up and ran over to the first cop he could find and kicked him in the shins. You should've seen it—he just hauled off and kicked. Wow! There was a photograph in the papers the next day of him being dragged away by two pigs. I guess the draft board took one look at the picture and that was the end of his student deferment."

Mariana asked Joyce if he wanted another joint and when he nodded she rolled one and lit it and pulled in the smoke and passed the joint to him. They smoked and talked for a long time. When the joint was gone the Poet looked around the room. "Who owns all this . . ." he motioned to the furniture.

"Not me. I rent the apartment furnished. I'll always rent furnished. I never want to own anything more than the clothes on my back. Property is theft. That's Proudhon."

"Well, I don't mind owning things if they're beautiful. A thing of beauty is a joy forever. That's Keats."

"You're a babe in the woods politically. In industrial societies, or their sequels, postindustrial societies, *things* aren't supposed to be beautiful; quantity is king, not quality."

"I don't know," Joyce said. "There must be a point where quantitative change becomes qualitative change."

"Shit, do you really believe that? That's what's known as the big lie. They'd like us to believe that. They'd like us to believe that if you make enough boob tubes and cars your life will change. But it just isn't so. You know what Lenin's last article was called, the last thing he wrote before he died? It was called 'Better Fewer But Better.' God, you really have a lot to learn. No wonder they made you an officer in *their* navy. You're brainwashed, you're propagandized, you're part of the Establishment, you're part of the problem. Maybe some day you'll do something to cut the umbilical cord. Maybe." And Mariana snapped the light off and went to sleep with her back to the Poet.

They woke once at dawn when two old ladies in an

apartment across a back alley started shrieking at each other. "The bitches," mumbled Mariana, "they never let me sleep," and she punched her pillow in irritation and slammed her head into it and went back to sleep.

In the morning Mariana got up first and pulled on her jeans. Halfway up the zipper stuck in her pubic hair. She tugged for a while, then tried putting soap on the zipper's teeth, then tugged some more. Finally she inched it closed. She tiptoed across the living room so as not to wake Bocth and took a carton of milk from the refrigerator to feed the cats. As she started to pour, the bottom of the carton split and the milk spattered over her feet and onto the floor. Mariana looked at the milk and burst into tears. Her crying woke Boeth, who sat up on the couch, and Joyce, who came into the room in his underwear.

"Why are you crying?" Joyce asked.

"I'm fucking crying"—she squeezed words out between sobs—"over spilt milk."

The Poet Nibbles at Some Food for Thought

The *Ebersole* heeled over sharply to port and the two young men in Main Plot braced themselves with their palms flat against the deck. The metal-bound loose-leaf book containing the *Rules of Engagement* slid across the top of the computer and thudded against the bulkhead. Then the ship steadied on a new course and Joyce and Boeth sat listening to the noises a ship makes at sea and the Brandenburg.

The Poet, who seemed emotionally drained, said softly: "I wish we could go to New York now. New York is a great town in the spring. God how I love the spring. It's the one thing I miss most at sea."

"It's the thing I miss the least," Boeth said. "I hate spring."

Joyce was genuinely amazed. "I never met anyone who actually hated spring."

"See, there you go again. That's what I mean by innocent. You make hating spring sound like an un-American activity. What you mean is you never met anybody who *admitted* hating spring. My God, millions of people hate spring, but they don't go around boasting about it because it makes them sound like a pervert or something like that."

"Why?" asked the Poet. "Why do you hate the spring?"

Boeth looked down at the deck, at the bits of eggshell spread out under his hand. He began to toy with the pieces, trying halfheartedly to jigsaw them back together again. "I hate spring because of the green. Green is for rebirth. Everything and everyone around is coming back to life—except me, and I detest that."

"They say April is the cruelest month," Joyce said. "You know the line?"

"I know it, but it's all wrong. August is the cruelest month."

"Why August?"

"That's when all the psychiatrists go on vacation, in August, leaving their patients stranded for four weeks without a couch. So to a lot of people August is the cruelest month."

Here it comes, the Poet thought, now he's going to tell me about it, about the hospitals and the psychiatrists and the physical scars they erased and the mental scars they couldn't do anything about. But Boeth only smiled bitterly and shook his head. He finished peeling the second egg and tossed it to the Poet. Then he picked up the first one and tossed it over too.

"Why do you peel them if you don't eat them?" Joyce asked.

Boeth shrugged. "I peel them to pass the time. Why do you write poetry?"

"I write poetry because I like poetry."

"Why do you like poetry?"

Now it was the Poet's turn to shrug. "I like poetry . . . I like it because the whole equals more than the sum of its parts."

Boeth laughed nervously. "I'd like to write about the war, but I don't know where to begin. Tell me something, Poet, how do you decide whether to use the present tense or the past?"

"You have to have a feeling for the difference," Joyce explained. "When you use the present—'He walks into the room and turns to the girl'—there is a real sense of immediacy. Nobody, neither the guy walking into the room nor the guy writing the line, nobody knows what will happen next. But when you use the past tense—'He walked into the room and turned to the girl'—it's obvious that the narrator knows, even if he hasn't said yet, what will happen next. He knows because the thing he's describing has already happened. See?"

"When you write about the war, which do you use?"

"The past tense. This creates the feeling that there are no surprises, that the narrator knows what's going to happen."

Boeth was interested. "What does the narrator know that the rest of us don't?"

Joyce thought a second. "I guess what he knows is that everyone who takes part in a war is a victim."

After a while Joyce asked casually: "You hear anything from Mariana?"

"I got a letter when we refueled from the *Taluga*. It started off with a headline in big red letters that said 'FOOD FOR THOUGHT.' Under that she listed half-a-dozen items. One said tombs for unknown soldiers glorify war. Mistrust anyone in uniform, soldiers, bellboys, Western Union messengers, that was another. And she quoted Henry James—about how a hotel spirit was coming to America which would make life like living in a luxurious hotel, with all the choices left to the management. Except for the part about luxury, it sounds like a description of the *Eugene Ebersole*, doesn't it?"

The Poet shook his head. "She never lets go, does she? Didn't she have anything personal to say—about us, about New York, about me?"

Boeth took a folded paper from the back pocket of his dungarees and began to read it to himself. "Yes, she says she hopes you're okay. She says . . ." Boeth's voice petered out.

"Come on, read it."

"She says you confuse her. One minute you put all your emotions on the table the way a child lays out cards for a game of solitaire. The next, you hold back part of yourself as if you were keeping a jerry can of gasoline in reserve. She says when you talk about politics your sentences sound like second pressings." Boeth looked up and shrugged. "That's what she says."

Joyce avoided his eye. "She's—"

"Very intuitive," Boeth supplied.

"I wasn't going to say that. I was going to say . . ."

But Boeth wasn't listening. He was back in New York waving and saying "Be my guest" and watching Mariana and Joyce disappear into the bedroom. He was slowly grinding the phonograph needle across the grooves and creating a sound that matched his emotions.

The Brandenburg tape ran out and Boeth got up and turned off the machine.

Joyce asked: "What do you think of this Sweet Reason business?"

Boeth responded too quickly, too lightly. "Whatever else he's doing, he's making time on this antiquated chicken-of-the-sea pass more quickly."

"That's what you said about peeling eggs."

"You have a good memory, Poet. It's one of the standards by which I measure things—eggshells, Sweet Reason leaflets, you name it. Every hour under the belt is another hour you don't have to worry about again." Boeth glanced at the clock on the bulkhead. It was five minutes to midnight. "Sometimes it seems as if all human activity is designed to make time pass more quickly."

"The trouble with Sweet Reason," the Poet said, "is he's not doing what he's doing well."

Boeth said: "Did you ever think, Poet, that if something is worth doing, it may be worth doing badly?"

YANKEE STATION

The Second Day

The Ship's Barber Sees Red

The ship's barber, a sour-grapes superpatriot from Detroit named Joe Czerniakovski-Drpzdzynski, spotted it first. His head thrown back, his Adam's apple bobbing against his taut neck muscles, he squinted up at the mast and poked Lustig in the ribs.

"Is it?" he asked angrily. "Supposed to be like that?"

Cee-Dee happened to be on the bridge as a result of a conversation he had with Lustig the night before in the barber shop, a converted paint locker back aft equipped with a used swivel barber's chair Richardson acquired in exchange for a potato-peeling machine and the musical services of Tevepaugh at another ship's picnic. The compartment was so cramped (Cee-Dee insisted on having some spare chairs and a small table for magazines) that there was no room to swivel in, so Cee-Dee danced around the barber's chair like a sparring partner, ducking and squinting and lunging and nipping nervously away as he went. A mirror hung from the bulkhead, along with an American flag, copies of the Declaration of Independence and the Gettysburg Address, a "God Is On Our Side" bumper sticker and a poster that said "Fuck Communism."

Arranged in a half-moon over the spare chairs—and looking like a homosexual's rogues' gallery—were eight framed pictures of various styles of haircuts clipped from a *Barber's World* Cee-Dee had swiped from the eighteen-chair shop on the Norfolk Naval Station. Actually, the pictures were there for atmosphere; Cee-Dee himself could only give one basic cut, a rounded-off, high-necked affair that left a tuft of hair falling across the forehead like the brim of a baseball cap. "Ain't nobody gonna take you for one of them friggin' college faggots when I'm through wit you," Cee-Dee would boast.

Cee-Dee always did the sideburns last—crossing the Ts after finishing the sentence, he called it. Standing directly behind the customer and squinting into the mirror to get the right angle, he would chop away with his mechanical trimmer, first on the right side, then on the left, then a touch on the right again, then a correcting smidge on the left until both sides had risen, like rungs of a ladder, to the top of the ears.

"Not too short on the sideburns," Lustig had said, trying not to move his head as he spoke. He was leafing through one of Cee-Dee's dirty magazines that, more than the haircuts, is what kept the customers coming back for more. The pages, worn thin and greasy from fingering, were full of garter belts and paraffin breasts—the kind of thing that turned Lustig off rather than on. But he studied them with the proper amount of intensity, grunting here or sneering there to keep up appearances.

"Enough, enough," Lustig had said, glancing at his exposed ears jutting out conspicuously from the sides of his head. "There's not much you can do with the ship rolling and pitching like this. I'll straighten them myself." ("What did you do—flunk sideburns?" Lustig thought to say when he reviewed the scene later.)

Cee-Dee had held a small mirror behind Lustig so that he could see the back of his head in the mirror in front of him. It was a touch that Cee-Dee had picked up from a $1.25 barber shop in Detroit and reserved for his officer customers.

"Looks great, just great," Lustig had said, studying the back of the head that was supposed to be his in the mirror. He didn't know what else to say.

"Whata cunt, huh?" Cee-Dee had said conversationally, nodding down at the girl peering up at Lustig from the magazine. "There's a cow on the cover, but inside is real good stuff. Well, they say you can't judge a book by the cover."

(Later Lustig thought to respond: "Some people can't even judge it by its contents.")

Cee-Dee had begun unpinning the sheet that kept some of the hair off the customer. "Hey, Mister Lustig, why did the XO put that note in tomorrow's plan of the day about no sightseers on the bridge?"

"Because the skipper was pissed by everyone and his uncle rushing up there when that plane went down today."

"I guess that means I'll never get to see the friggin' bridge," Cee-Dee had said.

"What do you mean never?" Lustig had asked. "Haven't you ever been on the bridge?"

"Nope, I never been. I been on the *Eugene Ebersole* a year come August but I never thought to go till I read you can't. Ain't that something. Closing the barn door after the horse's skedaddled." The aphorism was wildly inappropriate but Lustig didn't want to embarrass Cee-Dee, so he let it pass.

"Listen, Cee-Dee, I got the four-to-eight tomorrow morning. After reveille you grab a cup of coffee and come up and if anyone stops you, you say the coffee is for me, that I asked for it. And put three sugars in it, okay?"

"That's friggin' decent of you Mister Lustig, to go to all that trouble for me."

"Is it," Cee-Dee said moments after he arrived on the bridge, coffee in hand, "supposed to be like that?"

"Is what supposed to be like what?" Lustig asked. He and Cee-Dee were on the signal bridge along with two signalmen, Angry Pettis Foreman and Jefferson Waterman.

"The American flag—is it supposed to be like *that?* A friggin' disgrace, that's what it is."

Lustig followed Cee-Dee's gaze. He could see The Stars and Stripes shedding their wrinkles into the morning air. And he could see—"Oh my God Almighty"—that the flag was *upside-down*.

"What do you mean upside-down?" the XO yelled into the phone when Lustig woke him with the news.

"Upside-down! What do you mean upside-down?" Captain Jones fumed when the XO burst into his cabin.

"You know what an upside-down flag means," the Captain told the XO after the two of them had trooped to the signal bridge to see the apparition for themselves. "Good Christ, imagine if the people on the aircraft carrier had spotted it, eh? We'd have been laughed out of the war zone."

Jones covered his eyes to keep the vision at bay.

Captain Jones Puts a Foot into a Mine Field

"For your information," the Captain told the two black signalmen frozen in attention a few minutes later, "an upside-down flag is the international symbol hoisted by a ship in distress. More recently, it has become a symbol used by a small minority of sniveling, bleeding-heart, un-American fifth columnists for a country in distress."

Sitting at the edge of his bunk, Jones struggled to regain his composure. "This may be the work—" he began, trying to control the sudden twitching in his lower jaw. And he spat out the rest of the sentence: "—of Sweet Reason."

"Cap'n, can me 'n' Jefferson here say sumpin'?" Angry Pettis Foreman asked. He and Waterman had stood the four-to-eight signal watch, which made them, as the XO bluntly put it when he paraded them down to the Captain's cabin, "prime suspects."

Captain Jones thought of sending for Proper to conduct the investigation, then decided that they would take that as a sign of weakness. "Come ahead, son," he said.

"Cap'n, suh," Angry Pettis said, threading the brim of his white sailor's cap through his fingers. "Me 'n' Jefferson here we raised that flag, but we raised it right-side-up. I swear that we raised it right-side-up. Ain't that the actual situation, Jefferson?"

"That's correct, Captain," Waterman said. "We're not your Sweet Reason."

Captain Jones wanted desperately to believe that they had raised it upside-down by accident. That way he wouldn't be dealing with another Sweet Reason incident. "There are three possibilities," he had explained to the XO before confronting the two signalmen. "Either they raised it upside-down by accident, in which case the whole thing is simply an unfortunate mistake, or they raised it upside down on purpose, in which case one of them is Sweet Reason, or they raised it right-side-up but somebody else came along and switched it to upside-down, in which case we're right back where we started with this Sweet Reason business."

"There are three possibilities," Jones told the two black signalmen. And he ticked them off on the fingers of his left hand, careful to label them "one" and "two" and "three" so the blacks could follow the complexities of the situation.

Jones paced the cabin as he spoke and came to a stop squarely in front of his barbed-wire collection. For an instant his head looked as if it had been crowned with thorns. "Well," he said finally, "which is it?"

"Which is what, Cap'n?" Angry Pettis said blankly.

"Which is *it*— one, two or three?"

"Which was number tree again?" Angry Pettis asked, and when the Captain told him he said: "That's it, then. Number tree, Cap'n." To underscore the answer, Angry Pettis held up the third finger of his left hand.

Jones was about to dismiss them when he thought of something. "It was dark when you raised the flag, wasn't it?"

"Darker than a witch's tit, Cap'n," agreed Angry Pettis.

The Captain's eyes narrowed. "Then how could you be sure it was right-side-up, eh? Tell me that. How could you be sure?"

"Why Jefferson here, he held the flashlight while me, I clipped the flag to the halyard, Cap'n. I remembers them stars was up. Ain't that so, Jefferson?"

"That's correct, Captain," Waterman said coldly.

Jones took a turn around the room. Then he wheeled toward the two signalmen again and tried a new tack. This time he was looking for a motive. "Do you men think the navy is an equal opportunity employer?"

"An equal what?" Angry Pettis asked.

But Waterman understood the question. "No I don't, Captain. Most blacks in the navy end up as stewards or in the deck gang chipping and red ledding.

We don't get a chance at the technical ratings that could qualify us for good jobs when we return to civilian life."

"But you're not a steward—you're a signalman," Jones snapped.

"Sure, and when I return to civilian life I'll try and find a job teaching semaphore to Boy Scouts!"

Jones bristled. "Now just one moment. I'm not sure I like your tone."

At this point Angry Pettis figured it was time to get belligerent. Cocking his head, narrowing his eyes, relaxing into a spidery, loose-jointed slouch, he laid a restraining hand on Waterman's arm. "Cool it, baby," he said. Then he turned toward Jones and added quietly: "I told you we raised that flag right-side-up, Cap'n. Now there ain't no call for you to lean on us—*jus' cause we is black*."

Jones was instantly tentative; he began to select his words the way you choose footfalls in a mine field. "Your being colored has nothing whatsoever to do with your being under suspicion," he said, bringing his fingernails to his teeth. "I've dealt fairly and plainly with members of your race my whole career. There isn't a man aboard that doesn't know that, eh? I'm simply trying to get the facts in the case."

But Jones let the line of questioning drop.

Another Word from Sweet Reason

"I think it was Sweet Reason," Captain Jones told the XO when he and Proper turned up a few minutes later.

"I know it was Sweet Reason," the XO said, and he

handed the Captain a carbon (an original and four more carbons were eventually discovered) of Sweet Reason's latest leaflet. It had been found taped to the bronze "swift and sure" plaque in the midship's passageway.

Comrades in arms

("He must be a goddamn Commie, the way he keeps throwing that 'comrades in arms' crap up in our faces all the time," the skipper said when he and the XO went over the leaflet again later.)

For a while this morning, thanks to me, the *Ebersole* showed her real colors—an upside-down Amerikan flag. The *Ebersole* is a ship in distress. Yesterday morning we drew our first innocent blood, sinking a junk without warning and killing who knows how many innocent men, women and children. (Even Nazi subs let their victims get into lifeboats first.) Now our great Commanding ~~Lucifer~~ Officer, who risked this ship and the lives of all the men on board at Iskenderun (the tanker could easily have blown up when we were alongside) so he could advance his career, is ready to risk our lives again, is ready to kill again. And for what?

I ask you again, I beg you: Don't make war on innocent men, women and children. Don't let them make killers out of us!!! Let's put a stop to murder. Next time the pig captain of the *Ebersole* yells open fire, let him hear not the boom of cannon but the SILENCE of men who REFUSE TO KILL.

Remember, nobody can force you to pull a trigger!

The Voice of Sweet Reason

"By sweet Jesus, this time he's gone too far," Captain Jones said, crumpling the leaflet into a ball and flinging it into the wastebasket, a brass five-inch powder case with "DD722" engraved on it.

The reference to Iskenderun—which J. P. Jones considered, next to the action with the "patrol boat," his finest hour—stung. "Enough of this pussyfooting around, Proper. I don't care if you turn this ship inside out, I want Sweet Reason's scalp and I want it before the day is out. Do you read me, Proper, before the day is out."

The Captain was still shaking with anger after Proper left. "Except for Quinn's finger," Jones told the XO, "not a living soul from the *Ebersole* was scratched at Iskenderun. Risking the ship, he says, I calculated the odds. That's my job. They ordered me to render *all* possible assistance—those were the exact words, weren't they, XO?—*all* possible assistance. Well, I rendered *all* possible assistance and I put the fire out."

Jones clamped his eyes shut and lowered his voice to a tired whisper. "God, how I detest Sweet Reason," he said.

"Leave it to Proper," the XO said reassuringly. "He'll bring home the bacon."

More about the Incident at Iskenderun

With the help of a Turkish tug, the *Ebersole* had tied up alongside the burning tanker (the maneuver that cost Quinn the joint of a finger), and the crew had gone storming aboard to fight the blaze and keep it from spreading to the jet fuel bunkers. For a long while it was touch and go. Sailors had to hose down the tanker's deck plates, which were red hot in places, so that other crewmen could get close enough to hose down the flames. Working in relays they fought the blaze, which was confined to the tanker's engine spaces aft and the aftermost bunker, for fourteen hours. All the while the *Ebersole*'s searchlights, playing off the smoke and steam and flames and sheets of seawater and foam, gave to the scene the appearance of an erupting volcano.

In the early hours of the morning Ensign de Bovenkamp literally stumbled across the body of one of the tanker's crewmen killed in the original explosion. Shrunken to the size of a child's corpse by the flames, it was lying awash in oil and foam and seawater in a corner of the tanker's main deck. Only the penis, which was erect, seemed to belong to an adult. Glancing enviously at the erect penis, de Bovenkamp took two sticks and put them on the body in the form of a crucifix, then covered the dead man with a tarpaulin.

There was a bad moment at noon as the fire was beginning to come under control. De Bovenkamp was leading a crew into what had been the tanker's engine room. The smoke was still so thick that it was impossible to see the deck even with powerful hand-held lanterns. De Bovenkamp took a pole and began tapping like a blind man to find out if there was any deck left to walk on. For a few feet he could hear and feel the "tap-tap" of the pole; then suddenly he was hitting out at air. The deck grating had melted completely away. Just feet ahead was a sixty-foot drop into flames and molten metal. As de Bovenkamp shouted a warning he thought he saw one of the men on the hose lunge sideways and disappear into the smoke.

When word got back to the Captain he was furious—and frightened. He might have to account for his actions if someone had been killed in fighting the fire, and the second-guessers at the Pentagon could wreck a career on the strength of a lapse like that. Jones ordered an immediate head count. Fifteen minutes later the XO returned with the grim news that there were sixteen men missing. Almost catatonic with terror, Jones sent the XO back to count heads again. This time the Executive Officer found eight sailors and Chaplain Rodgers asleep in various bottom bunks around the ship, which brought the number of missing men down to seven.

"Jesus," said the Captain. He was in agony now, pacing the cabin and sweating even though the air-conditioning unit in the bulkhead was on full blast. "Pull everyone back from the tanker, muster them at abandon-ship stations and count again." This time the XO came back with good news: all 255 officers and men on the *Ebersole* were present and accounted for.

No one ever did find out what de Bovenkamp had seen out of the corner of his eye.

With the fire reduced to embers, another destroyer joined the *Ebersole* in Iskenderun and started pumping all the seawater out of the tanker that the *Ebersole* had pumped in. Amid a deluge of congratulatory telegrams, the *Ebersole* weighed anchor for the war zone. Later the crew learned that a seaman from the other destroyer had died of asphyxiation while showing a Lloyds of London man through the burnt-out fuel bunker in the tanker's hull. The second destroyer was relieved by a Turkish salvage vessel that came down from Istanbul. Two days after that, with the salvage ship tied up precisely where the *Ebersole* had been, the tanker blew sky high. The Turkish press, which printed some remarkable action photos of the tanker in midair, reported that the explosion sank both ships and killed sixty-two men. The Turkish government explained that somebody had apparently struck a match in the wrong place and awarded twenty-seven dollars to each of the new widows.

Until Sweet Reason brought the subject up again the last word on the episode at Iskenderun had been supplied, as usual, by Wallowitch. "What the hell a twenty-two-hundred-ton destroyer crammed with ammunition was doing alongside a burning tanker full of aviation fuel I'll never know," he told some of the junior officers in the privacy of the after wardroom. "If she had blown when we were alongside, all the P.R. guys in the Pentagon wouldn't have been able to put the Captain's career, not to mention his body, back together again."

Proper Comes Up with a Rain Check

A quarter to the hour had come and gone and the reliefs were nowhere in sight.

"Shit, fuck, fart, piss and corruption," shouted "Striker" DeFrank, a stringy, nineteen-year-old apprentice boilerman whose main regret in life seemed to be that he only had to shave once a month. Stimulating the sparse stubble with the back of his hand DeFrank added: "Shoot, how much longer they gonna keep us roasting down here?"

"We set till they tell us to get, then we get till they tell us to set again," Duffy yelled back good-naturedly. The senior man in the after boiler room and the oldest chief petty officer on the *Ebersole*, Duffy ran the watch with a firm, fatherly touch and an uncanny sense of the limitations of both men and equipment.

"Well, balls on Sweet friggin' Reason for causin' all this trouble," DeFrank yelled, but the sting had gone out of his voice and he smiled the ear-to-ear grin that always flashed on, like a neon sign, when the going got rough.

Snipes, which is what the engineering people are called, were like that—patient, plodding, not normally given to griping. They had become more or less used to conditions that made duty in any other part of the ship seem like a seaside vacation; temperatures that seldom dipped below 130 degrees even when the huge blower system that was the last word in air conditioning in 1945 was working; a noise level (when the boilers were not "down" for repairs) that forced them to yell directly into someone's ear to be heard; a workload that had them standing four hours on, four hours off, round the clock; and a water shortage that made it practically impossible to wash off the grime and grease and sweat that crusted on the skin like a scab.

But there was one thing that could set off a snipe. That was when the reliefs failed to show up on time. For four hours the most important thing in the boiler room to the men on duty was the large-faced electric clock on the bulkhead. The men made the time pass as best they could, baking potatoes stolen from the spud locker on the main deck in the water drum casing (where the temperature reaches 489 degrees) and wolfing them down with warm Cokes, taking a turn around the boiler room to check levels and temperatures and pressures. All the while their eyes kept darting back to the electric clock—to the hour hand and finally to the minute hand inching toward the moment when the hatch two decks up would be flung open and feet would show at the top of the ladder. Psychologically speaking, the high point of the watch was the end point of the watch.

Today, of course, there was no relief in sight. Soon after the eight-to-twelve people trooped on deck, Ohm's voice had come grinding over the loudspeaker. "Now all hands will" he said—breaking the sentence in the wrong places—"remain at their stations due to a"—break—"search of the ship being"—break—"conducted to turn up the"—gulp of air—"person or persons unknown responsible"—break—"for the seditious"—break—"leaflet."

Relief time, not to mention chow time, had come and gone, then noon, then 12:15. Finally at 12:25, a foot swung over the lip of the hatch and Proper started down the ladder. He had already worked his way through the after spaces—after steering, the after crew's quarters, the after magazines and storage spaces, Mount 53 and its handling room, the after head, the first-class lounge, the barber shop, the after wardroom, the post office, the damage control office and half-a-dozen other compartments that had no names but only letter and number designations. As the search progressed, Proper seemed to grow more confident. He knew the typewriter was out there somewhere; it was merely a question of narrowing down the area to be searched. In his mind's eye he saw himself, not as the uniformed cop directing schoolchildren at rush hour, but as a plainclothes detective, a faint "I've seen it all" smile playing on his lips, a forty-four-and-a-half ounce Smith and Wesson .357 Magnum in his spring-assisted shoulder holster, telling a suspect in a slightly bored monotone: "In keeping with the Supreme Court decision in Miranda versus Arizona, we're required to advise you of your rights, and that's what I'm doing."

"The Captain ordered me to search the ship and that's what I'm doing," Proper said matter-of-factly when his foot touched bottom in the boiler room.

"You'll have to speak louder," Duffy called back, funneling his words directly into Proper's ear with cupped hands.

"I said, the Captain ordered me to search the ship and that's what I'm doing," Proper yelled. "I want to start at one end—"

"One what?"

"One end—E as in echo, N as in November, D as in delta—one end, and work my way systematically through to the other. I want to check every space where someone could stash a typewriter."

"Help yourself," Duffy yelled, and turned back to study the dozen or so dials that told anybody who understood them how ridiculously inefficient the boilers really were.

"I'll start here," Proper yelled, pointing to a wooden footlocker wedged behind the access ladder. "Who has the key?"

"It's hanging on the hook over your head," shouted Striker DeFrank.

"If the key is right out here in the open, why do you lock it?" yelled Proper.

"Why shoot, so them's that don't know where the key is won't get into the box," DeFrank explained as if it were the most obvious thing in the world.

Crisply, professionally, Proper unlocked the box and threw back the lid. Inside were the boiler room's mess stores—forty or fifty spuds, a dozen or so onions (a boilerman on the midwatch made a fantastic onion soup), a few half-rotten stalks of celery, two jars of instant coffee and a coffee pot, seven cans of anchovies, a small plastic bag of truffles, a jar of chives, another of peanut butter, assorted knives and spoons and can openers and a well-thumbed copy of *The New York Times Cookbook*.

"What's this?" yelled Proper, fingering a small package of what looked like herbs and tobacco mixed together.

"Herbs and pipe tobacco mixed together," said DeFrank with a straight face. Duffy kept his back turned, oblivious to everything but the dials in front of him.

Proper had his orders about "tobacco." So far he had turned up at least a dozen satchels that the owners described as tobacco or snuff or "a kind of Italian sugar." Proper had also uncovered three revolvers, at least a dozen containers filled with whiskey or vodka or brandy, a small box of Spanish fly, a life-sized inflatable female doll, a seven-foot African spear and a shopping bag full of assorted women's underwear. He had come across his biggest haul—film shot through a peephole in a Piraeus bar called the "Black Cat Inn" showing a number of the *Ebersole*'s officers in compromising positions—hidden in a hollowed-out fire extinguisher in the barber shop.

"Whatcha gonna do wit them?" asked Cee-Dee, who had arranged for the films to be shot and was showing them at five dollars a head whenever he could get his hands on the crew's movie projector.

"I'm gonna come see them—gratis—as soon as you send me an engraved invitation," Proper had said pointedly.

"Sure, anytime, anytime at all," Cee-Dee had said, smiling broadly. "Take a rain check. Whatcha doin' tonight?"

Proper knew what he was after and he covered every inch of the boiler room searching for it. He looked behind the generators and made DeFrank unscrew the casing on the reduction gear. He poked into obscure corners over the steam pipes and dragged a stick through the bilges to make sure there was nothing there but water. Then he had Duffy shut down the blower system and crawled into the main duct to make sure there was nothing there but air.

Twenty minutes later—soaked in sweat, his face and hands and clothes grease-streaked, his head splitting from the unaccustomed heat and noise—Proper emerged from the boiler room to tell the XO: "That space is clean." And he plunged into the after engine room with another "In keeping with the Supreme Court decision" look on his face to continue the hunt.

McTigue Puts a Word in for Quinn

The XO looked up from his desk at McTigue. "What can I do for you, Chief?"

"It's about Keys Quinn, XO. I promised him I'd—"

The phone rang and the Executive Officer snatched it off the bulkhead bracket. He listened for a second. "Who's this Haverhill?" He listened again. "And who's Filmore?" The XO nodded. "Okay, I'm on my way."

Grabbing his hat, the XO brushed past McTigue and raced from the cabin.

"About Quinn—" McTigue called after him.

"The answer is no."

"But—"

But the XO had disappeared.

The XO Thinks of All the Angles

At long last the chickens were coming home to roost, J. P. Horatio Jones thought, and he took the steps three at a time and burst straight into the radio shack— breaking one of his cardinal rules about giving warning so he would not be confronted with the sweet smell of pot.

"Well, what they say, eh?" the Captain asked. "Is he coming? How long have we got? Did they say why us? Did he pick us himself? Or were we assigned? Goddamn it, XO, fill me in, will you?"

"From what I gather from Commander Filmore, who is the Pentagon P.R. guy handling the whole thing—"

"You spoke with this Filmore fellow?" Jones interrupted.

"Not actually, Skipper. But I spoke to his aide, a Lieutenant Commander Haverhill, on the single sideband here. He says that Filmore says that the Congressman specifically asked to include us in the itinerary when he heard about the business with the Commie patrol boat yesterday."

"Wow!" said Jones, his enthusiasm bubbling to the surface. "All I can say, XO, is it couldn't happen to a nicer guy, eh?"

A few minutes later, in the privacy of the Captain's cabin, the two began making plans.

"How do we get him?" the CO asked. "Helicopter?"

"Haverhill says Filmore says he wants to be highlined over. It'll give them some good film footage."

"When? When do we pick him up?"

"They want us in approach position at thirteen-fifteen. They're recovering a strike group at thirteen-hundred and as soon as that's out of the way, we're to haul ass in and get him. They want to get off another strike at thirteen-thirty."

"Thirteen-fifteen—Christ Almighty. That doesn't give us time to pipe chow. What'll we do if he finds out the crew hasn't eaten, eh?"

As usual the XO had a scheme. "Listen, Skipper, people like that don't do much talking to ordinary sailors. When they do they always ask them what state they're from or what football team they root for or crap like that. And ordinary sailors know better than to do any belly-aching"—the XO chuckled at the appropriateness of the phrase—"in public. In any case, if he gets wind of it all we've got to do is let on the crew skipped lunch and donated the money to some war orphans. He'll eat it up."

"But the men don't pay for lunch."

"He won't know that, Captain."

"XO, irregardless of the obstacles you think of all the angles. Remind me to polish my superlatives when I write up your fitness report."

Both men were all smiles.

"Anybody else coming with him—a governor or a senator or an actor or anything like that?"

"Haverhill says that a journalist named Kobb (with a 'K') is coming over too. But there's nothing to worry about because he's on our side. That's what Haverhill says Filmore says. Oh, and Haverhill says he and Filmore are coming over too. Haverhill says Filmore will field anything that's tricky and for us not to worry. He says all we have to do is put the men into clean dungarees and have them smile and everything will be four-oh. Those were his exact words—clean dungarees and smile. Sounds like the pot of gold at the end of the rainbow to me, Skipper."

"Okay, XO, get up on the bridge and give me a course to put us astern of the carrier by thirteen-fifteen on the dot. And don't forget about the dungarees."

The Executive Officer was halfway out the door when the Captain thought of something else.

"About Proper—you'd better call him off for a while. We don't want him underfoot at a time like this, eh?" And Jones nodded to indicate he was making an important point.

Ohm Passes the Good Word

His lips moving imperceptibly, Ohm scanned the slip of paper the XO had handed him.

"Can you read my writing?" the XO asked.

"All except this BIPs," Ohm said. "What's BIPs?"

"That's VIPs," the XO explained patiently. "It stands for Very Important Persons."

"VIPs," Ohm repeated. "VIPs."

Ohm pulled the microphone close to his lips and flipped on the switch. "Now relieve the watch," he said, his stomach growling as well as his voice. "Now the twelve to sixteen is on deck." Then Ohm started to read from the slip of paper. "Now all hands are"—break— "informed that the ship is"—break—"expecting BIPs on board this"—break—"afternoon. All hands are further"—gulp of air—"informed that they are to change into"—break—"clean dungarees, clean"—break— "workshirt and clean white hats before"—another gulp of air—"thirteen hundred hours." Click.

The Ebersole *Plays Host to Some Very Important Personages*

The Kobb with a "K," it turned out, was the syndicated Washington columnist Lizzy Kobb ("Kobb's Korner"), and the first words out of her mouth as she stepped from the bo's'n's chair onto the *Ebersole's* deck were: "Hey, sailor, where can a lady pee around here?"

The sailor she was addressing was none other than the Executive Officer, and he was startled by the question as well as the questioner—a slightly heavy but handsome woman in her late thirties or early forties dressed in combat boots and marine fatigues clingy enough to make it apparent that she wore no bra and had reasonably solid breasts.

"I beg your pardon," the XO said, flustered and coloring. And for lack of anything better to do he saluted and repeated the question: "Where do you pee around here?"

"Pee," Lizzy Kobb explained sweetly, "as in natural bodily function."

Not a moment too soon Filmore, the Pentagon's P.R. specialist, came to the rescue. Sliding off the bo's'n's chair right behind Lizzy Kobb, he patted her on the ass with his left hand and offered the XO his right.

"Don't let her intimidate you," Filmore said. "She's got the fastest typewriter and the dirtiest mouth in Washington, but she knows the score. Don't you, Lizz old girl? I take it you're the XO. You've got four more coming: the Congressman's Filipino steward, a navy photographer, one of my lackeys named Haverhill and last but by no means least, the senior representative from the sovereign state of North Carolina, Everett Oakwood Partain."

Commander Whitman Filmore came equipped with an imposing personality and a deft touch; he was, he often told friends, a guy who could put English on anything. A bluff, heavy-boned three-striper with cheeks the color of polished apples, Filmore thought of himself as the last remaining sovereign in the world—a public relations man on assignment. In sixteen years in the navy he had never served on a ship, but he had been around the Pentagon so long he was not awed by admirals or senators, an attribute that left him a leg up in dealing with line officers of whatever rank. As for non-navy types, Filmore spent arduous hours studying their personalities and figuring out how to handle them. Lizzy's weakness, he had long ago discovered, was that she wanted to be taken at face value; she despised anyone who tried to dig under the surface to search for the woman beneath. And so Filmore, taking her at face value, treated her as one of the boys.

"If you have to pee, Lizz old girl, then rub your pretty legs together to keep up the circulation and hang in there. Now, XO, if you can prevail on these men here to take their eyes off Lizzy's boobs, we can bring the rest of the contingent across and put this show on the road. What d'you say, fella, huh?" And Filmore clapped the XO on the back to establish the fact that they were, after all, on the same team. "My philosophy and my modus operandi are the same," Filmore had once lectured a group of junior Pentagon P.R. staffers. "Make 'em feel like teammates and you're bound to score."

Ten minutes later the senior representative from North Carolina made his entrance.

"Hold it about two yards out," Filmore shouted, directing the sequence from the *Ebersole's* deck. "Right there. Okay, Yancy, start shooting." With Haverhill on the sound equipment and photographer's mate Yancy on the movie camera, Partain jiggled over on the highline. In the thirty-five-second tape that the Pentagon later distributed to the networks, the moment came across with dramatic intensity. "Somewhere off the enemy coast, Representative Partain—on a special fact-finding tour for the President—visits one of the greyhounds of the fleet," the voice-over intoned. There, slightly out of focus behind the Congressman, was the aircraft carrier with its jets poised on the flight deck for the next strike against the enemy mainland. And in the background the audience could hear the sound of Tevepaugh's electric guitar rippling off a cacophonous hard-rock rendition that was recognizable—but only barely—as "Dixie."

"On behalf of the officers and men of the *Eugene F. Ebersole,* welcome aboard, sir," the XO said, saluting smartly as the bo's'n's chair deposited Partain on the deck.

"Mighty fine, son, mighty fine," replied Partain, smiling broadly and shaking every hand in sight—the camera was still grinding—as if he were priming pumps.

"Mighty fine what?" prompted Filmore, who was off camera and knew that his voice could be edited out.

"Mighty fine to be a-visitin' the fightin' men who so recently and so heroically been in the thicka action."

The smile on the Congressman's face evaporated and he looked around with a skeptic's eye. "This heah is a God-awful small vessel, Filmore. You-all sure we want to commence with this?"

The camera was still recording the scene, but Representative Partain knew every bit as much as Filmore about editing.

"Congressman," said Filmore—applying English, "this ship's been floating since nineteen forty-four, which if I recall correctly was your fourth year in the House of Representatives. I suspect it will be floating long after you've left too, and I don't expect *that* to happen for quite a while yet."

"Well, Ah reckon," chuckled Partain, pleased with the compliment. "Let's git on with it."

Everett Oakwood Partain's Curriculum Vitae

North Carolina's senior Democratic representative was sixty-two or sixty-three years old, he didn't know which. His father, a small-time still operator who had worked the reaches of the Catawba near Asheville in the Great Smoky Mountains, could never remember whether Everett had been born before Lucius and after Calvin, or before Calvin and after Georgina. "Ah reckon it was 'roun' the time that this heah Willum Bryan lost out to McKinley," was the closest that the old man could come when his son tried to pin him down.

"Don't mattah none," the Congressman always told reporters. "Ah had horse sense afore Ah was knee-high and that's all that counts in mah cornah of God's green earth."

Partain, who had gone on record recommending the use of nuclear weapons to end the war, was one of the best friends the military services had on Capitol Hill. He was, accordingly, wined and dined and toasted and chauffeured around in air force jets and army limousines and navy yachts; in the course of three decades in Washington, he had developed backslapping relationships with practically every flag rank officer in the Pentagon. Yet during all those years nobody ever quite figured out what made Everett Oakwood Partain run. "Ah had to hustle to stay alive when Ah was a mite," he once explained. "Why do Ah keep a-hustlin'? Ah guess you-all could chalk it up to force-a habit."

He believed in God and country and free enterprise, that much was clear, but there was considerable controversy over what order he put them in. He grew up with the notion that competition was a law of nature, and meandered through adulthood more concerned with the pecking order than the social order. "If'n theah was no peckin' ordah," he told a local chamber of commerce group, "everybody and his uncle would be a-pushin' and a-shovin' 'roun' the barnyard. Now is some cornahs of the world that theah goes undah the name of chaos."

Economically, Partain leaned toward the belief that the United States was a meritocracy in which success was determined by strength of character and hard work. When pressed, he allowed as how the basic unit of American life wasn't so much the family as the factory, as how the essential institution of American life wasn't so much marriage as the marketplace. To critics who argued that the marketplace was no longer relevant because the country had turned into an uncontrollable corporate state, Partain replied: "Bull."

Above all Everett Oakwood Partain was a firm believer in America, a bouillabaisse whose ingredients he identified as "radio evangelists shoutin' 'Glory be to Jay-sus' and Rural Free Delivery and plain folk rockin' on the front porch and dollah watahmellons and bullfrogs and collards and 'C' for colored after names in the phone book."

Filmore Asks the Captain for a Favor

With Captain Jones, the XO, Lizzy Kobb and Filmore in tow and Yancy's camera grinding away, Partain started out with a turn around the main deck, chatting amicably with the sailors, including the black ones, he passed along the way.

"What state you-all from, son?" he would ask.

"Texas, sir."

"Great state, Texas," the Congressman would say, pumping the man's hand. "Ah suspect that makes you a Dallas Cowboy fan. Great team, the Dallas Cowboys." And on to the next man, who turned out to be Gunner's Mate First Quinn, fresh from repairing Mount 52.

"What state you-all from, son?"

"Beg pardon, sir?" said Quinn.

"The Congressman asked what state you're from, Quinn?" prompted Jones.

Quinn glanced uneasily at the Captain as he spoke to the Congressman. "I'm not really from any state, sir. I live on the *Ebersole*. When the ship's in Norfolk, I'm from Virginia. When she's in Newport, I'm from Rhode Island. When she's in for repairs at the Brooklyn Navy Yard, I'm from New York. When she's in—"

"But when you leave the ship, where do you go?" Partain interrupted.

"I never leave the *Ebersole*, sir—at least I haven't up to now. I haven't been off except for a beer or a movie in twenty-four years."

"Cut," Filmore ordered Yancy.

Partain stared at Quinn as if he were insane, shook

his head imperceptibly and stalked off in search of another sailor to ask: "What state you-all from, son?"

"It takes all kinds," Lizzy Kobb whispered to the XO, pressing her breasts into his arm as she leaned toward his ear.

"Can I see you a second, Captain?" Quinn asked as the skipper started down the deck after Partain. "It's about my keys and my application for—"

"Later, Quinn," hissed Jones, "see me later." And he raced after the Congressman.

Filmore spent a good deal of time organizing the photographic end of the visit. He set up one shot of a beaming Captain Jones handing a blue "Swift and Sure" baseball cap to the Congressman under the muzzle of the five-inch gun that fired the shot that sank the enemy patrol boat. And he turned up a couple of sailors who claimed to be from North Carolina, borrowed a few medals and had the Congressman pin them on their chests. Then there was the obligatory footage of Partain, tray in hand, waiting his turn on the chow line like any other person on the ship. ("Fawh as Ah'm concerned, being a *U*-nited States congressman don't rate me the privledge of going to the head of the line, not when the line is composed of American fightin' men, nosirree," Partain was quoted as saying.) Since dinner was still a long way off Filmore had to round up some off-duty sailors and stick trays in their hands to pose the scene.

"All this seems a mite tame," Congressman Partain complained to Filmore after the chow line take. "Ah mean we don't stand much of a chance with a chow line shot, do we? Now if'n we could mosey up to the coast and squeeze off a few pot shots at the enemy . . ."

"He wants to what?" Jones said when Filmore brought up the idea.

"Captain, let me fill you in on the facts of life,"

Filmore said. "The Congressman isn't here for his health. He's committed to the military, and he wants to demonstrate to the people back home the vital role the military plays out here. But to get into the living rooms of the people back home, to get into those homes during prime time, we've got to get past an effete corps of impudent snobs—that small clique of eastern television executives, most of whom are against the war and suspicious of the military. These executives are like a turnstile. To get past them we've got to stick the right coin in. And the right coin is film footage that has action with a capital 'A' in it."

"But I can't simply haul ass and fire at the coast," Jones said. "I have to get permission and a target assignment and coordinates and a spotter helicopter and some standby jets in case we run into counterfire and need to call in a protective reaction strike. It's an involved production requiring a considerable amount of preparation."

"Captain, believe me, I can arrange it—as long as I can say you're willing."

"Willing? Jesus Christ, I'm delighted."

Filmore Pulls a Few Strings

"Flanks," Whitman Filmore was fond of saying, "are every bit as crucial in public relations as they are in war." Accordingly, the first thing he did on any operation was to protect them.

"Now the Congressman doesn't want you to lay on anything special just for his sake, you understand," Filmore radioed the flag operations officer. "But he thought if you have something lined up for this afternoon, you might be able to let the *Ebersole* go in and do the firing, huh, so he could get a first-hand idea of what we're up against out here. Over."

"Roger, Filmore, I read you," the operations officer replied. He had one of those monotonous "This is your captain speaking" voices common on commercial aircraft. "We usually shoot in the morning to keep the sun at our backs, but I'm sure something can be worked out without too much strain. Stand by, will you? Over."

"Roger, standing by," Filmore said.

The long, tedious process of selecting a relatively safe target so as not to endanger the Congressman's life, working up the coordinates, getting permission from higher authority for the shoot, dispatching a helicopter to spot the fall of shots and positioning an aircraft carrier so that it could provide jet fighter cover on short notice took seven minutes.

"Like I said, Filmore, no sweat," this-is-your-captain-speaking radioed back. "The Admiral is happy to be of service."

Jones Puts the Show on the Road

Things moved rapidly once the target assignment came in over the teletype. As the *Ebersole* heeled over and headed toward the thick gray smudge on the horizon that was the coastline, an OH-6 "Loach" recon helicopter, its rotor blades beating the air like a panicky sparrow, hovered over the destroyer's fantail to pick up the spotter.

"Since when do we supply the spotter?" demanded

Lustig when the XO told him to assign someone to the job. Usually the helicopter pilot or one of his crewmen did the spotting.

"It was the P.R. guy's idea," explained the Executive Officer. "He wants some footage of the chopper lifting off one of our men. Says it will dramatize how close we are to the war. Listen, I have enough trouble as it is. Now don't *you* give me a hard time."

"Jesus fucking shit, why me?" demanded Chief McTigue, who didn't have the slightest desire to get that close to the war.

"Because you're the only one around here who knows how to spot the fall of shot, Chief," Lustig explained. "Come on, don't give me a hard time."

And so, as Yancy's camera took in the scene, McTigue was strapped into a canvas harness, plucked off the *Ebersole's* fantail and cranked up through the trap door into the helicopter, which rocked off like a pendulum toward the coastline.

"What-all we gonna be shootin' at heah, Cap'n?" Partain asked. The Congressman, Lizzy Kobb, and Filmore were standing on the signal bridge peering after the helicopter, now only a flyspeck blending into the thickening coastline.

"The target assignment, Senator—"

"He's not a senator yet, Captain Jones," Lizzy Kobb said drily. The Captain had stumbled across an old joke.

"Don't wanna be either," muttered Partain. "Only advantage is you don't hafta mess with the voters so often. Ah'd as soon mess." Partain hadn't had a serious political opponent in his district since he won his first election in 1940. Nowadays, with fifty percent of the district payroll coming from military installations or civilian defense plants filling lucrative government contracts, he didn't even bother to campaign anymore.

"I beg your pardon, Congressman. No offense intended," said Jones.

"Don't fret, son," said Partain. "None taken."

Jones began again. "The target, Congressman, is—— ——, a small town that straddles route ten, which is one of their main thoroughfares down south. I say that so you can see how important this assignment is. According to our intelligence information, there is a truck depot at the western end of the town just beyond some thatched huts. It's incredible, I know, but that's how most of these Communists live, in thatched huts. Now what we're going to do is stand off the coast about three miles and overshoot the town and then walk the spotting shots back on down till they're smack in the middle of the depot. That way we'll avoid the civilians— or at least most of them. When the spotter tells us we're hitting the depot, we'll open up with everything we have. That's called firing for effect."

"Will we be able to see the target, Captain?" asked Lizzy Kobb.

Jones shook his head. "—— ——is four miles inland, so we won't be able to see or hear the shells land. That's what the spotter's for. He radios back when they land and tells us where they land. I'm afraid it's all rather workaday dull, but it's the kind of job you've got to tackle, glamour or no, to keep the pressure on the enemy." Jones nodded to underscore the point.

"Well, seein' those gray barrels a-pointin' at the shore and a-shootin' will be excitin' enough for me."

The coastline loomed larger now and features began to stand out in the landscape—a two-story blockhouse on top of a rise, a pale-green swamp at the edge of the sea, a solitary white cloud hovering like the top of a mushroom over a mangled tree.

"Perhaps the Captain here can give us an idea of the

technical end of the shoot," said Filmore. "For example, who gets the information the spotter sends back? And who actually pulls the trigger?"

"We'll hear the spotter's voice coming over a speaker on the bridge, of course," Captain Jones explained. "But essentially his information is for Main Plot. The firing is done in Main Plot—"

"Don't the people in the gun mounts pull the trigger?" asked Lizzy Kobb. "I always thought the people at the guns pulled the trigger."

"They can, Miss Kobb, but in this instance they don't. Generally speaking, when we see what we're shooting at—such as the Commie patrol boat yesterday morning—we get the range and bearing to the target from the director which is right over your heads, right up there. And the director officer, that's our Mister Wallowitch, pulls the trigger which fires all six of our five-inch guns at once in salvo. But when we don't see the target—which is the case this afternoon—the range and bearing to the target are taken initially from a navigational chart and fed into the computer in Main Plot, which then keeps the guns pointing at the target as we move through the water. On the order to commence fire, the Main Plot officer—in this case a young seaman—pulls a remote control trigger firing the spotting rounds. When the spotting rounds are on target we open up in salvo. That's roughly how we operate."

"Ah see," said Partain.

"Uh huh," said Filmore.

"We're getting close to the coast, Captain," said Lizzy Kobb. "What's next on the agenda?"

"My navigator, who is also my Executive Officer, will advise me to come right to a course paralleling the shore. He's probably already taken the initial range and bearing to the target from the navigation chart and sent it down to Main Plot. When we come right and steady on the new course, we'll load the guns. My gunnery officer—Mister Lustig there, the one with the headset—will tell me when the mounts are ready to shoot. And I'll order them to commence fire."

"Captain, this may sound insanely naive, but how do guns shoot?" asked Lizzy Kobb.

"I'm not sure I understand?" said Jones. "They shoot when someone pulls the trigger."

"No, no. What I mean is what actually happens when you pull a trigger? What makes the bullet go all that way and explode when it gets there?"

"Captain, sir," the XO called, sticking his head out of the pilot house. "About four minutes." He winked at Lizzy Kobb and she winked back.

"Right, XO. Just have the helmsman come around when you're ready, eh?"

Jones squinted at the coastline. "What makes guns shoot? Ever use a pressure cooker, Miss Kobb?"

"Are you kidding? There were always stories in the newspapers about the damn things exploding."

"Yes, that's it exactly. Our guns are something like pressure cookers. We put a twenty-four-pound powder case in the barrel of each gun behind the projectile, or bullet, if you will. Then we detonate the powder case with a 440-volt electric spark. The guncotton and gunpowder in the powder case disintegrate, generating a large volume of hot gas in a confined space. The gas has no place to go but straight out the barrel, and so that's where it goes—pushing the fifty-four-pound projectile ahead of it. Something like when the pressure built up in your pressure cooker—remember, a lot of gas in a confined space—and shot off that weighted gadget on the cover into someone's face. If we want to we can lob one of these five-inch projectiles nine and a half miles, though for accuracy's sake we like to keep the ranges down to around eight or even less. Now when the projectile reaches the target it can detonate on contact, or it can be detonated by a preset fuse in its nose. Either way the projectile explodes—again, disintegration and hot gases pushing off, this time in all directions— showering a considerable area with shrapnel. Not very complicated, eh? Even a child can grasp the fundamentals."

As Jones was talking the *Ebersole* swung to starboard and steadied on a course parallel to the shore, which was plainly visible now.

"Permission to load?" called Lustig.

Jones nodded and Lustig spoke into his sound-powered headset: "Stand by." It was the signal for the powder men to heft the powder cases onto the loading trays.

Three miles away the swampy stretch of coast that was under water at high tide lay quiet, still, like a mirror to the sky. Beyond came the ridge. And four miles behind the ridge, out of sight of the *Ebersole*, the helicopter with Chief McTigue on board flew in lazy circles around the rim of the target town.

"You know, of course," the Captain continued, "that modern cannon are rifled. Ours have forty-five lands and forty-five grooves to the inch. The rifling, which is something like the threads of a screw, gives the projectile a right-handed spin as it leaves the barrel. Actually—"

"Permission to open fire?" called Lustig.

Jones, intent on finishing his sentence, ignored Lustig. "Actually, the only gun in the entire United States Navy that gives a bullet a left-handed twist is the forty-five caliber pistol."

"Is that right?" said Lizzy Kobb.

"Um," said Congressman Partain. He was learning, as he later confided to Filmore, something more about guns than he cared to know.

"Captain, sir," called Lustig. "Request—"

"Wait one," Jones ordered sharply, and turned back to his guests. "The rifling is what separates our modern guns from the old smooth-bore cannon that the navy used to use," he went on. "Of course the quality of the powder and the fire control equipment have changed enormously. But the rifling is what really makes the difference. We give the projectile a spin as it leaves the barrel"—Jones demonstrated with a twist of his wrist—"and this is what stabilizes it in flight. Makes the trajectories more accurate and more predictable."

Jones suddenly remembered that Lustig was waiting for the order to open fire. "Well," he said, "I hope that answers some of your questions. Now let's put this show on the road, eh?" He closed his eyes for an instant and saw himself standing on the embattled quarterdeck, pressing his three-cornered hat to his head, coolly leading his man-o'-war into harm's way. Jones opened his eyes and shook the daydream out of his head and barked: "Okay, Mister Lustig, let 'em have it."

"Commence fire, commence fire," Lustig called into the sound-powered phone.

"SHOOT, SHOOT," Tevepaugh yelled into the squawk box.

The dull boom of a single shot reverberated across the water as Mount 51 kicked out a spotting round. The hot brass powder canister clattered onto the deck.

"Spotting round en route," Lustig said into the hand telephone to McTigue in the helicopter.

McTigue's voice, excited and garbled, came back: "Jesus shit, you're short—you're . . . ort . . . you're in

. . . thatch . . . d'you read . . . huts . . . thought you . . . gonna overshot and walk . . . over."

"How short, dammit?" Lustig asked.

". . . are on fire . . . up five hund . . . read me over."

"Ah reckon you bagged somethin', Cap'n," said Partain. "Looka-there."

A thin wisp of brown-black smoke spiraled up from behind the ridge line.

Lustig spoke into the sound-powered phone connecting him with the mounts and Main Plot. "Up five hundred and shoot again."

"UP FIVE HUNDRED AND SHOOT," Tevepaugh echoed into the squawk box.

Another hollow boom from Mount 51, another brass canister clattering around the deck.

". . . still in . . . fuckin' huts," screamed McTigue. "Burning . . . tinder . . . up . . ."

"Up what?" yelled Lustig into the headset. "Say again, up what?"

". . . hundred . . . ver."

"What-all's he sayin'?" asked Partain.

"You're garbled," yelled Lustig. "Say everything twice, over."

"Up up . . . three hundred hund . . . d'you read me, d'you read . . . ver."

"Up three hundred and shoot again," Lustig ordered Mount 51 and Main Plot. Another shot boomed out.

". . . on tar . . ." said McTigue.

"I think we're on target," said Captain Jones.

"Okay, all mounts fire for effect, fifteen rounds of VT frag per barrel, commence fire, commence fire," said Lustig.

"FIRE FOR EFFECT. SHOOT, SHOOT," yelled Tevepaugh.

All six of the *Ebersole's* five-inch guns belched fire
and smoke. The boom of gunfire, the hiss of recoil, the
clatter of brass canisters rolling onto the deck filled the
late afternoon air.

"Skipper," the XO called between salvos. "I think
we'd better come around again. I don't think we can get
all ninety rounds off on this run. We're too far down the
track."

The voice of McTigue, intermittent bursts of excitement and static, came over the bridge speaker again.
"Jesus shit . . . shooting short . . . huts . . . inferno
. . . what . . . raise . . . deaf . . . up."

Jones began to nibble on his cuticles. "Raise your
sights, Mister Lustig," he ordered, glancing nervously at
his visitors to see what kind of impression the show was
making.

By now the *Ebersole* was so far past her target that
Mount 51 on the bow could no longer swivel its guns far
enough back to bear and stopped firing. The port barrel
of Mount 52, angling back into the stops, was dangerous-
ly close to the Plexiglas windows on the open bridge.

"You'd better cease fire on Fifty-two," yelled the
XO. "The business end of the barrel is almost—"

He never finished the sentence.

In the port gun of Mount 52 a 440-volt spark ignited
the mercuric fulminate in the detonator which ignited
the guncotton and gunpowder in the powder case which
disintegrated, generating hot expanding gas which ex-
pelled the high explosive projectile from the barrel. A
fraction of a second later the concussion from the shot
shattered the Plexiglas on the bridge, showering the two
lookouts, Lustig, the Captain, Congressman Partain,
Lizzy Kobb and Filmore with glass.

Jones picked himself up off the deck and saw the port lookout walking toward him, his face a mask of bleeding scratches.

"Oh my God, my God, my God," moaned Lizzy Kobb when she saw the blood on the lookout's face.

"What the heyell happened?" cried Congressman Partain.

"Keep that camera going, Yancy," yelled Filmore. "Stay down, Congressman, stay down there. Let him get you getting up. That's it, that's it."

"WE'VE BEEN HIT," screamed Captain Jones, his jaw jerking spasmodically, his voice reaching for octaves reserved for sexual ecstasy. "WE'VE TAKEN A HIT. THE BASTARDS ARE SHOOTING AT US. RIGHT FULL RUDDER. ALL ENGINES AHEAD FLANK. TURNS FOR THIRTY KNOTS. GIVE ME EVERY-THING YOU'VE GOT. WE'VE BEEN HIT."

Jones bounded to the radio-telephone. "McTigue, d'you hear me, we've been hit, we've taken a hit. Do you see any counterfire?"

But McTigue had problems of his own. ". . . hit in rotors . . . day . . . mayday . . . going . . . God's sake help . . . help . . . hel . . ." There was a burst of static that sounded like a yelp of pain.

"What-all can Ah do to hep?" Partain said directly into Yancy's camera.

"Isolated Camera, Isolated Camera, do you read me, this is Elbow Room," Jones yelled into the handset. He was calling the aircraft carrier patrolling over the horizon. "We've taken a hit from shore fire. I repeat. We've been hit by shore fire. Request protective reac-tion strike. Do you read me? Over."

Three minutes later, wagging their wings playfully, the first jets flew over the *Ebersole*'s bridge toward the coastline. For the next two hours they came on, in flights of twos and fours, jets and prop planes with names like *King Kong* and *Devil's Advocate* and *Monday Morning* stenciled on their noses, each with its own assortment of technological ingenuity: bombs that exploded on contact and others that waited for the village firemen to try and dislodge them, rockets with infrared homing devices, machine guns that could saturate an area the size of a football field in a single burst, napalm that could sear a strip of land and incinerate every living thing on it. The whole thing was reasonably systematic. First the planes swept the swampland at the edge of the sea. Then they worked over the ridge, leveling the two-story block-house and the mangled tree. After that they moved on to the rolling meadow between the ridge and—— ——, cutting football-field-wide strips across it as if they were mowing a lawn. Finally, guiding on the blazing thatched huts, the planes zeroed in on—— ——itself.

"Ah declare," mused Congressman Partain as he watched the performance through binoculars from the bridge of the retreating *Ebersole*. "If'n only the folks back home could see this, they wouldn't say Ah been wastin' their tax money on *hardware*."

The XO Ignores the Handwriting on the Wall

The Executive Officer locked his cabin door, switched on the desk lamp and switched off the over-head, unbuckled his belt, dropped his trousers and jockey shorts down around his shoes and stretched out, face up, on his bunk. Lizzy Kobb stripped off her tailored fatigues, her wash-and-wear underpants and her combat boots and climbed on top, spiking herself on his member as if she were a receipt for services rendered.

There was some confusion at first as she went one way and the ship went another, and she had to spike herself back on again. But in no time at all she got the hang of it. Matching grunt for groan, the XO and the female VIP relaxed and let the destroyer work for them. They came off in salvo when the *Ebersole* plunged into and out of a particularly deep swell.

"Oh God," shrieked Kobb as she fell breathlessly against the bulkhead, where she found herself face to face with the only piece of art in the XO's cabin—a handwritten poster that said "Make War Not Love."

Lizzy Kobb Takes a Survey

Partain skipped the business about the "C" for "colored" in the phone books when he ticked off the glories of America to the *Ebersole's* officers at dinner that night.

"Y'all're out heah defendin' the American way-a-life: radio evangelists shoutin' 'Glory be to Jay-sus' and Rural Free Delivery and plain folk rockin' on the porch through long nights of smotherin' heat and poundin' rain and explodin' thundah. Good Lord, Ah can smell the damp air full of honeysuckle and wisteria and pine needles and cicadas right heah on the *Eugene*—"

"*Ebersole*," prompted Filmore.

"*Eugene Ebersole*," the Congressman went on without missing a beat. "And Ah fur one feel mighty damn proud to be heah, to share this meal with y'all, to tell you that behind the strident voices of dee-sent back home theah is the low, throaty rumble of people who say: 'God bless our fightin' men, God bless 'em one and all.'"

("Any questions?" the Congressman asked when Lustig re-enacted the scene in his mind later. "Sir," Lustig heard himself say, "just what is it that we-all are defending—the American way of life or the southern way of life?")

Sitting on the right of the Captain, Partain peered around the table as if he had misplaced something. "Ah wonder," he said, "if Ah could trouble one of you fine gentlemen to pass ovah the Russian dressin'?"

Before any of the *Ebersole*'s officers could lay a finger on the bottle of prepared dressing, the Filipino steward supplied by the Pentagon snatched it from the table and set it in front of the Congressman.

For a long while the officers toyed with the food and forks and knives and napkins and napkin rings in silence. Except for the snacks from the pantry refrigerator they had gone without anything to eat since breakfast, but the excitement of the late afternoon fireworks had drained their appetites. True Love served coffee. The Filipino, always alert, got position on True Love and placed the cup in front of Partain.

Filmore coughed.

The XO cleared his throat.

At the other end of the table, Lizzy Kobb smiled at the XO and then turned to Ensign de Bovenkamp. "They tell me you were a basketball star in civilian life— pretty well known one too they say."

De Bovenkamp fingered a stick of gum and began unwrapping it slowly. "Heck, I'm not nearly as famous as you."

Lizzy Kobb laughed. "What school did you lead to triumph?"

"It was Yale."

"Yale! Now that's interesting. Tell me, as someone out here with his neck on the firing line, what do you think of all those antiwar types who are raising such a ruckus back at your old alma mater?"

De Bovenkamp smiled self-consciously. "If I were back there there'd be one heck of a lot less of them, that's all I can tell you."

There was some appreciative laughter around the table.

"How long have you been in the war zone?" Lizzy Kobb asked.

"This is our second day," de Bovenkamp replied. "We arrived on Yankee Station early yesterday morning."

Miss Kobb waved her hand in surprise. "My God, with your record, I thought you'd been here months. Tell me"—she placed the tips of her fingers on de Bovenkamp's wrist and looked straight into his eyes—"what do you think of the war?"

The stick of gum was unwrapped now. De Bovenkamp slid it into his mouth as if it were a tongue depressor and began to work it around thoughtfully. "I feel we have a job to do out here, and it's not my place to ask about the whys and wherefores, but to get on with the job. I mean, the way I understand it, these Communists want to take over the world and right now they're picking on a little guy and it's our job to—we have treaty obligations that—heck, what I'm trying to say is—"

"I think I understand," Lizzy Kobb said sweetly. She pulled out an envelope and began to scribble on the back of it. "How do you spell your name?"

"De Bovenkamp, with a small d-e, then a new word, capital B, small o-v-e-n-k-a-m-p."

Lizzy Kobb turned to Lustig, sitting across the table from her, and asked him what he thought of the war.

"I really don't think about it much," he said noncommittally. "If the government says this is what we ought to be doing, I guess that's good enough for me."

"You trust your government then?"

Lustig looked startled. "Sure. Doesn't everybody?" ("I trust it—as far as I can throw it," Lustig thought to say later.)

Miss Kobb scribbled some more notes and asked Lustig how he spelled his name.

"L-u-s-t-i-g."

She finished writing and looked up into the deep-set eyes of the young man next to Lustig. "What's your name?" she asked.

"I'm Joyce," said the Poet. "J-o-y-c-e."

"You look like an awfully alert fellow," Lizzy Kobb said. "Tell me what you think about the war?"

Suddenly it seemed as if everyone were hanging on Joyce's answer.

"To tell the truth, Miss Kobb, some of us—maybe I should only speak for myself—*I'm* confused about what we're doing out here."

Lizzy Kobb scratched a line through the word "Joyce" and put her envelope and pencil away. "You hear that, Filmore?" she said. "You guys spend millions putting out the word and here is someone who doesn't know what he's doing out here. My God, wait till they hear about this back at the Pentagon." And she laughed at his embarrassment. "Come on, Filmore, why don't you tell him what he's doing out here." And she laughed again.

"Ah'd be proud to answer that question if'n Ah can." All heads turned toward Congressman Partain, all that is except Captain Jones who, cuticles to teeth, sat glaring at the Poet.

Nobody was better equipped to enlighten Joyce than the Congressman. He was on his fifth fact-finding trip to the war zone in five years—the last four at the express request of the President of the United States. After each tour Partain returned home to tell the network reporters about how "the tide is a-turnin'" or how he could see "a specka light at the end of the tunnel" or something of the sort. ("Stick to the clichés," Filmore always advised him. "It reassures people to hear familiar phrases.") In the privacy of the White House, Partain was more candid. "Ah reckon, if'n the pantywaists and bleedin' hearts would get off'n our back, we could hold out another year or so," he had reported after his fourth trip.

Partain was nobody's fool. He had read every scrap written on the current war he could get his hands on, he had attended secret war college briefings and think tank seminars. The Congressman knew the scenarios and options backward and forward. He understood as well as anyone what the President hoped to achieve, or at least what he would settle for. It was a grim insight into foreign policy and the Congressman usually kept it to himself. Today, for no good reason, he felt like calling a spade a spade and seeing what the reaction would be.

"Now I know you-all are housebroken, Lizz," Partain started out, "but for the record this is off the record. If'n anybody quotes me, Ah'll deny it, but Ah believe in the domino theory. Ah really do. Ah believe that if'n we back off heah, we'll have to defend ourselves on a line closah to home—and closah—and closah, till we stop 'em dead in their tracks."

"So we must have victory here, then?" the Poet asked.

"Ah believe we're obliged to, yes," the Congressman said. "Isn't that right, Lizzy?"

Lizzy Kobb smiled. "Would the gentleman care to define victory?"

"What she means, son, in her sardonic way, is that theah is no such thing as victory out heah," Partain said. "Lord knows we're a generous people." ("We're generous because we have so fucking much," Lustig thought of putting in—as always, later.) "But this heah is your proverbial bottomless pit, and theah is a limit to how much even we can provide without drainin' our vast resources. All things considered, we'll be Godamighty lucky to keep from sinkin' in any deepah."

"I don't understand," the Poet said. "If we can't win, what do we hope to accomplish?"

"Now see here, Joyce," the Captain interrupted, chewing the inside of his cheek.

"That's all right, Captain," Partain said, waving off Jones's interruption. He turned back to Joyce. "When anyone asks me what we hope to accomplish heah, son, Ah usually talk about defendin' freedom or aidin' a peace-lovin' people to fight off aggression, but between you, me and the wall ovah theah, that's pure bull. Buyin' time. That's what we're about. Buyin' time. What we're aftah is a decent interval—say two or three years—between our disengagement and the Communist take-ovah. That'll give us time to get the American people used to the ideah we got to defend the next line."

"Decent interval?" said the Poet.

"Decent interval," repeated Partain.

"More coffee, sir?" asked True Love, and he turned on the empty, mechanical smile of those who are programmed to serve by standing and waiting.

Proper Cashes in a Rain Check

Five men were squatting in the crowded barber shop. Four of them—Angry Pettis, Waterman, Tevepaugh and Ohm—had paid five dollars a head for the privilege of being there. The fifth, Sonarman Third Dwight Proper, hadn't paid a cent. Cee-Dee, the impresario of the show, was threading the film through the projector and telling about the Italian who had figured out a new way to beat the draft.

"How soon the fuckin' thing gonna start?" demanded Angry Pettis.

"Why don't you jerk off—makes the time go quicker," said Ohm.

Angry Pettis spun around to Ohm. "Watch your fuckin' ass, whitey," he snapped.

"Yeah, watch yourself," giggled Tevepaugh, "or Proper here will get the bright idea you're some kind of nut, like—what's his fuckin' name?—Sweet whatcha-ma-call-it."

Ohm, only too happy to sidestep a confrontation with Angry Pettis, glared at Tevepaugh. "Nobody accuses me of being Sweet Reason."

Cee-Dee pushed Ohm away from Tevepaugh. "Pick on someone your own size, Ohm," he said. "That's the American way. If you pick on somebody, you pick on somebody your own size."

Cee-Dee turned back to the projector. "Okay, okay, here it comes," he said finally. "Get the lights, will you, Proper?"

Proper switched off the overhead light. The emer-

137

gency bulb next to the fire extinguisher remained on, bathing everything in eerie red. The movie projector started up, spattering its image of the Black Cat Inn on the far bulkhead.

"She-it," said Tevepaugh. "Will you look at de Bovenkamp go. This here is almost as good as being in Pireaus."

The way he pronounced the name of the Greek port city that Socrates once frequented, it sounded like a venereal disease.

De Bovenkamp Laughs Last

Angry Pettis and Waterman were heading forward along the inboard passageway when they met de Bovenkamp coming aft. Waterman kept a straight face but Angry Pettis couldn't contain himself. As he stepped to one side to make way for de Bovenkamp, he started giggling, then burst into laughter. The mood infected Waterman and he burst into laughter too.

"What's so humorous?" de Bovenkamp demanded. But the two blacks, holding their sides now and gasping for air and words, just laughed harder.

A crowd began to collect. Suddenly de Bovenkamp found himself trapped inside a circle of laughter.

"I won't be made fun of," de Bovenkamp said, his voice rising in anger. The two blacks laughed still harder.

"Gawddamn, enough is enough," de Bovenkamp yelled. He was furious now. "I'll give you something to laugh about. I'm writing you two men up for insubordination. Let's see if you're still laughing when you're in front of a court-martial."

Angry Pettis and Waterman stopped laughing instantly. "You've got to be kidding?" said Waterman.

"You'll see if I'm kidding or not," de Bovenkamp sneered as he pushed through the circle.

"Motherfucker," Angry Pettis yelled after him, but de Bovenkamp retreated into the after wardroom and slammed the door on the insult. "Motherfucker," Pettis yelled again and started to follow de Bovenkamp into the wardroom. Waterman grabbed his arm and pulled him back.

"He'll get his," Waterman said.

Proper Comes Up with Another Suspect

Captain Jones was on his way back to his cabin from the radio shack when Proper, standing in the shadows, buttonholed him outside the chart house.

"Beg pardon, Captain. Can I see you for a—"

Jones threw up his hands to fend off a would-be mugger. "Who's there? Who is it? Come out of there." He backpedaled as he spoke, ready to turn and flee if the face that emerged from the shadow looked as if it were still in a shadow.

"It's me, Proper," Proper said, stepping hat in hand into the light. "I only wanted to see you for a second, Captain."

"Ah, you gave me a fright, Proper. What do you have to report? You've brought home the bacon, eh?"

"The bacon, sir?"

"That's a manner of speaking. What I mean is have you found the fatal typewriter? You did finish the search when the Congressman left?"

"I sure did, Captain. I been through every compartment in this ship, from after steering to the chain locker up forward. You know what I found in the chain locker, right under the anchor?"

"A typewriter?"

"A dead seagull."

"A dead seagull?"

"Squashed dead, with maggots and all."

"Uck," said Jones, and he turned his head away to hide the fact that it really didn't bother him all that much. He turned back. "So you didn't find the fatal typewriter, eh?"

"No sir, but I accomplished a lot, because now I know where it isn't."

Proper was beginning to wear thin. "Two days ago, damn it, you promised me you'd find out where it is, but all you seem to have accomplished, if I read you correctly, is to've found out where it isn't."

"In police work, Captain, that's a very crucial step. I've narrowed down the area where the typewriter could be."

"Since you've searched the entire ship and haven't found it, I'd say you narrowed it down to zero."

"No sir, not quite. There are a few places I haven't searched yet, and that's where the typewriter will be. I'll stake my reputation on it."

"As far as I'm concerned, Proper, you're risking nothing if you stake your reputation. Where is it you haven't searched?"

Proper leaned toward the Captain and lowered his voice. "There are eight spaces that were locked when I went around the ship, Captain—places like the after paint locker and the ship's store."

"Why didn't you open them?"

"Either the men who had the keys couldn't be found, or the keys themselves were missing."

"And so now you propose to search these spaces, eh?"

"Yes sir, that's what I'd like to do, Captain," Proper said. "The fatal typewriter is sure to be in one of them, and the man who has access to the space is sure to be Sweet Reason."

"All right, Proper, I'll give you one more shot at it," Jones said. "After the shore fire exercise tomorrow morning, get the XO to give you Quinn's key ring. You should be able to open the doors with that. And this time you'd better come up with something, eh?"

"Aye aye, Captain," Proper said. As Jones turned to go Proper tugged at his sleeve. Jones looked down at his sleeve with a pained expression on his face. "Are you trying to attract my attention, Proper?"

"Beg pardon, Captain, no offense intended. I wanted to tell you one more thing." Again Proper lowered his voice to a conspiratorial whisper and leaned toward Jones. "I got another prime suspect, Captain. I thought you might like to sound him out, sort of, the way you sounded out Ensign Joyce."

"Who is it this time, Proper?"

"It's . . ."

"Speak up, man, how do you expect me to hear something when you whisper like that?"

"It's Cee-Dee, sir."

"Who the hell is Cee-Dee?" Jones asked.

"Cee-Dee is Czerniakovski-Drpzdzynski, the ship's barber, Captain. I suspect him for two reasons. One is I personally heard him talk about draft dodging in such a way as to indicate he approved of it."

"And the second?"

"The second what, Captain?"

"Jesus Christ, Proper, the second reason."

"Oh, that. The second reason is because he's the least likely suspect on the entire ship, and in police work it's very often the least likely suspect that committed the crime. This Czerniakovski-Drpzdzynski goes way out of his way to show how pro-American he is. He even has a—begging your pardon, Captain—'Fuck Communism' sign up in his barber shop. Now it seems to me that anybody who is really innocent wouldn't have to go to all this trouble to appear innocent, if you get my drift."

Jones nodded slowly. "What kind of a name is—"

"Czerniakovski-Drpzdzynski."

"Czerniakovski-Drpzdzynski," the Captain repeated. "What kind of name is that? He's not colored, is he?"

"Oh no, sir, it's nothing like that. Czerniakovski-Drpzdzynski's a *foreign* name."

"A foreign name, eh? All right, send him on up and I'll see which way the wind is blowing."

Cee-Dee Comes Through with Flying Colors

Cee-Dee turned up fifteen minutes later carrying a sheet and his barber utensils in his right hand and one of his sex magazines in the other. "Evening, Captain," he said, offering the magazine to Jones. "Makes the time pass more quickly." And before the Captain could say a word he plunked the magazine on his lap, draped the sheet over his shoulders and started trimming the hair away from his right ear.

Jones was a split second away from yanking the sheet off and leaping out of the chair and giving Cee-Dee a piece of his mind when he remembered he needed a haircut and decided this was as good a time as any to get one. So he sat back and watched Cee-Dee, who was ducking and weaving around him, darting in with a clackety-clack-clack of the scissors, then leaning back and tilting his head to observe his handiwork. All the while Cee-Dee kept up a running conversation.

"Pleasure to give you a haircut . . . you know some of us think you're doing a bang-up job . . . big difference since you took over command . . . could you turn a little more toward me, that's it . . . friggin' Commies will rue the day the *Eugene Ebersole* turned up off their friggin' coast . . . hear you been recommended for a silver star . . . bend your head forward, please . . . some shellackin' we—"

"Tell me something," Jones interrupted. "What do you think of this Sweet Reason character?"

Cee-Dee stopped cutting and stepped back from the chair and stared at the Captain in astonishment. "You asking me what *I* think of Sweet Reason?" he demanded, brandishing his scissors. Jones sank back into his chair, afraid that Cee-Dee was about to lunge at him.

"You don't have to answer the question if it disturbs you," he said in a thin voice. His lower lip was quivering and he put his hand against the side of his face to stop it.

"No offense intended, Captain, but this faggot who calls himself Sweet Reason should be boiled in friggin' oil."

"In oil, eh?" Jones said, and the quivering in his lower jaw stopped.

Cee-Dee went back to cutting hair. "There's a rotten Commie apple in every barrel, Captain."

Jones had regained his composure by now. "I'll remember that, son," he said. "You feel pretty strongly about Communism, don't you, eh; what do they call you, Cee-Dee?"

Cee-Dee darted in and snipped away at the hair over the Captain's collar. "I sure do, Captain sir. I got a poster in the barber shop that tells it like it is. It says— excuse the expression—'Fuck Communism.' That's how I feel about it. I'd like to fuck—beg your pardon, Captain—I'd like to have *sexual intercourse* with every one of those filthy, atheistic Commie sons of bitches, every man, woman and child. They're all the same if you ask me. Scratch a Commie and you find a friggin' bastard."

Now Cee-Dee started in on the sideburns, raising first one side, then the other, then the first side again, then back to the other until there was nothing resembling sideburns left on the Captain's face. With a flourish he reserved for officers Cee-Dee whisked the sheet off the Captain's shoulders, and Jones promptly began fishing with two fingers under his shirt collar for loose hair. "Let me ask you one more thing, Cee-Dee. Someone—I won't say who—someone mentioned to me that you made some remarks about draft dodging in which you more or less indicated your approval—"

"Draft dodgers are scum of the earth in my book, Captain," Cee-Dee interrupted. "I don't hold with no friggin' draft dodging."

"So irregardless of what he thought he heard, whoever heard you must have been mistaken, eh?"

"Captain, the only thing I know about draft dodging is what I heard from this sailor in Naples. Like I say, this sailor has an Eye-talian cousin, see, who was drafted into the Eye-talian army. Well, it seems there's a law in Italy that mutilated soldiers from the war are entitled to the permanent company of an enlisted man, so this guy that was drafted, his father, who runs a brassiere factory, he

hires the mutilated veteran and puts him on the payroll
and this mutilated guy, see, *he* puts in for the kid to
accompany him all the time. So then the kid is drafted
and first thing you know he's ordered back home to keep
this old man company. Some deal, huh?"

"And the government let him get away with this?"

"The government didn't do nothing to stop him,
yeah."

"Well, if you ask me," Jones said, "it's still draft
dodging."

"With all respect," said Cee-Dee, "it ain't draft
dodging, it's just Italy."

Captain Jones Gets a Glimpse of Something Larger than Himself

It was evening penumbra—that space of time when
the sun has set but not yet extracted all the light from the
day. At sea this is star time—the few moments when the
navigator measures the angle between the horizon and
the celestial bodies. Any earlier and the stars would not
be visible; any later, the horizon would be lost in
blackness.

Sextant in hand, the XO was waiting for the first
stars to appear in the sky—Alioth or Dubhe in the Big
Dipper; Polaris, the Pole Star, in the Little Dipper;
Schedar or Caph in Cassiopeia; Sirius in Canis Major;
Procyon in Canis Minor.

"Nothing yet, eh?"

"Nothing yet, Skipper."

"That was pretty handsome, what he said before the
chopper lifted him off, eh?"

"Goddamn handsome, Captain," the XO said. "Sounded like he meant every word of it too."

"Sure doesn't hurt a man's career to have someone like that put in a good word with the Admiral, does it?"

"Worth its weight in gold," the XO agreed.

"See anything yet?"

Searching the sky as if he were looking for rain, the XO shook his head. "Few minutes more," he said.

"What do you think he meant by 'give credit where credit is due'?" Jones asked. He reached under his shirt collar and rubbed his neck. "Do you think he meant us in particular or the navy in general or what?"

"Hard to say, Captain. He's a smart cookie, the Congressman. Hard to say exactly what he meant. But he was pleased, that's for sure. Even Filmore was tickled pink. Did you see his face when they lifted off the cans of film? If one of them had fallen into the drink he would have dived in after it."

"Filmore said he'd get at least twenty seconds on Huntley-Brinkley and Cronkite with the stuff he had."

Captain Jones took off his baseball cap and threaded his fingers through his hair. As usual after one of Cee-Dee's haircuts, it felt as if there was none left. "Do you suppose he heard about, well, about our little problem?" he asked the XO.

"How could he have, Skipper? One of us was with him almost every moment. I'll lay a month's wages he never got a whiff of Sweet Reason on the *Ebersole*."

"I hope you're right, XO, that's all I can say. I hope you're right."

Both men were lost in thought for a few minutes. Then the XO laughed out loud.

"What?" the Captain asked.

"No, I was just thinking what would have happened

if the Congressman had been wounded. Christ, we're lucky, Captain."

"Filmore said he wouldn't have minded a scratch or two. Good for a few minutes of conversation at one of those Washington cocktail parties, eh?" And he and the XO laughed knowingly.

"Goddamn shame about McTigue, huh, Captain?" the XO said.

"Goddamn shame is right," agreed Jones. "Which one was he?"

"Lustig's chief—tall, tough, regular navy. Looked like one of those actors you see all the time in those old westerns. He ran Mount Fifty-one. Lustig says he heard the jets spotted the helicopter outside of the town. It was a burnt-out wreck."

"McTigue," Jones said thoughtfully. "I remember him now. He's the one who came back from the dentist with all the gaps between his teeth."

"That's him, Skipper. Lustig talked him into taking all the tartar out."

"Do I write his next of kin now?" Jones asked. "Christ Almighty, how I hate this drill."

"I got some missing-in-action forms in a BuPers pamphlet somewheres," the XO said. "It's got a lot of great phrases in it about how you knew the guy personally and respected him and stuff like that. With your permission, Captain, I'll work up a draft for your signature."

"Thanks, XO, you're a lifesaver. Hey, there, there, over there, see it—the first star, eh?"

The XO raised his sextant to his eye and, through a system of mirrors, brought the light of the star down so that it rested on the horizon. "Mark," he called, and read off the angle to the yeoman who was standing, stopwatch in hand, in the pilot house door.

The star was Betelgeuse, a giant red that is so vast you could fit the sun, Mercury, Venus, the Earth, Mars and all the space between them into it and still have room to spare.

YANKEE STATION

The Third Day

Proper Hears an Ominous Echo

An hour into the midwatch Sonarman Third Dwight Proper put the sonar on automatic scan and settled back in his imitation leather swivel chair with a paperback detective novel. He was up to the part where the beautiful young heiress answers the doorbell wearing a gold bracelet around her left ankle and nothing else. "'Yes, I'm Cynthia Crespin,' she told Mullins in a throaty, almost hoarse, half-whisper. She brushed her long blond hair away from her breasts with a snap of her head. 'Won't you come on up.' 'Baby, I already have,' he answered and followed her into the house."

Proper crossed his legs over his own erection and started to turn the page when he heard the first "brrrrrrrrp-*brp*." "*Je*-sus," he said and snapped off the overhead light to cut the glare on the sonar scope.

From a small dome attached to the keel of the ship pulses of sound shot into the surrounding water at the rate of one a second. If the sound waves struck nothing all you heard was the "brrrrrrrrp" of the outgoing beams. This time, however, there was a short, sharp echo to indicate that the sound waves were bouncing off something. Proper adjusted the electronic bug and measured the range and bearing to the echo, which registered as a white blip on the sonar scope. Then he flipped the 21MC on the bulkhead to "bridge" and yelled: "Bridge, this is

151

sonar. I have a sonar contact bearing 180, range 1200 yards."

"A what!" the Officer of the Deck, Lieutenant junior grade Moore, called back. "You have a what?"

"A sonar contact," Proper said excitedly. "I'm in the sonar shack looking at the scope and there's a contact bearing one eight zero at twelve hundred yards."

"My God," Moore shouted down, "what do you think it is?"

Proper bent his head and concentrated on the sound. "Brrrrrrrrp-*brp*. Brrrrrrrrp-*brp*. Brrrrrrrrp-*brp*." The echo had a distinct down doppler—a slightly lower pitch than the outgoing sound beams—indicating that the target was heading away from the *Ebersole*. "Well," Proper yelled back up to the bridge, "it sounds suspiciously like the ass end of a submarine to me."

Concentrating on the steady "Brrrrrrrrp-*brp*" that filled the small sonar shack, Proper hardly heard the tingling ripple of the general alarm peeling through the ship. He didn't look up when Ensign de Bovenkamp, the sonar officer, came charging into the shack.

"Hot damn," said de Bovenkamp. He was wearing silk pajamas and chewing away rhythmically on a stick of gum. "Hot gawddamn."

Ensign de Bovenkamp's Curriculum Vitae

"Give me a Y."
"Y."
"Give me an A."
"A."
"Give me an L."

"L."

"Give me an E."

"E."

"What does it spell?"

"Yale."

"I can't hear you."

"YALE."

"I still can't hear you."

"Y-A-L-E."

Bedlam broke out in the gymnasium. The coach laughed and waved to two trustees and then bent back into the huddle. Instantly the expression on his face changed. "Awright now, here we go," he yelled, dealing out sticks of gum. "I told you men once, I told you a thousand times, the trick is you got to think of 'em as enemy."

"We'll kill 'em," said the right guard.

"We'll murder 'em," said the center.

"We'll maim them," said de Bovenkamp, working the gum around in his mouth and nodding in anticipation.

"Awright, awright," the coach yelled. He glanced at the other team with pure hate in his eyes. "They're not opposition, get that straight, they're enemy, see, and you guys are gonna mop up the court with them as a matter of self-defense. Awright, you got the message, what are you waiting for, an engraved invitation? Now what I want you to do is I want you to get on out there and fight—for yourself, for your school, for your coach."

"Hot damn," said de Bovenkamp, and he slapped his hands onto the coach's hands and other hands slapped down on top of his. With the cheers ringing in his ears, de Bovenkamp burst from the huddle and led the team to victory.

As far back as he could remember de Bovenkamp

had been a winner. From the age of eight, when he walked away with a spoon and egg race, he knew what all winners know: everybody hates a winner. Or more precisely, everybody hates a winner who wins the way de Bovenkamp won—easily, casually, with a "Look Ma, no hands!" expression on his face.

There was only one flaw in this picture of the supersuccessful American: for the life of him, de Bovenkamp couldn't score. Sexually, that is. Oh, he could get it up all right, but he couldn't keep it up; at what is commonly called "the crucial moment" he always wilted. Various female acquaintances, turned on by the challenge long after they had been turned off by de Bovenkamp himself, had tried any number of "cures," but he had never been able to rise to the occasion and achieve actual penetration. "Gawd, I'd consider premature ejaculation a triumph!" he confided to the psychiatrist he finally took his troubles to.

De Bovenkamp talked guardedly at first, then opened up and they made some progress; the doctor traced the problem to de Bovenkamp's Caspar Milquetoast of a father and his soaring eagle of a mother. Armed with a fistful of sixty-dollar-an-hour insights, de Bovenkamp went out and fell in love with the first girl he could find who didn't remind him of his mother.

Her name was Evangeline and she taught chemistry in a high school. She was soft and womanly and walked around with bare feet indoors. What really attracted him to her was that she had a very low opinion of herself, a brilliant flash of a smile and stunning Irish eyes. But when the romance reached the point where coitus uninterruptus was the next dish on the menu, de Bovenkamp panicked. Without a word he packed his matched Gucci duffel bags and hightailed it to Officer Candidate School in Newport, Rhode Island. Desperate, she wrote him: "I love my family, I love teaching, I love my godchild Jennifer. I still love them now but I love you more than all of them. All you have to do is say you want me with you and I'll be there in less than two hours. Nothing else matters to me."

De Bovenkamp wired back: "Think of this separation as a test."

She answered with a post card: "Dummy—the real test is being together, not apart."

Much to his relief he never heard from her again.

From the start of his navy career de Bovenkamp seemed destined for great things. No matter that he wound up eighth from the bottom of his class at Officer Candidate School; more to the point, his contemporaries voted him the man who *looked* most like an officer.

After graduation a computer in Washington assigned him to the *Eugene Ebersole* out of Norfolk. Standing on a long pier in the destroyer base in Norfolk on a bright Monday morning, de Bovenkamp caught sight of the sun glinting off rust. It was the *Ebersole*. His heart sinking, he lugged his matched Guccis across the gangway to the quarterdeck, drew himself up to his full height and snapped off the salute he had perfected in Newport. "Request permission to come on board?" said de Bovenkamp.

Tevepaugh, all blackheads where his dirty white sailor hat met his forehead, lazily returned the salute. "Why not," he said. "You must be the new George, right?"

"George?"

"George is what we call the junior ensign on the ship," Tevepaugh explained.

"Who's the Officer of the Deck?" de Bovenkamp demanded.

"That'd be Mister Lustig."

"Well?"

"Well, what?"

"Well what *sir!*"

"You don't have to call me sir," Tevepaugh said. "Me, I'm not the Officer of the Deck, Mister Lustig is the Officer of the Deck."

There were tears of frustration behind de Bovenkamp's mask of imperturbability. "Where is this Mister Lustig?" he asked.

"Taking a crap, where else?" Tevepaugh said.

De Bovenkamp never did get to see Lustig until after dark when the free-for-all broke out on the mess deck over which channel to watch on the single television set. It seemed that the white sailors wanted one program and the blacks another. De Bovenkamp discovered Lustig kneeling at the top of the ladder leading to the mess deck (he was, he later admitted, afraid to descend into the pit) screaming, with no visible effect, for everyone to stand at attention. De Bovenkamp took the practical step of commandeering another television and setting it up on the other side of the mess deck. And that's how he came to meet the man who was to have such a great impact on his life, Captain J. P. Horatio Jones.

"If you ask me it was a clear case of high spirits," Jones told Lustig the next morning when he muttered something about a race riot. Jones turned to de Bovenkamp. "But *you* certainly used your head, my boy. Keep it up and I'll write up a fitness report on you that'll knock your eye out, eh?"

Spurred on by this early success de Bovenkamp set out to endear himself to the Captain. He organized an *Ebersole* basketball team (with himself as player-coach), exhorted it to victory with phrases borrowed from *his* coach ("think of them as enemy") and in short order picked up a gold basketball from the Commander

Destroyers Atlantic. Much to the Captain's delight, a photograph of the Admiral congratulating Jones and the *Ebersole* team made the Norfolk papers, and that was followed by a personal letter from the Commander Destroyers Atlantic, Jones's ultimate boss, complimenting the Captain of the *Ebersole* on coping with the problem of morale in an active and thoughtful manner. "In this day and age of drugs and long-haired pansies," the Admiral wrote, "it is a pleasure to see a destroyer Captain who can draw inspiration from American basics such as basketball."

In the months that followed de Bovenkamp turned out to be the Captain's staunchest ally on the ship. At Iskenderun it was de Bovenkamp who, alone of all the officers, supported Jones's decision to go alongside the burning tanker and fight the blaze. Later, during the first war council after the *Ebersole* arrived on Yankee Station, it was de Bovenkamp again who responded wholeheartedly to the Captain's pep talk. And it was de Bovenkamp who came up with the idea of using Proper, the ex-cop, to catch Sweet Reason. "My God," Jones told the XO, "if all my officers were like young de Bovenkamp, I could put my career on automatic and retire to my sea cabin."

If de Bovenkamp was Jones's favorite, Jones in turn filled an important need for the young ensign—he became his surrogate father. De Bovenkamp had never really seen a *man* give orders before and it affected him profoundly. He began to feel that he had a lot in common with the Captain—the one isolated (as Jones never tired of telling him) by the loneliness of command, the other isolated (as de Bovenkamp explained when he got to know the Captain better) by the loneliness of being a winner.

Gradually de Bovenkamp began to think of himself

as something more than a winner. He was, as he confided to Jones late one night, "a captain too—the captain of my fate." De Bovenkamp in fact began to sense the sap rising within himself. He actually managed a premature ejaculation in the Black Cat Inn in Piraeus—a sequence, incidentally, which anyone on the *Ebersole* could see, for five dollars a head, on Cee-Dee's late, late show. Sexually speaking de Bovenkamp still tended to wilt at crucial moments, but he felt that in time, given the inspiration of working for Captain Jones, he could hold up, if not his member, at least his head.

De Bovenkamp Sights Sub, Sinks Same

De Bovenkamp peered over Proper's shoulder at the sonar contact. Three other sonarmen had joined them in the shack. They stretched and craned, peering over de Bovenkamp's shoulders. Proper turned up the volume—the "Brrrrrrrrp-*brp*" filled the small room—and pointed to the small blip on the scope.

"Hot damn," said de Bovenkamp, chewing away on a stick of gum. "You think it's a you-know-what?"

"Sure looks like it," said one of the other sonarmen.

"Sure sounds like it," said another.

"I think it is," said Proper. "She's got down Doppler—hear it?—so she's heading away from us. Why would she head away from us unless she had something to fear from us. You get my meaning? Range is holding pretty steady at twelve hundred yards."

Captain Jones's voice came over the 21MC. "Well, Mister de Bovenkamp, what do you make of it, eh? Is it or isn't it, a sub I mean?"

"We're pretty sure it's a sub from the sound of it," de Bovenkamp called up confidently. "Let me track it for a few minutes."

De Bovenkamp switched on the electro-mechanical computer in the corner of the sonar shack. Instantly the sonar set began to feed the range and bearing to the target into the computer, and in a few seconds the dials on the face of the computer showed that the echo was tracking on a southerly course at eight knots. De Bovenkamp snapped on the 21MC and called up to the bridge again. "She tracks like a sub, Captain—she's moving south at eight knots. What do we do now?"

"We attack, my boy," Jones said. "According to our operation orders there are no American subs in Yankee Station, so it's a free-fire zone. It's probably some Commie Chink sub poaching in our waters. Attack, Mister de Bovenkamp. Try not to think about the enemy down there drowning when the sub's bulkheads cave in on them. The trick is to think of this as a game—to think of them as the opposing team. Then go on out there and give it the old college try, eh?"

"Aye aye, Captain," de Bovenkamp called. He turned to the sonarmen gathered in the shack and began handing out sticks of gum. The last stick he unwrapped and stuck in his own mouth. "Hot damn, he wants us to attack! Okay, the trick is to think of them as enemy. If every man does that it'll go like clockwork."

Adjusting the headset that connected him with the pilot house, de Bovenkamp began to bark out orders. "Load hedgehogs. All engines ahead full, turns for twenty knots. Helmsman steer one eight zero."

One of the sonarmen plugged the cable trigger into the bulkhead and handed de Bovenkamp the business end. On the firing panel a small red light came on indicating that all forty-eight hedgehogs—small antisubmarine rockets—were on the firing pins and ready to go. The dials on the computer began to generate a solution. Chewing away on two sticks of gum and nodding rhythmically, de Bovenkamp kept his eyes glued to the one that would tell him the instant to pull the trigger.

"Target coming slightly left," Proper called. "Son of a bitch's trying to wriggle off the hook."

"Come left to one seven zero," de Bovenkamp ordered the helmsman over his headset.

"Bearing steady, sir," said Proper. "Looks good."

"Stand by to fire," de Bovenkamp called.

"The echo's getting kind of mushy," Proper said. "Target appears to be breaking up into a lot of small echoes, Mister de Bovenkamp. *Je*-sus, what the hell is going on?"

De Bovenkamp turned on Proper. "Well, should I shoot or shouldn't I?" he yelled.

"Hell, what have you got to lose?" Proper said uncertainly.

The dial on the computer indicated that the bow of the *Ebersole* was almost 300 yards from the target. It flashed through de Bovenkamp's mind what it would be like to be in a submarine, to hear the explosions, to see the bulkheads cave in, to cringe as hundreds of tons of water gushed through the hole, to feed the overpowering terror of certain death by drowning. And he jerked the trigger.

Three decks above the sonar shack, the forty-eight hedgehogs—each with an explosive charge in its nose— flew off into the night and splashed into the water in a figure-eight pattern ahead of the *Ebersole*. If one of them struck something solid on its way down it would explode, and the explosion would set off the other forty-seven hedgehogs.

On the bridge of the *Ebersole*, Captain Jones

peered into the blackness listening for the explosion that would indicate they had scored a direct hit on the "Commie Chink sub." Just when he thought none would come there was a sharp underwater "thud" from one of the hedgehogs. Then the sea churned as the other forty-seven exploded also.

"WE GOT THE BASTARD!" screamed Captain Jones, dancing up and down.

The XO started giggling gleefully. "WE GOT HIM, WE GOT HIM," he screamed back at the Captain.

Moore, who was the Officer of the Deck during General Quarters, and Lustig, who was standing by to control the guns, laughed and pounded each other on the back.

In the sonar shack de Bovenkamp listened to the explosions with a smile on his face. "Hot damn," he said. "Hot gawddamn."

As the explosion subsided, Captain Jones flicked on the ship's public address system and spoke into the microphone. "Officers, men, this is the Captain speaking. This is an historic moment, eh? We have just become the first American naval vessel since World War Two to sink an enemy submarine in action." There was another cheer from the men on the bridge. Back aft the crew of Mount 53 climbed on top of the mount and waved their hats. "I especially want to congratulate Mister de Bovenkamp and his crack sonar team down there for a bangup job." This brought more cheers from various corners of the ship.

The XO tapped Jones on the shoulder. "Captain, why don't we illuminate the area with a flare and pick up some pieces of the sub as evidence, in case anyone should doubt us?"

"You're always thinking of the angles, XO," Jones said. He turned to Lustig. "Grab hold of that flare pistol, will you, Mister Lustig, and shed some light on the subject."

Lustig loaded the Very pistol with a white cartridge, pointed it straight up in the air and fired. A few seconds later there was a "plop" high over the *Ebersole*, and the entire area was suddenly bathed in daylight. Lustig kept firing flares as Jones brought the *Ebersole* around full circle and stopped at the spot where the hedgehogs had exploded.

"There, there," the XO shouted, "see it? There's something in the water."

Jones and the XO leaned over the railing to watch the sailors on the main deck retrieve pieces of wreckage with long boat hooks. There was some yelling, which the Captain took for cheering.

Jones beamed at the XO. "Nobody will be able to say we're exaggerating now, eh?"

There was some more yelling on the main deck. Jones turned to Lustig. "Ask the talker down there what they've picked up, eh?"

Lustig said a few words into his headset, listened, then looked up at the Captain.

"Well?" asked Jones.

"It's—"

A sickening odor wafted up from the sea around the *Ebersole*. The XO turned his face away and covered it with a handkerchief.

"It's whales, Captain," Lustig said. "We sank a bunch of whales!"

Jones sank dejectedly into the Captain's chair. "Goddamn de Bovenkamp." He shook his head sadly. "What's this world coming to, XO? That's what I want to know. What's this world coming to?"

Lustig Sees a Ghost

The deck gang was still hosing down the fo'c'sle when the helicopter from the aircraft carrier flew in over the fantail, hovered and lowered a man onto the *Ebersole*. Lustig, back aft to supervise the transfer, grabbed his legs as he swayed above the pitching deck and hauled him in.

"My God, you look like a ghost—I never thought I'd see *you* again," Lustig yelled, but his voice was drowned out by the roar of the helicopter.

With Lustig leading the way, the two men walked forward along the port side of the main deck to the sick bay.

"I tell you they checked me out on the carrier, Mister Lustig," Chief McTigue was saying. "I'm mostly dirty and tired and scared shitless."

"You know we got a shoot scheduled for sunup," Lustig said. "If you aren't up to it—"

"A few hours in the rack and I'll be as good as new."

"Must have been rough, huh?" Lustig asked.

"Jesus shit, it was plenty rough," McTigue agreed. "That's the last fucking time I go out spotting, you understand?"

Lustig was offended by McTigue's tone, but he decided he had to make allowances because of what the chief had been through. "You're not holding a grudge, are you?" he asked. "It wasn't me that offered to supply a spotter. I was only following orders."

Doc Shapley, the hospital corpsman who fainted at the sight of blood, bustled into the sick bay and started to undo the bandages around McTigue's head. A small patch of hair over his left ear had been shaved off. The bare scalp was covered with gauze. The hair around the gauze was matted with dried mud and dried blood.

Shapley started in on the bandage. Three layers down he came across some blood that hadn't completely coagulated. Swallowing hard, he quickly wrapped McTigue up again. "I think what you need more than anything else, Chief, is a dose of rest and relaxation. What you got on will hold fine till morning. Here, take two of these"—he thrust a small envelope of red pills into McTigue's hand—"and one of these"—this envelope was full of yellow pills—"every four hours." And Shapley turned on his heel and disappeared.

"Two red and one yellow every four hours," McTigue repeated. Holding his head, he made his way down to the chief's quarters forward. Everyone was asleep except Duffy, the engineering chief, who was studying a reduction-gear manual by flashlight.

"Holy Mackerel, you're supposed to be dead!" Duffy whispered. "You look like hell warmed over. What happened?"

"Jesus shit, don't ask," McTigue said glumly. "Don't ever fuckin' ask."

He washed down the two reds and the yellow with straight vodka. Then he stretched out on his bunk and tried not to dream.

McTigue's Curriculum Vitae

The pilot, an olive-skinned lieutenant junior grade with the name "Ruggieri" stenciled on his candy-striped flight helmet, had glanced suspiciously at McTigue. "First time in a chopper, Chief?" he had asked over the intercom.

McTigue had nodded sourly and had said "Yeah" without depressing the transmit button on the flight panel. Ruggieri had thought "Holy Jesus—why me?" and had pointed impatiently to the button and McTigue had pushed it. "Yeah, it is," McTigue said, and he heard the "Yeah, it is" over the earphones in his helmet. "I been in planes a lot, but I never been in a chopper before."

"Difference between a plane and a chopper," Ruggieri had said, "is a plane is aching to fly and these eggbeaters just naturally want to crash." It was a harmless enough line, but Ruggieri had seen the flash of fright on McTigue's face. "Don't sweat it," he had added quickly, "you'll get to love it."

Ruggieri had swiveled his joy stick and the helicopter had banked toward the coast in a great rocking motion that lifted McTigue's heart to his mouth.

Feeling cramped and uncomfortable and out of his element, McTigue had sat stiffly in his seat and had watched the ground roll out like a carpet under the helicopter. First came the swells of the sea, then the water turned choppy and suddenly there were breakers and a curve of coast and a flat stretch of swampland. Ruggieri had tapped McTigue on the shoulder and had pointed with a gloved finger, and McTigue had followed the finger and had seen the shadow of the helicopter racing along the ground slightly in front of them and off to one side.

"I always get a kick out of that," Ruggieri had said, hoping to distract McTigue, who looked as if he were about to throw up.

McTigue had nodded to indicate that he got a kick out of seeing the helicopter's shadow too.

The shadow raced along the ground for a while. Then it rose to meet the helicopter and McTigue saw that they were flying over a ridge with a blockhouse and a mangled tree on it. A tuft of a cloud hovered over the mangled tree.

"What d'you say I give the blockhouse a burst?" one of the door gunners asked on the intercom.

"Negative," ordered Ruggieri. He turned to McTigue. "My theory is live and let live," he explained.

After the ridge came a rolling meadow and McTigue watched the shadow helicopter cut across the grassland until suddenly it was lost in a maze of dirt lanes and thatched huts and tents.

"That's —— ——," Ruggieri motioned with his finger, and he put the helicopter into a long, lazy arc that took it around the rim of the town.

McTigue could make out dozens of children in the town and in the fields that surrounded the town. The ones in the fields stopped work to look up at the helicopter. Some started gesturing. Some started running. McTigue could see that there was panic in the way they ran.

"Jesus shit, the place is full of kids!" McTigue said on the intercom.

One of the door gunners laughed into the intercom. "Them dinks look like ants to me."

"It's the angle," the pilot assured McTigue. "From up here everyone looks like kids."

—— ——was sliced into two unequal parts by a paved highway that ran from north to south. On the seaward side of the road the town was tents and thatched huts and small backyard vegetable gardens. On the landward side there were a few dozen one-story cement buildings, a two-story building alongside a soccer field, more cement buildings, then a tangle of thatched huts and then on the edge of town an old truck depot with three dilapidated trucks in it.

Except for children running in all directions and someone hastily hoisting a white flag with a faded red cross on a pole in front of the soccer field,—— —— looked peaceful enough.

"Looks peaceful enough, don't it?" McTigue asked over the intercom.

"They always do," Ruggieri said.

The radio-telephone crackled into life and McTigue heard a familiar voice in his earphones.

"Spotting round en route," is what the voice said.

Suddenly it dawned on McTigue, "Jesus shit, that's Mister Lustig!"

Ruggieri pulled the helicopter up, with its bubble nose angled down, for a grandstand view.

The first spotting round exploded in the tangle of thatched huts on the landward side of the town, about five hundred yards short of the truck depot. There was a burst of bright yellow, like a flashbulb going off, then a spreading blaze and a wisp of brown-black smoke spiraling into the sky.

"Jesus, they're firing short!" McTigue told Ruggieri.

"Don't tell me, tell them—that's what you're here for," Ruggieri said, and he pointed to another button on the panel marked "external transmit."

McTigue depressed it and shouted into his microphone: "Jesus shit, you're short, you're firing short, you're in the thatch, d'you read me, you're hitting the huts, I thought you guys were gonna overshoot and walk the stuff back down, over."

"How short, damnit?" Lustig asked.

"Jesus shit, the fuckin' huts are on fire, you've got to come up five hundred at least, do you read me, over."

Another spotting round landed three hundred yards short of the truck depot.

"Jesus, you're still in the fuckin' huts," McTigue shouted into the microphone. An area about the size of a football field in the middle of the tangle of huts was ablaze. People were scurrying in all directions. "The huts are burning like tinder," McTigue yelled, "up three hundred."

"Up what?" called Lustig. "Say again, up what?"

"Up three fuckin' hundred, don't you understand English, over."

"You're garbled," radioed Lustig. "Say everything twice, over."

One of the door gunners came on the intercom. "What the fuck they holding—a dink roast?"

The other door gunner laughed into the intercom: "Hey man, that's good—a dink roast."

Ruggieri tapped McTigue on the arm. "You're cutting out because the angle of the antenna keeps changing. Just say every word twice, get it?"

McTigue nodded and punched the "external transmit" button with his fist. "Up up three three hundred hundred, d'you read me, d'you read me, over over."

The next shot fell short of the depot again.

"Jesus shit, you guys still aren't on target," McTigue yelled.

A few seconds later, to McTigue's astonishment, the

Ebersole opened fire in salvo and the rounds of VT frag began to hail down on the already blazing tangle of thatched huts. An ancient fire engine with an army jeep in front of it and another behind came chugging into town from the north and pulled up on the fringe of the fire. Instantly dozens of children surrounded the jeeps and the fire engine. Those around the fire engine pointed to the flames; those around the jeeps pointed to the helicopter.

McTigue punched the transmit button again. "Jesus fuckin' shit, you guys are shooting short, you're shooting into the huts, the whole fuckin' place is an inferno, what the fuck you think you're doing, you got to raise your sights, you hear me, what are you, deaf or something, up, up, up, UP, UP, UP." Now McTigue was screaming the word "up" into the microphone over and over.

One of the door gunners interrupted him. "Hey *Lou*tenant, I think one of them there jeeps down there has a machine gun mounted—"

McTigue never heard the machine gun, only the cold metallic sound of steel shredding steel. Ruggieri's eyes, bulging with terror, scanned the dials on the panel in front of him; the needles seemed calm enough. The rotors were still turning and the engine sounded as it did before. Ruggieri relaxed and pulled back on the stick to gain altitude.

The helicopter didn't respond.

"Dear mother of God—" from Ruggieri, pulling back harder on the stick with his gloved hands.

A mild explosion shook the helicopter and McTigue looked back into the smoke and wiped his eyes and saw the two door gunners on the floor holding their stomachs as if they had cramps. Then the seat seemed to drop out from under McTigue. Like a bird heavy with buckshot the helicopter began to settle, rotor blades flapping, toward the earth.

"We're going in," Ruggieri shouted. "Jump as soon as we hit—"

"What about them?" McTigue gestured toward the door gunners.

"If they're alive, they'll fend for themselves," Ruggieri said.

The static-decayed voice of Captain Jones bit into McTigue's earphones. "McTigue, d'you hear me, we've been hit, we've taken a hit. Do you see any counterfire?"

McTigue punched the "external transmit" button. "Mayday, Mayday, we've been hit in the rotors, Mayday, Mayday, we're going in Captain, for God's sake help, oh Jesus shit, help, help, help, heeeeeeeeelp."

The helicopter jarred onto a flat stretch of ground some 800 yards beyond the truck depot, pitching McTigue forward into his shoulder harness. When the helicopter motor cut out, McTigue could hear the crackling of flames in the back section of the craft. He saw Ruggieri tugging wildly at his shoulder straps and he did the same. An instant later both Ruggieri and McTigue leapt from the helicopter, each on his own side, and raced for a small rise forty yards away.

"Dear mother of God," panted Ruggieri.

"Jesus fuckin' shit," gasped McTigue.

Crouching on the rise, breathing heavily from exertion and fright, the two men looked back at the blazing helicopter. They could hear the roaring of the flames and the crackling explosion of firecrackers.

"Ammo's—cooking—off," Ruggieri said between gasps of air. He yanked off his gloves and his candy-striped helmet and threw them as far as he could and ran his fingers through his thick hair, which had been pasted down by the weight of the helmet. Through the film of smoke and heated, wavy air McTigue could see some movement at the edge of the town near the truck depot. He pointed at the movement and Ruggieri drew a blue-black .45 caliber pistol from his holster, threw a round into the chamber and flicked off the safety. "Come on," he said, and tugging at McTigue's sleeve, he pulled him along. Bogged down by flight suits and heavy boots, the two men lumbered across a brush field and sank out of sight into a clump of bushes.

While they were trying to regain their breath the first flight of jets came in from the sea at rooftop level, dropped some canisters on the town and soared into the sky like roller coasters. Great beautiful red-black balls of smoke and fire billowed up after them.

"What the fuck we gonna do?" McTigue asked after a while.

"We're going to get rescued," Ruggieri said.

"How we gonna do that?"

Ruggieri pointed to a small leather-covered box, about the size of a transistor radio, strapped to his belt. "Transmitter," he explained. "It puts out a signal. Soon as they've taken care of the opposition"—Ruggieri motioned with his head toward the flaming town—"they'll home in on the signal and pick us up. All we got to do is lay low."

A flight of prop planes swept in from the north and strafed the truck depot. Another flight came from the east. The last plane peeled off toward a cluster of children scampering away from the depot. The plane seemed to pull up without dropping anything. For an instant McTigue thought the pilot must have seen that they were children. Then there was a ball of fire where the group had been.

"They're sure putting on one hell of a show," Ruggieri said.

But McTigue was thinking about something else. "What happens if there isn't no rescue chopper?" he asked.

Ruggieri looked at him. "There will be."

"But what if there isn't?" McTigue insisted. "What if?"

"There will be." Ruggieri turned back to watch the show.

Long after Ruggieri thought the town was neutralized the planes kept coming—from different directions, at different heights, with different armaments. Finally, halfway through the second hour, there was a pause.

"Maybe we should surrender?" McTigue said. "You think we should surrender?"

Ruggieri jerked himself around toward McTigue. "Surrender! Dear God, you must be out of your mind. You know what some choppers did around here a few days back? They lassoed this gook in a field and stripped him naked and put a rope around his neck and started out slowly with the gook running like crazy to keep up. After a while the gook can't keep up and his neck snaps. You get the picture, Chief?"

"What the fuck they do that for?" McTigue asked.

"What do they do anything for? Me, I live and let live, right, but these gooks here, how they going to know that, huh, how they going to know I live and let live?" Ruggieri fingered his pistol. "If they catch us, they'll lynch us," he said. "Go ahead and surrender if you want to; me, I'll put my money on this." And he hefted the pistol.

Another wave of jets came in from the sea, and then another, and still another. After a while it seemed to McTigue like an endless wave of planes and he lost all sense of time. Every now and then he peered out between the bushes at the town, but the town was disappearing before his eyes. The part of—— ——that had been cement buildings was nothing but dust and rubble now. The truck depot had ceased to exit. Beyond McTigue's line of sight, where the thatched huts had been, there was a wall of flame.

As McTigue watched, two teenage boys carrying a baby carriage between them dashed from the rubble of the truck depot and headed into the field. A prop plane with teeth painted on the nose darted in and dropped a canister of napalm behind the running boys. The canister hit and the flame spread forward in a sweeping arc; the boys abandoned the baby carriage and ran faster but the flame caught up with them and passed them.

The grass and brush were burning now and the fire was moving across the fields, away from—— ——toward McTigue and Ruggieri. Just when it looked as if it had burned itself out, four more children popped up near the small rise between McTigue and the downed helicopter. A prop plane detached itself from a flight and dropped the canister too far behind them and they got away into a wooded area to the north. But the napalm rekindled the brush fire and it moved closer to the clump of underbrush that hid McTigue and Ruggieri.

"We'll have to run for it," Ruggieri said. He pulled a large piece of silk from a pocket on his calf and spread it on the ground. On one side was a map of the enemy's country and a few dozen phonetic phrases such as "Don't harm me—I was only following orders." The other side was an American flag. "When we run, I'll stream the flag, just in case one of those jet jockeys up there gets any bright ideas. Okay, you ready?"

McTigue glanced at the brush fire, which was only a few dozen yards off now, and nodded and heaved himself to his feet to follow Ruggieri, who trotted ahead streaming the flag. Suddenly Ruggieri stopped short and McTigue almost ran into him, and then he saw why

Ruggieri had stopped; thirty yards dead ahead five teenage boys armed with long-handled axes waited for the two American airmen.

"Holy mother of Christ," Ruggieri said, and he turned to his right and ran parallel to the fire, with McTigue trailing after him, but the boys trotted along on a parallel course waiting for the brush fire to bring the two Americans to them. McTigue noticed the fire had burned out ahead and to the right and he yelled to Ruggieri and the two Americans lumbered toward the hole in the wall of fire with the five boys in pursuit, the five gaining on the two Americans, closing the gap on the Americans, then McTigue saw that Ruggieri wasn't running anymore, that Ruggieri had dropped to one knee the way he had been taught in survival school, had dropped to one knee and gasping for air had steadied his pistol with two hands and had started shooting, had hit one of the teenagers, had hit a second, then the boys were up to Ruggieri, were on top of Ruggieri, hacking at him, he covering his head with the silk flag the way a child crawls under a sheet, he screaming from beneath the sheet "Mother of God don't harm me—I was only following orders" in English because he can't remember the phonetic translation. Then one of the teenagers looks up and sees McTigue and starts toward him, sure of catching him, McTigue too winded to move, McTigue mixed up, not sure what is happening, sure only that it is happening to him, thinking Jesus shit this is happening to me, the teenager in front of him swinging his ax in an arc, the ax just catching the side of McTigue's head as he lunges sideways, then a burst of machine-gun fire that rips away the teenager's chest and left arm and flings him back, flings him away from McTigue. Then a curious beating sound and the wind hammering against McTigue and something, he's not sure what, thuds onto the ground directly in front of him and hands pull him

roughly into a cave only it isn't a cave it's a helicopter and
the helicopter rises a few feet and hovers while the door
gunner furious about the American lying out there under
the flag cuts down the other teenagers. Then the
helicopter pendulums off toward the sea in a motion so
comforting it brings tears to McTigue's eyes.

Lying face-down on the floor next to the open door,
next to the booted feet of the door gunner, feeling the
blood ooze from his matted hair, feeling the wind on his
face, McTigue gasps for air and watches the ground roll
out like a carpet underneath. First come the fields
charred by the brush fire, then the smoke and dust and
rubble where the cement buildings had been, then
nothing but embers where the thatched huts had been,
then the pockmarked road with the charred remains of
the fire engine and the two jeeps, then bits and pieces of
tents and burnt-out, bombed-out vegetable gardens,
then the rolling meadow that looked naked and mown,
then the ridge with the ruins of the blockhouse and a
stump where the mangled tree had been, then the curve
of coast and beyond, the whitecaps and the ground
swells and the sea.

"Jesus shit," moans McTigue. "*Je*-sus fuckin' shit."

McTigue Hears a Few Words of Wisdom

Soaked in sweat, the figure in the lower bunk tossed
and turned as if he were trying to throw off a shroud or a
sheet that covered his head.

Tevepaugh bent over the figure and whispered:
"Mister Lustig says for you to start breaking out the
ammo, Chief."

The figure stopped jerking and lay still, breathing heavily.

"Jesus shit, what time is it?"

"After five, Chief."

"Who says?"

"What d'you mean 'who says?'? It's after five, Chief, I swear it is."

McTigue was lying on his back staring straight up. "After five," he repeated.

"Yeah, Chief, it's after five." Tevepaugh pointed to the bandage on McTigue's head. "I'll bet you didn't have no picnic on shore, huh, Chief?"

McTigue ignored the remark. "You're sure it's after five?" he asked again.

Tevepaugh pulled up the sleeve of his foul-weather jacket and exposed his wristwatch. "Like I says, Chief, it's after five. Mister Lustig says for you—"

"I got it the first time around, kid. Now you haul your ass back up topside and you tell Mister Lustig—"

The night light in the bunk over McTigue's snapped on. Half a dozen men curled up in their bunks turned their faces to the bulkhead or buried them in blankets. Chief Duffy, a stocky man wearing skivvy shorts and a T-shirt and white sweat socks lay propped up on an elbow under the light. "Okay, Tevepaugh, you just mosey on back to the bridge and inform Mister Lieutenant junior grade Lustig that everything's under control, you understand? Tell him the ammo is being broken out. Now you got that?" The man in the underwear spoke quietly but with unmistakable authority.

"Sure thing, Chief, I got that." Tevepaugh was still whispering. "Chief McTigue's breaking out the ammo, right? I get the idea."

Tevepaugh flashed what he thought was an ingratiating smile and scampered out of the compartment.

"Jesus shit, I've had it up to here, Duffy," McTigue said hoarsely. His skin was drawn back tightly over his gums in a frozen half-grimace, an expression that revealed gaps between his teeth where the navy dentist had chiseled out the tartar. "You know what was in that fuckin' town we hit yesterday?" McTigue swallowed hard. "I'll tell you what was in that fuckin' town. There was nothin' but fuckin' kids there, that's what there fuckin' was. Jesus fuckin' shit."

Duffy slid his feet over the edge of his bunk, dropped heavily to the deck and sat down on the edge of McTigue's bunk. "Forget what you seen," he said earnestly. "You never seen it. If you pull something now you'll wreck your career. You got three more years till your twenty is up. You got maybe one more year, a year and a half at most, sea duty. You got it made. Don't blow it all, Tom. Don't let it all go down the drain because you seen some dead slopes."

"You shoulda seen what they done, them jets," McTigue said. "Jesus shit, the napalm—"

"It wasn't you that did it, Tom," Duffy said. "Anyhow, you was only following orders."

"Yeah," McTigue said. "Don't harm me—I was only following orders."

McTigue Lets Quinn Down Gently

His face still frozen in a grimace, his eyes looking as if they had been in—or seen—pain, McTigue made his way up to the galley where the night baker, a meaty black named Seldon Saler, was pulling the last batch of loaves out of the oven.

"Good Lord, I never thought I'd see the likes of you again," Saler said, as always breathlessly cheerful. "Here—let some of this melt in your mouth." He handed McTigue a fistful of piping-hot bread. The sound of Nat King Cole filled the galley. Saler, who according to mess deck rumor, had once worked as a cook in an Uncle John's Pancake House on the Santa Ana Freeway, boasted that he had all of Nat King Cole on cassettes, and he played them over and over during the night to prove the point.

With the odor of freshly cooked dough and the sound of Nat King Cole trailing behind him, McTigue climbed down the ladder to the forward crew's quarters under the mess deck. Munching the bread, he stood next to the ladder waiting for his eyes to become accustomed to the darkness. Then he walked over to Quinn's bunk against the bulkhead.

"Rise and shine, Quinn," McTigue whispered, shaking the first class gunner's mate by the shoulder.

"Jesus, Chief, I never thought I'd see you again!" Quinn shook himself awake. "What time is it?" he asked.

"After five, Quinn. Get some of the men up, will you, and start breaking out VT frag for Fifty-two and Fifty-three. Sixty-two rounds a mount. I'll do Fifty-one myself. And get Boeth up to the handling room to stack for me."

"Sixty-two rounds of VT frag. All right." Quinn sat up and McTigue turned to go.

"Chief," Quinn said.

An angry voice called from a nearby bunk: "Knock it off, will you?"

"Chief," Quinn repeated in a whisper.

"Yeah, Quinn."

"I don't s'pose you got a chance to speak to the XO about my keys and my application?"

"I spoke to him, yeah," McTigue said. "Forget the keys, will you. As for the other thing, the XO says the Captain wants you off the ship. He thinks you need to broaden your horizons. You been on one ship too long, he says." McTigue shrugged. "That's what he says."

"Did the thing in the Captain's cabin have anything to do with it?" Quinn asked. "I'll apologize, I'll be glad to apologize—in front of everybody. I'll tell him I found the fuckin' electro servo coupler. Only I got to stay on the *Ebersole*."

"Jesus shit, Quinn, you got it made and you don't know it. You may even get one of those new cans with air conditioning and a real first-class lounge and fully automatic mounts you don't have to lay a finger on. You got it made." McTigue remembered that Duffy had said the same thing to him moments before. "We all got it made," McTigue added.

Before Quinn could say anything he turned and climbed down another ladder to the forward five-inch magazine under the crew's quarters.

McTigue Passes the Ammunition Without Bothering to Praise the Lord

The magazine was one of the few spaces on the *Ebersole* that was always kept antiseptically clean, as if cleanliness were really next to godliness. Every handle or lever was painted bright red and marked for easy identification. A sign above the largest wheel, smack against the bulkhead next to the access ladder, said: "To flood magazine, turn wheel clockwise." The wheel was locked shut with a bicycle chain and a red padlock. Next to the padlock was another sign that said: "The following named men have the key to this padlock." McTigue's name headed the list, Quinn's came next. Hand-stenciled signs saying "No Smoking" were painted on every bulkhead. In one corner was a large plaque entitled "The Ten Commandments of Damage Control" which began with "1. Keep the ship watertight" and ended with "10. *Don't give up the ship!*" underlined in red.

Under normal circumstances, with a full wartime complement of 345 officers and men aboard, five seamen would be stationed in each of the destroyer's magazines during General Quarters to keep the projectiles and powder flowing to the handling rooms, two decks up, and eventually to the three five-inch mounts that were directly above the handling rooms. But the *Ebersole* had not had a full complement of officers and men on board since 1945, when the race began to demobilize. With only 255 officers and men assigned, the *Ebersole* didn't have enough warm bodies on board to man all battle stations. So every time the destroyer had to shoot any of its guns someone climbed down into the magazines beforehand and counted out the projectiles and powder cases and sent them up the dredger hoist to the handling rooms.

McTigue, who never asked the men under him to do anything he himself didn't do, had climbed down into the magazine and passed the ammo up hundreds of times. But he had never felt odd about it until today. Suddenly it seemed to him as if he were spooning out death as casually as Saler measured out flour in the galley.

"You there?" McTigue called up the dredger hoist to the handling room.

The trap door in the overhead slipped open. "Come ahead, Chief," called Boeth, the seaman who ran Main Plot. "How many cheeseburgers do you have coming?"

"Cheeseburgers! Jesus shit!" McTigue muttered. Then he yelled back: "Sixty-two."

McTigue pushed the foot pedal that started the hoist and began to feed the five-inch projectiles into it, watching them disappear through the hole in the overhead like bottles on a dumbwaiter. He wondered who decided on the number sixty-two? McTigue had been in the navy seventeen years; he'd been on the *Ebersole* for seventeen months. But he didn't know where the number originated. With Mister Lustig, the gunnery officer? With the XO? The Skipper? Rear Admiral Haydens, who was in command of the Task Force of which the *Ebersole* was but one small unit? Some unnamed and unidentifiable vice admiral in the basement of the Pentagon? Or even one of his junior aides who, scanning the *Ebersole*'s target assignment for the morning, turned to the first class petty officer pouring coffee into a playboy mug and said: "Sixty-two rounds of five-inch from each mount should be about right." Who was responsible? And why not sixty-three or seventy or a hundred and seventy? Why not shoot the works—all 2000-plus rounds left on the ship? Why not ram the ship into the target? Why not—

"That's it, Chief." Boeth hollered down. "I count sixty-two."

"That's it," McTigue called back, and the trap door in the overhead clanged shut.

Ohm Sounds Reveille

Reveille sounded minutes later—a long shrill blast of Ohm's bo's'n's pipe, followed by his grating voice speaking so close to the microphone everyone could hear him suck in air between phrases. "Now hear this, reveille, reveille, reveille, all hands heave out and trice up. Now the smoking lamp is lit in all authorized spaces. Sweepers, man your brooms. Make a clean sweep down fore and aft."

The *Ebersole* came alive with electric lights and yawning sailors and flushing toilets and aerosol cans of shaving cream and cigarettes and mess trays with one not quite rectangular compartment full of lukewarm scrambled eggs.

Topside, deck apes in rubber boots scrubbed down the weather decks. As he did every morning, Boeth took a turn around the main deck checking for flying fish. The dead ones, their frail bluish wings folded stiffly back in rigor mortis, he tossed over the side; the live ones, squirming weakly from side to side, he gripped just behind their heads and banged sharply, cruelly against the railing. Then he tossed them overboard too.

McTigue Feeds in the Ballistic Data

With half an hour to go before General Quarters, McTigue made his way to Main Plot off the scullery on the mess deck. Main Plot housed the brain of the destroyer's fire control system—an electro-mechanical computer that allowed the *Ebersole's* main battery of six five-inch, .38 caliber guns to lob projectiles toward distant and generally unseen targets with a remarkably good chance of hitting them.

The computer, designated Mark One Able in the navy idiom, was an old warhorse that had been directing the *Ebersole's* guns since the first shells left their barrels back in 1945. Its components were so intricate that only Seaman Boeth, who had a scientific cast of mind to begin with and who had taken a four-month course on the Mark One Able before reporting aboard the *Ebersole*, really knew what went on beneath the green casing.

McTigue understood the essentials. A delicate gyro kept track of the ship's roll and pitch and made sure the guns compensated for them. Another gyro put in the destroyer's course and speed, two other ingredients in the puzzle. But there was other ballistic data to feed into the computer and McTigue did that now. First he dialed in the temperature of the gunpowder, which he had noted in the magazine. The temperature affected the speed with which the powder burned, which in turn affected the distance the projectile would travel as well as its speed. Then McTigue called the chart room and got the morning readings on wind velocity and barometric pressure, both of which had a bearing on the performance of the projectile. The final pieces of information that would allow the Mark One Able to solve the problem of how to end the lives of enemies of the United States six or eight miles away—the range and bearing to the target—would be fed in later directly from the optical range finder on the main director.

Richardson Makes an Exception for True Love

In the wardroom the last of the officers were finishing breakfast. Hovering over them like an unobtrusive angel, True Love poured coffee from a plastic pitcher.

Sipping lukewarm cocoa, Ensign de Bovenkamp thumbed through a copy of the charges he had brought against Angry Pettis and Waterman. "Charge:" (it read), "willful insubordination. Specification: In that Pettis Foreman, 337 93 33 USN and Jefferson Davis Waterman, 660 70 92 USN on board the *Eugene F. Ebersole* DD722 on or about————were willfully insubordinate toward Ensign de Bovenkamp by subjecting him to ridicule and contempt . . ."

Across the table Chaplain Rodgers, who had fought down his seasickness long enough to take breakfast in the wardroom, listened uneasily to Ensign Wallowitch. "My whole life," Wallowitch was saying, muttering into his breakfast plate and toying with the cold scrambled eggs on it, "my whole life I've been asking, 'Where were the good Germans?' Well, I know where they were. They were paying taxes, that's where they were." Rodgers rested what he thought was a comforting palm on Wallowitch's arm—it was a gesture he had picked up at chaplain's school—and said encouragingly: "Listen, Wally, people get killed in war—that's what war is all about. Besides, the other side has a record of atrocities as long as your arm—"

Wallowitch shook off the Chaplain's comforting palm. "The *other* side always has a record of atrocities as long as your arm. What else is new?"

Just then the Executive Officer, breakfasting in the Captain's chair, burst out laughing at something in the latest COMDESLANT all-ships directive, and Wallowitch, looking for trouble, told him, "You know something, XO, you laugh in all the wrong places."

The XO's laughter dried up. The two men eyed each other across the table. Then the XO sidestepped the confrontation by taking Wallowitch's comment as a joke too. "You're really a card, One Shot, you really are," he said lightly.

"I told you to lay off that 'One Shot' business," Wallowitch said quietly. Scraping back his chair, he walked heavily out of the wardroom.

"What's got into him?" the XO asked innocently. Without waiting for an answer, he started to complain about True Love emptying the dustpan into his urinal. True Love smiled like a child caught in the act of a not very serious crime and filled the XO's cup with coffee.

De Bovenkamp suddenly discovered a typing error in the charge sheet. "Heck, you'd think they—"

De Bovenkamp was half out of his chair when the *Ebersole* rolled heavily to port. He clutched at the table and missed and went flying across the wardroom toward the couch. En route his flailing left arm knocked the model of the *Ebersole* off the shelf. The bottle smashed on the deck, and as de Bovenkamp sat up on the couch his foot came down on the model, shattering it into tiny pieces.

"Gawddamn," he cried, "I sure didn't mean to do that." De Bovenkamp looked around the room. "You guys won't tell the Skipper it was me, will you?"

True Love was sweeping up the pieces when Ralph Richardson, the supply officer, rolled up his napkin and inserted it into a plastic ring. "Excuse me, will you, gents," he said, and headed aft.

Just aft of the midship's passageway Richardson pushed open the supply office door and settled into the upholstered easy chair he had acquired from a bumboat in Santo Domingo in return for some boxes of moldy beef. Richardson spread a batch of requisitions out carefully, overlapping them enough so that the line for the signature showed, and picked up his pen.

Suddenly there was a sound at the door—a sound so vague that at first Richardson thought someone walking down the inboard passageway had inadvertently brushed against it. But the sound came again and Richardson recognized it as a knock and called for whoever was there to come in.

The door opened a crack and a single worried eye appeared. Then, hinges squeaking, the door swung back, revealing True Love. He was wearing a white ankle-length cook's apron over his dungarees and a tall, floppy chef's hat that the other wardroom stewards had given him for his nineteenth birthday. They had intended it as a joke but he wore it as if it were a Congressional Medal of Honor.

"Mistah Richardson," True Love said. Smiling shyly, shifting his weight from foot to foot, he stood on the threshold with his head angled down so that his eyes had to peer through his lashes to see the supply officer. "Do you think Ah . . . do you think Ah could . . . could . . ."

"Could what?" prompted Richardson. "Do I think you could what?"

"Could talk . . . talk to you?" asked True Love.

"Sure I think you could," Richardson said. "Sure I do." And he smiled warmly and motioned True Love in.

Because True Love was black, Georgia-born-and-raised, the only boy in a family of nine girls and had an IQ of eighty-four, Richardson made allowances for him. And because he made allowances for him he was able to cope with True Love's peculiar mixture of exquisite sweetness and exquisite slowness. When True Love (to cite one example) had infuriated the Executive Officer by emptying the sweepings from his cabin into his urinal, Richardson had approached the situation calmly. "True Love," he had told him, "you can't just dump the sweepings into the XO's urinal—that clogs it up and causes the XO's urine to overflow onto the deck, where it collects in small puddles and gets into the XO's shoes. Do you think you understand?"

True Love had nodded vigorously and had promised not to do it again. The very next day there were more sweepings in the XO's urinal. When Richardson pointed this out True Love shook his head at the oversight and said, "Oh, Ah fergot, suh," and promised not to do it again.

It was a promise he had a great deal of difficulty keeping.

Not surprisingly, True Love was an easy touch for the other wardroom stewards. It was True Love, for instance, who always lugged the fifty-pound crates of frozen hamburger up from the freezers below deck. And whenever the *Ebersole* hit port it was True Love who somehow wound up with the duty that first weekend. Actually, he didn't mind the duty—it gave him a chance to parade around with his chef's hat on and a cleaver in one hand. Because he didn't know where to begin when it came to making a dinner, True Love had to borrow precooked meat and mashed potatoes and vegetables from the crew's mess, reheat them in the wardroom platters and serve them as original creations. The officers knew where the food was coming from. But since everyone (except the Captain and the XO) liked True Love, they went out of their way to make appreciative noises. "Who cooked this dinner?" the Poet demanded on one such occasion. True Love's worried face appeared in the serving window leading from the wardroom to the pantry. "Me, suh," he said nervously. At which point Joyce said, "My compliments to the chef"—a comment that left True Love grinning from ear to ear.

"Well, True Love," Richardson was saying, "what can I do for you?"

After a few false starts True Love explained that he had come to Richardson to confirm a rumor he had heard on the mess deck—the rumor being that the *Ebersole* had received a directive from BuPers ordering, as part of an economy drive, the immediate release of all navy personnel with IQs under ninety. When Richardson confirmed the rumor, tears welled up in True Love's eyes.

"Mistah Richardson, suh, what'll Ah tell 'em, mah folks, if'n you *de*-mote me back to a civilian. Las' time Ah wen' home, why, everyone fer two streets turned out, me in mah dress blues wid mah boondocks all spit-polished an' shinin' like they was solid gold. Ah can't never show mah face there 'gain if'n Ah'm not in mah uni-form." True Love wiped the tears away from his eyes with his hand and then dried his hand on his apron. "Mah pa . . ." he began, and broke down completely.

Richardson stood up and put an arm around True Love's shoulder. "Listen, True Love, the BuPers directive says that sailors with IQs under ninety are to be discharged unless they perform a job crucial to the operation of a ship or shore station. Now as far as I'm concerned the *Ebersole* wardroom can't function without your services, and if the wardroom operation falls apart, they might have to take the ship off the line."

"You mean . . ."

"I mean you can stay in the navy as long as I'm supply officer here. By the time the next supply officer takes over from me that BuPers directive will have long since been filed and forgotten, along with the hundreds of other directives we get every month. All right? You feel better now?"

Nodding vigorously, True Love took Richardson's hand and shook it. Then, with a smile beginning to find its way back onto his boyish face, he backed out of the supply office and closed the door.

Richardson sat down and looked at the requisitions lined up on his desk. He was about to begin signing when, from force of habit, he reached down to the office safe and gave the combination lock a spin. Instead of running free it clicked to a stop. The door was closed but the safe was unlocked; it had been unlocked all night.

A cold fright pushed Richardson back hard in his chair. The ship's operating funds, which Richardson used to pay wages every two weeks and buy food and fuel in foreign ports, were in that safe. Trying to fight off an image of his navy career ending in jail, Richardson gingerly opened the safe door, afraid of what he wouldn't find.

The money was there all right—but was it all there? What with this Sweet Reason business, he couldn't be too careful. Obviously he would have to count it, all $322,648.73 of it. Richardson bolted the door to the office from the inside, scooped up the requisitions and put them in a file basket. Then, still in a cold sweat, he piled the bound bundles of bills on the table. First came the seventy-three cents—two quarters, two dimes and three pennies. That much was fine. Then, trying to moisten his fingertips on his bone-dry tongue, Richardson started in on the bills: "Ten, twenty, thirty, forty, fifty, sixty, seventy, eighty, ninety, a hundred, a hundred ten . . ."

The Ebersole *Goes in for the Kill*

The clock in the pilot house showed four minutes to General Quarters when Captain Jones stepped onto the bridge.

"Now the Captain is on the bridge," Ohm growled into the ship's loudspeaker system.

"Morning, Captain," Lustig said through the pilot house porthole. "I have land on radar dead ahead at sixteen miles."

"Very well, Mister Lustig," the Skipper said. He started toward his sea chair on the starboard wing of the bridge. "I trust you'll give us a good shoot today, my boy," he called to Lustig. "We've come a long way to deliver the goods, so let's deliver them expeditiously and accurately, irregardless of the obstacles, eh?" His eyebrows shot up to underscore the point.

"Aye aye, sir," Lustig said noncommittally.

"A cup of pilot house java, Captain?" Ohm asked, pointing to the coffee pot on a small electric burner.

Chewing nervously on the inside of his cheek, Jones ignored the offer and settled into his sea chair. The sun edged over the horizon now and Jones put on a pair of Polaroid sunglasses.

"Morning, Skipper," said the XO, saluting his image in the Captain's sunglasses. "I'm sorry to have to tell you this, but de Bovenkamp knocked over the model of the *Ebersole* at breakfast this morning."

"Can it be repaired?"

"I don't think so, Captain. After he knocked it over he more or less stepped on it and, well, frankly, there isn't much left to piece together."

Jones shook his head angrily. "I expected more from that boy," he said. "First the whales, now this."

The Executive Officer coughed nervously. "It's zero seven twenty, Skipper," he said.

"Fine, XO, let 'er rip."

The XO walked across the pilot house to the alarm boxes and pushed down the handle on the general alarm. Again the DONG DONG DONG DONG DONG DONG DONG DONG reverberated throughout the *Ebersole*.

Ohm put the betting sheet on the morning's shoot into his breast pocket (his rule was "all bets closed once GQ sounds") and clicked on the microphone: "Now this is *not* a drill. This is *not* a drill. Now all hands, man your battle stations. Now set condition one Able throughout the ship." Then he raced off to his battle station in Main Plot.

The Executive Officer unlocked the cabinet under the navigator's pilot house desk and passed out sidearms to each of the officers on the bridge, including the Captain.

"Six minutes thirty-two seconds," the XO said, punching his stopwatch as Wallowitch, looking particularly grim, disappeared into the Main Director.

Jones fidgeted in his chair. "Heads up now, XO," he called, "I don't want to go inside the ten-fathom curve."

The XO studied the navigation chart, which showed the enemy coast from someplace called—— —— ——to someplace called—— ——.

A fathometer reading—"11.5 fathoms"—came up from the chart house.

"Recommend we come right to course zero two zero in, oh, three minutes, Captain," the XO said. "That'll put us parallel to the shore and six miles off target. You should be able to see—— ——light dead ahead soon as we turn."

"Mister Moore, come right to zero two zero in three minutes," the Skipper ordered.

"Quartermaster, log this," the XO called. "Zero seven twenty eight, crossed into free-fire zone."

Jones seemed to relax perceptibly.

"Zero seven thirty, Captain," said the XO. "Recommend we come right."

"All right, Mister Moore, you heard the man, come right," the Skipper said. He was starting to get excited now; the feeling of his own racing pulse imparted a rhythm to events.

"Right standard rudder, come to zero two zero," called Moore.

"Rudder is right standard, sir, coming to zero two zero. Steady on zero two zero."

"What speed you want, XO?" Moore asked.

"What speed do you want, Captain?" the XO asked.

"Give me twelve knots. With a following sea that should be enough to keep her steady on for the guns. But make sure the engine room has those superheats up in case they shoot back like last time and we need to hightail it out of here, eh? If I ring up flank speed I *want* flank speed."

"Turns for twelve knots," Moore ordered.

As the *Ebersole* steadied on its new heading, the

early morning mist that had obscured the shore thinned and broke.

"Can you see the target yet, Shrink?" Lustig asked, speaking into his headset that connected him with the Main Director, Main Plot and the gun mounts.

"Affirmative, I can see the target," said Wallowitch, perched overhead on the tractor seat in the director, his eyes pressed against the twenty-four-power eyepiece of the optical range finder. He twisted a knob and brought the split image of the target together so that he could find the range and shell it and split it into pieces again.

"What's the matter with you, Wally?" Lustig asked. Something in Wallowitch's tone was not quite right.

"I said I can see the fucking target, what else you want?"

("Some human decency," Lustig thought to say later.)

On the port wing of the bridge, Lustig, Moore and the Captain steadied their binoculars on the target; a small hamlet named—— —— ——clustered around either end of a steel and concrete bridge that straddled the—— ——River a hundred yards up from its mouth. On the right or higher side of the river were a handful of two-story cement buildings; on the left or lower side a score of thatched huts and a brick church. There was no movement in the town except for some streaks of sunlight glinting, like sparks from an anvil, off the single bell in the church tower and an old man and two small children fishing from the girders of the bridge. The old man seemed to be shading his eyes with his hand, leaning forward slightly, squinting out to sea toward the rising sun, toward the *Ebersole*.

—— —— ——was listed in the target assignments as a "key road junction."

"Let's get on to that church right away, eh?" the

Captain ordered, his voice betraying his excitement. "They probably have their observation boys up there. Don't want to give 'em a chance to zero in on us again."

"Surface action port," Lustig called into his headset. "Spot on the church, Shrink."

The two forward five-inch mounts on the *Ebersole* jerked into life, fidgeted back and forth, then swung around to port. Mount 53 on the fantail, under the command of Ensign de Bovenkamp, started to starboard by mistake. "Jesus Christ Almighty," Lustig screamed into the headset, but before he could say anything else the offending mount froze and, like a mischievous child caught in the act, sheepishly began to make its way back around to port.

The computer in Main Plot, taking its range and bearing to the target from the Shrink's optical range finder, generated a solution and sent it out automatically to the gun mounts.

"Solution," Seaman Boeth, in charge of Main Plot during GQ, said tensely.

"Solution," Ensign Joyce, who was standing next to Boeth, repeated into his headset.

Across the room Ohm unfolded his betting sheet and got ready to identify the winner.

"On target, Captain," Lustig called. "Main Plot is generating a solution."

The six five-inch guns, each 190 inches long and rifled to spiral projectiles out like footballs, seemed to take on a life of its own, moving up and down and back and forth in small, squared-off figure eights. Actually they had locked on the target; it was the 2200-ton destroyer that was moving around the guns.

The sun was full up now, shining squarely into the face of anyone ashore who might be looking out to sea.

Biting his nails, Captain Jones nodded toward Lustig.

"Stand by," Lustig called into the headset. "We'll put out a spotting round from the port barrel of Fifty-one."

In the forward five-inch mount Chief McTigue nodded grimly and helmsman Carr hefted a twenty-eight-pound brass powder case, with the word "flashless" stenciled across it in large black letters, onto the port gun tray.

Cee-Dee, standing directly in front of Carr, stomped on a red pedal, bringing VT frag projectiles crammed with fifty-four pounds of TNT up the hoist from the handling room. The system was so integrated that the fuses in the noses of the projectiles were set automatically at 14.4 seconds as they came up the hoist on the basis of target information generated from Main Plot. Traveling at 2500 feet per second, the projectiles would take precisely that long to cover the distance between the *Ebersole* and—— —— ——. Seventy-five feet over the target the projectiles would explode, killing every living thing in the open within 100 feet.

The Captain, the XO, Mister Moore and the other men on the bridge stuffed small cotton wads into their ears; Tevepaugh, the messenger of the watch during CQ, was afraid he wouldn't be able to get the cotton out again so he pressed his palms against the sides of his head.

Overhead the American flag and the *Ebersole*'s thin, tattered commissioning pennant snapped from the fore-top. The air search radar antenna, an ancient apparatus that looked exactly like a bedspring, squeaked as it scanned the skies.

"All right, Mister Lustig," the Captain said, doing a jig on one foot. *"The hell with Sweet Reason—let the bastards have it, eh?"*

"Commence fire," Lustig called into his headset. "Commence fire."

Tevepaugh took one hand away from his ear and pushed down the lever on the 21MC marked "Director." "SHOOT, SHOOT, SHOOT," he screamed, and clamped the hand over his ear again.

Richardson Tries to Figure Out What It All Adds Up To

Two decks below Richardson worked his way with a single minded concentration through another stack of bills. "Twelve thousand eight hundred sixty; twelve thousand eight hundred eighty; twelve thousand nine hundred."

And he reached over and put another tick in the hundreds column.

Lustig Invokes the Love of God

"Well, what are you waiting for, Shrink," Lustig yelled into the sound-powered phone, "an engraved invitation? Commence fire, huh."

"What's the trouble?" the Captain asked impatiently. "What now?"

"We only have six minutes on target on this course, Captain," the XO called from the pilot house.

"You can't what, Shrink?" Lustig asked into the phone. "What do you mean you can't?" As Lustig listened to the answer, his mouth fell open and his eyebrows arched up.

"Well?" asked Jones.

Lustig turned to the Captain and stared at him until Jones said, "Spit it out, my boy."

"The director's out, Captain. Probably the, eh, firing circuit. We had trouble with the firing circuit in the Caribbean last year, remember?"

"Jesus, this is one hell of a moment for the director to go out." Jones glanced nervously toward the shore as if he were afraid the target would get away. "Can you switch to local and fire from the mounts?"

"Can you switch to local, Shrink?" Lustig asked. A pleading note crept into his voice. "Can you let the mounts do the firing?" Instantly Lustig brightened and nodded. "Okay, stand by Fifty-one," he called into the phone. "We'll fire the spotting rounds in local control. It's your baby, McTigue. Commence fire. Commence fire."

Tevepaugh punched down the lever on the 21MC marked "Mount 51" and yelled: "SHOOT, SHOOT, SHOOT."

Still no sound came from the port barrel of Mount 51.

"What now?" Jones whined. Beads of perspiration collected on his forehead and dripped into his eyes, then continued on down his cheeks as if they were tears of frustration.

Lustig paled. "Could you repeat that again, Chief?" he called into the phone. Then, softly, he said: "I suppose you know what you're doing."

Lustig turned back to the Captain. "McTigue says the local control firing mechanism contacts have burned out, Captain. He says you can only fire Fifty-one from remote."

"What in God's name is going on here?" Jones said. He was biting his nails now, jerking his head around from one face to the other. He darted into the pilot house, pushed Tevepaugh aside and depressed the "Mount 52" lever on the 21MC. "Listen, Fifty-two, this is the Captain speaking. I want you to put out a spotting round. I don't care which barrel you use. Just load and shoot. You got that, load and shoot."

There was a burst of static, and then Quinn's voice filtered through the crackling. "I'm sorry, Captain, but Fifty-two's crapped out. I think it's the electro servo coupler. Yeah, it must be the electro servo coupler—the servo just don't seem to want to couple."

"I know your voice, Quinn—I know it's you. I'll see you rot in hell for this, in hell, you hear me, I'll see you rot—"

"Three minutes left on this course, Captain," the XO called from the chart desk.

His jaw quivering, Jones flipped down the "Mount 53" lever on the 21MC. "Who's in charge there?" he asked.

"I am," de Bovenkamp called back over the squawk box.

"Who the hell are you?" Jones yelled.

"It's me, Captain—Ensign de Bovenkamp."

"Ah, de Bovenkamp." Jones wiped the perspiration away from his eyes with the back of his shirt-sleeve. "Listen, my boy, I want you to load one of your barrels and fire off a spotting round. Do you understand?"

"Hot damn," de Bovenkamp called back. "Port or starboard?"

"Port or starboard what?" Jones asked. He was making a visible effort to control himself.

"Do you want me to load the port gun or the starboard gun, Captain? Lustig always specifies."

"Load the port gun, Mister de Bovenkamp, and if for any reason that doesn't function, load the starboard gun and shoot that one." Jones leaned closer to the mouthpiece and lowered his voice. "You know, Mister de Bovenkamp, I've always had a special trust and confidence in you. I want you to know I'm prepared to forget about the unfortunate business with the whales this morning. And I won't hold it against you about breaking the model of the *Ebersole*—accidents can happen to anybody. I simply want you to shoot. You're a good officer, a good American, and I expect you to do your duty."

"You can count on me, Captain," de Bovenkamp said. "I'm ready to shoot, ready and willing."

Jones nodded at Lustig, who spoke into the sound-powered phone. "Commence fire, commence fire," he called. Tevepaugh leaned over the Captain's shoulder, pushed down the "Mount 53" lever and yelled: "SHOOT, SHOOT, SHOOT."

On the bridge, everyone craned toward Mount 53 back aft. De Bovenkamp's guns gyrated for a moment as if they were about to shoot, then lost their erection at the crucial moment and wilted to the deck.

Sobbing, half-hysterical with fear, de Bovenkamp's voice crackled over the 21MC. "Captain, sir, they won't let me. I tried, I swear to God I tried, but they won't let me."

Shaking violently, Jones stood in the pilot house door staring out across six miles of ocean at—— —— ——.

Lustig tapped him on the elbow. "I can try Main Plot, Captain. Fifty-one is still loaded. McTigue said you could shoot from remote. We'll get Boeth to fire from Main Plot." When Jones didn't respond Lustig spoke into the phone. "Joyce, are you there? Joyce? Hey, Poet, are you on the line? Where the hell are you, Main Plot? Why don't you answer?"

Lustig turned back to Jones with a defeated look on his face. "Main Plot doesn't seem to answer, Captain," he said in a whisper.

"One minute more on this course," the XO called. "One minute left."

Jones exploded. "It's this goddamn Sweet Reason," he shrieked.

"Sweet Reason has nothing—" Lustig started to say, but the Captain drowned him out. "You're the gunnery officer here," he screamed. "Your career is riding on getting those guns operating."

"For the love of God," Lustig cried into the headset, "somebody shoot."

"I'm trying, I'm trying," de Bovenkamp shouted back.

Locked on target, Mounts 51 and 52 continued to twitch as if they had life left in them. But the only thing the *Ebersole* bombarded the shore with was silence.

Ohm Passes the Buck

"Thirty-eight thousand six hundred, thirty-eight thousand six hundred ten—"

There was a loud knock on the supply office door. "Hey, Mister Richardson?"

Richardson didn't look up. "Thirty-eight thousand six hundred twenty—"

"Mister Richardson, it's me, Melvin Ohm."

"Thirty-eight thousand six hundred thirty—"

"You in there, Mister Richardson? Open up, will you?" Ohm knocked again.

"What is it, Ohm?" Richardson called. "What do you want?"

"I got to see you a second, Mister Richardson—it's about the bet you laid on the shoot this morning."

"Don't tell me I finally picked a winner?"

"Nobody picked no winner, Mister Richardson. We never shot—didn't you not hear it?"

"I've been tied up in here all morning," Richardson said. "What happened?"

"Search me," Ohm said. "I keep my nose clean, right. All I know is there wasn't no shoot."

"Well, if we didn't shoot what you come down here for?"

"I come to give you your buck back," Ohm said unhappily. "No shot means no bets. No bets means I got to give the bread back. Open up so I can let you have your buck."

"Listen, Ohm, I'm really busy. Just slip it under the door, will you?"

Ohm squatted and pushed a dollar bill under the supply office door, along with the betting sheet. "Would you mind putting your initials next to your name. You're in square number forty-one. Got to keep this all legal and aboveboard, right?"

Richardson pocketed the dollar, scribbled his initials alongside his name in square forty-one and slid the sheet back to Ohm under the door.

"Thanks, Mister Richardson," Ohm said.

"Sure thing," Richardson said, swiveling around to the money stacked on his desk. "Now where was I? Thirty-eight thousand six hundred fifty, thirty-eight thousand six hundred sixty . . ."

Captain Jones Takes the Bait

Captain Jones was sitting at attention on the closed toilet seat between the metal washbasin and the stall shower. His feet were flat on the deck inside his unlaced Adler elevators. His head was angled back like a praying mantis's. A wet washcloth covered his eyes. Every few minutes the Captain would wring it out under the cold-water tap and fold it over the top half of his face.

The door to the cabin was jammed open with a wedge of wood. The Executive Officer and Sonarman Third Dwight Proper had pulled over two seats so they could talk to the Captain through the open door.

With his head tilted back and his eyes blindfolded, Jones seemed to take on the mannerisms of a sightless person. He listened without turning his head toward the speaker; he spoke to the space between the two chairs.

"You sure you don't want me to call the Doc?" the Executive Officer asked again. The ship's clock had just struck ten—the signal for him to head up to the bridge with his sextant to take a morning sunline. But the XO didn't have the slightest interest in the sun this morning; the way he saw it, his career would be riding on what happened in the next few minutes.

"No, no," Jones said to the space between the two chairs. He waved his hand impatiently. "Let's get on with it, Proper."

"Like I was saying, Captain, I figure we can get Mister Wallowitch, McTigue, Quinn, the Negroes in Mister de Bovenkamp's mount and Mister Joyce for

202

violation of the Uniform Code of Military Justice, article—"

"Never mind the article," Jones snapped. "What precisely can we pin on them?"

"Mutiny," said Proper. "We can get them for mutiny, which carries a maximum sentence in times of peace— which is the category we're in—of life imprisonment."

"Just life?" complained Jones. "What a pity it's not wartime, eh?"

"Mister de Bovenkamp is another kettle of fish altogether, if you get my meaning, Captain. Him we can nail for dereliction of duty, which is worth five years if it's worth a day. Let's see"—Proper glanced at his notes— "that leaves Mister Lustig and Boeth. Mister Lustig we should be able to tag with knowingly falsifying verbal or written reports."

"In simple English, lying to his commanding officer," the Captain summed up.

"That's it in a nutshell," agreed Proper. "I'm sorry to report that the most that carries is three years. But I want to hold out the possibility that with further investigation—you realize I've only been on this for two hours—I may be able to come up with something more substantial. Now as for Boeth—well, the particulars of Boeth's case are more complicated."

Jones peeled away the washcloth and blinked open his eyes. They were shining with fever. His face was covered with red blotches, as if the blood had rushed to his head and not all of it had rushed back again. Between the blotches the Captain's skin looked like beeswax that was just beginning to melt, a state of affairs that gave his face a vaguely blurred quality. His lower jaw worked when he wasn't talking.

"Good police work, Proper," Jones was saying. "You're a credit to this ship, a credit to your country. Isn't he a credit, XO? All right, let's go over them one by one. We'll take Boeth in his turn, Start with that clown Wallowitch."

"Aye aye, Captain," Proper said. He glanced at the XO, then at his notes. "Wallowitch has—"

"*Mister* Wallowitch to you," Jones snapped. "Let's not forget he's an officer and a gentleman by act of Congress."

"*Mister* Wallowitch it is, Captain. No offense intended. *Mister* Wallowitch has confessed everything."

"He admits it wasn't a malfunction?"

"He admits he didn't follow a lawful and express order to open fire, yes, sir. He admits it had nothing to do with the equipment not working."

"Does he give any excuse?" the XO asked.

"I guess you could call it an excuse, but I doubt whether it'll stand up even in a civilian court. What he says is he didn't shoot—now get this—he didn't shoot because he wasn't physically able to contract the muscle in his trigger finger."

Jones nibbled on his cuticles, his eyes wide with astonishment. "He wasn't able to contract the muscle in his trigger finger?" he repeated, contracting the muscle in his own trigger finger several times to show how effortless the motion was.

"Sounds like—no offense intended, Captain— sounds like a crock of shit, if you get my drift. Even if it's true he still had nine other fingers he could have tried."

"And ten toes," the Captain chimed in. "Don't forget the ten toes. Did Wallowitch tell this to Lustig over the sound-powered phone?—tell him about the finger not contracting?"

"He sure did, Captain."

Jones slowly lifted his body off the toilet seat, shuffled over to his desk chair and carefully lowered himself into it. The XO and Proper turned their chairs around to face the Captain. The XO's chair scraped against the deck and the noise sent a shiver up the Captain's spine.

Jones chewed away on a particularly stubborn cuticle for a few moments, then thoughtfully shifted to another finger. Finally he said: "So when Lustig told me the firing circuit was on the fritz he was covering for Wallowitch?"

"Right as rain, Captain. Wallowitch—I mean *Mister* Wallowitch told *Mister* Lustig he couldn't shoot because he couldn't contract his trigger finger, and Mister Lustig told you the firing circuit was out of order. Which adds up to an open and shut case of knowingly falsifying a verbal report if I ever saw one. We can nail him to the cross on this."

Jones nodded enthusiastically. "All right, now McTigue—what happened on Mount Fifty-one?"

"McTigue claims that the local control firing mechanism contacts burned out. I checked out his alibi personally, Captain. The contacts were burned out just like he says, but they were still warm—and so was a soldering iron I found stashed behind the port hoist in the gun mount. When we examine the iron for fingerprints I'm pretty sure we'll find McTigue's all over the handle."

"A warm soldering iron, eh?"

"Right, Captain. I can show it to you if you want, but naturally it isn't warm anymore."

"That won't be necessary, Proper. Now about Fifty-two—how about that man"—Jones unaccountably smiled—"Quinn?"

"Quinn swears on a stack of Bibles he pushed the firing button when you ordered him to, Captain. He says the reason the guns didn't go off"—Proper checked his notes—"is because something called the electro servo coupler burned out, making the mount inoperative. I looked at the index of the maintenance handbook on a five-inch, .38 caliber gun mount and couldn't find anything that sounded like"—Proper glanced again at his notes—"electro servo coupler. Apparently there is no such animal." The Captain stole a look at the XO, but he was staring out the porthole as if he were lost in thought. "Besides that," Proper went on, "I got a signed statement from the hot-case man in Fifty-two. He says that Quinn said, 'Shit, if nobody shoots, they can't lay a fucking finger on me,' or words to that effect. Sorry about the profanity, Captain."

"We'll see if we can't lay a finger on him, eh?" Jones said. "What about Mister de Bovenkamp? What the hell was he doing in Fifty-three in the first place?"

"You assigned Mister de Bovenkamp to Mount Fifty-three two weeks ago, Captain, because he's supposed to take over from Mister Lustig as gunnery officer eventually and has to qualify as a mount captain first. When you ordered him to open fire, he passed the command on to the two powder men and two projectile men whose job it was to load the guns. Now you'll be interested to know, Captain, that all four of these men are colored." Proper glanced quickly at his notes. "Two of them are the signalmen you suspected of having raised the flag upside-down—Pettis Foreman and Jefferson Waterman. The third is the night baker, Seldon Saler. The fourth is Truman Love—"

"He's the dumb steward who keeps clogging my urinal," the XO reminded Jones.

"Waterman seemed to be the ringleader, Captain. When Mister de Bovenkamp ordered them to load, Waterman said they wouldn't follow the orders of a racist officer, or words to that effect."

"Did he mean me or Mister de Bovenkamp?" Jones asked.

"That's a good question, Captain. I'll have to interrogate him again and check that out. Anyhow, it's my feeling that their refusal to load notwithstanding, it was Mister de Bovenkamp's job as mount captain to shoot one way or another. And his failure to do so constitutes, according to a strict construction of the appropriate statutes, dereliction of duty."

". . . think you can. . ."

"Beg pardon, Captain?" Proper said, cocking an ear.

"I said, do you think you can make it stick?"

"Do I think I can make it stick? Jesus, coming against the background of this Sweet Reason business it'll look as if we're handling him with kid gloves, if you get my meaning, Captain."

Jones nodded twice. On the second nod his head stayed down, lost in his cuticles.

Proper waited until he saw that Jones wasn't coming up for air. "Begging your pardon, Captain, but do you want to hear what happened in Main Plot? The Poet was in Main Plot." When Jones hesitated, Proper added: "He was the one with all those subversive pictures on the bulkhead."

"What was the Poet doing in Main Plot?" the Captain asked. "He's supposed to be my Communications Officer."

It was the Executive Officer who answered. "The *Rules of Engagement* specify we've got to have an officer in Main Plot during General Quarters, and Joyce was the only officer we could spare, so I assigned him there, Captain. Course Seaman Boeth actually runs the show down there—Boeth's been to navy fire control school, you remember—so we put Mister Joyce on the sound-powered phones where he couldn't do any harm." The XO chuckled at his own ingenuity.

"Sounds reasonable," said Jones.

"Like I was saying, Captain, it seems that Mister Joyce more or less followed what was going on over the sound-powered phones, so when Mister Lustig called down to him thinking to get Boeth to shoot, Mister Joyce yanked the phone jack out of its socket. You remember Mister Lustig wasn't able to raise anybody on the phone? Well, that's why the line went dead."

"I remember," Jones said bitterly.

"Now here's where the plot thickens. When Mister Joyce pulled the plug, so to speak, Gunner's Mate Third Melvin Ohm—"

"Ohm's the one who organizes the betting pools," the XO reminded the Captain.

"That's the man," Proper said. "Ohm tried to plug the phone jack back in, and in so doing wrestled Ensign Joyce to the deck—"

"He attacked an *officer*?" the Captain asked incredulously.

"Don't forget he attacked an officer to prevent him from committing mutiny, Captain."

"I suppose you could look at it that way," agreed Jones. "Well, at least there's one man on board who was loyal to his Captain and his country."

"Now all the while he had Mister Joyce pinned to the deck," Proper continued, "Ohm kept shouting, 'You fuck, I'll have to give back all the—' or words to that effect."

"Give back all the *what*?" asked the XO.

"Don't know, XO. He never got to finish the sentence. Just at that precise exact instant he was struck on or about the right eye with the *Rules of Engagement* thrown by Seaman Boeth, who then landed on Ohm and pummeled—begging your pardon, Captain—the be-Jesus out of him."

"But that means we can file mutiny charges against Boeth too!" exclaimed Jones.

"With all respect, not so fast, Captain. I told you before that Boeth's case was complicated. On the one hand we could get him for assault with a deadly weapon, the deadly weapon in question being the *Ebersole's* copy of the *Rules of Engagement*, which tips the scales at eight and eight-tenths pounds—it's bound, as you remember, with metal covers so we can jettison it in case the ship falls into enemy hands."

"Deadly weapon, eh?"

"The trouble is," Proper went on, "that Boeth's defense would probably stand up in court. Boeth says he heard a commotion and spun around to find an enlisted man attacking an officer, so he instinctively came to the assistance of the officer in question, unaware—this is Boeth talking, mind you—unaware that the said officer was in the act of committing mutiny."

"So that's it, eh?" Jones reached down and began lacing his Adlers, which were covered with scuff marks. Both the XO and Proper noticed that the Captain's cuticles were bleeding and that his hands were shaking.

"Yes, sir, that's about the size of it. You can see for yourself we got every one of them, with the possible exception of Boeth, right where we want them. And when we get our hands on this Sweet Reason character, we'll have more on him than unlawful posting of personal messages or inciting—we'll get him for mutiny."

Jones shook his head regretfully. "This is the last thing in the world—" he began, "—the last thing in the world I wanted, XO. You know that. Dealing with a mutiny inevitably taints all the officers in the same command no matter how loyal they are. Wherever we go after this, they'll be whispering, 'He was on the *Ebersole*.' But painful as it may be, I've got to do my duty." A smile inched its way onto the Captain's face. "Of course," he added, "there will be compensations," and he closed his eyes and saw himself on the quarterdeck of a man-o'-war, saw the mutineers spreadeagled on the shrouds below him, saw himself nod once, saw Proper raise the cat behind his ear and bring it down with a "phhhhit" across the bare vertebrae of Ensign Joyce. Seeing it all, the smile spread across the Captain's face in all its glory now.

"Yes, compensations," Jones said, opening his eyes.

Once he saw which way the wind was blowing, the XO normally would have run before it. Instead he turned to Proper. "Would you mind," he said, indicating the door with his head. "I want a word with the Captain."

When the door clicked closed, the XO turned back to Jones. "Captain, I think you know that I share your dedication to duty one hundred percent. But the question, as I see it, is, what is duty in this case? Of course, we can draw up charges and specifications against these men—"

"I'm not sure I understand—"

"Captain, you and I are professionals. With us duty has always come before everything—before our families, before our personal likes and dislikes, before you name it—even when doing our duty would hurt our own chances for promotion. Neither of us, it goes without saying, would shrink from doing our duty for personal motives. But I think there is another duty, a larger duty—"

Jones leaned forward. "Stop beating around the bush, XO."

The Executive Officer took a gulp of air. "Captain,

you know as well as I do that when the balloon goes up, the United States is obligated by treaty to come to the assistance of forty-two separate nations around the face of the globe. And we have strong moral obligations to another two dozen or so. What's the key to fulfilling these obligations? I'll tell you what the key is, Captain. The key is seapower. To get down to the nitty gritty, what I'm saying is that we can't report this mutiny because it will undermine confidence in the U.S. Navy and, ultimately, in the United States itself. My god, if it becomes common knowledge that one of the greyhounds of the sea failed to do its duty—more than failed, but mutinied in the face of the enemy—the Ruskies will start poking their bows right smack into our sea lanes, right smack into Norfolk Harbor maybe." Having planted the bait, the XO tugged gently at the line. "I know what I'm asking is the harder course to follow, Captain—"

"You're asking the impossible, XO—you're asking me to let these"—Jones racked his brain for the right word—"these—" He couldn't find it.

"I'm asking you to weigh which is more important, Captain—the fate of a few bleeding-heart yellowbellies or the credibility of the United States of America."

Jones's teeth gnawed on a nail. "I have to hand it to you, XO—you think of all the angles," he said. "But I don't see how we can simply ignore what's happened. What the hell would I put in my action report to Admiral Haydens?"

The XO pondered the problem. "I suppose," he said finally, "you could always tell him what he wants to hear."

The Captain's Batteries Run Down

The Poet expected the worst when he learned the Captain wanted to see him.

"About what?" Joyce asked Tevepaugh, who brought the summons.

"Search me," said Tevepaugh. "He just said for you to bring your message blanks."

"Tevepaugh says you want to see me," the Poet said a few minutes later.

The Captain was sitting with his back to the door, hunched over his desk, writing. He was wearing a dark blue terrycloth bathrobe with the letters "CO" stenciled on the back and a "Swift and Sure" emblem under the letters. "With you in a second," he said. For the next few minutes the only sound in the cabin came from the Captain's felt-tip pen—soft brush strokes underlining sentences. Finally Jones turned around.

"Come in—close the door behind you. I see you have your message pad, eh? Good. Good. I want you to encode this and send it off to Admiral Haydens. You'll have trouble making out my handwriting so I'll read it to you." Jones scanned what he had written, reached for his pen and changed another word, looked at it for a moment and then restored the original. Again the Poet heard the brushing of the felt tip.

"All right, here we go. 'From Commander *Eugene Ebersole*. Action report follows. Complying with Op Order three seven charlie romeo, fired one hundred eighty-six rounds of VT frag at—— —— ——. Damaged pilings and roadway of bridge straddling—— ——River.

Destroyed four armored personnel carriers, twelve trucks, a barrack compound and a fuel oil storage facility. Enemy casualties estimated at two hundred fifty-five.'" Jones looked up. "You have that, Mister Joyce?"

In a toneless voice Joyce read the message back again, ending with "Enemy casualties estimated at two hundred fifty-five." Then it struck him. "But that's the number of men on board the *Ebersole!*"

"Is it, Mister Joyce?"

"You know it is," the Poet said. "You're trying to tell me something."

"I could never tell you anything," the Captain said. "You know why? Because I'm professional navy and you're professional civilian. And professional navy has no language in common with professional civilian. I went to sea when I was seventeen, Mister Joyce. I traded a sea of wheat for a sea of water. You wouldn't understand when I say I've never regretted it."

"I realize there are pleasures in going to sea," the Poet conceded. "The sunrises—"

Jones laughed out loud. "Sunrises! I've seen the sun rise so many times in my life, Mister Joyce, it's become an everyday occurrence."

The Poet was suddenly very moved. "I'm sorry—"

"Don't be sorry, Mister Joyce. Whatever you do, don't be sorry. The professional navy doesn't need sympathy from a professional civilian. I'm telling you the facts of navy life, that's all. If I had a choice I'd want you to understand rather than not understand, but I don't hold out much hope for you."

"I'd like—" the Poet began, but the Captain interrupted.

"I made my friends by the time I was seventeen and spent the rest of my life losing them. The navy ruined my friendships, my family—my wife divorced me twelve years ago because I couldn't get a shore assignment. I haven't seen my sons in three years."

"But why did you stick it out?"

"Because," Jones said—his eyes fell on the barbed-wire collection on the bulkhead—"because it didn't seem as if there was anything left after the war except my country and my career."

"Those are two different things, Captain."

"That's a professional civilian point of view, Mister Joyce. I've always found them to be the same thing, my country and my career. If I serve one, I serve the other."

The Poet and the Captain looked at each other for a long moment, looked at each other squarely in the eye. "But you used the number two hundred fifty-five," Joyce said finally.

The Captain's gaze fell away now and he began talking in short sentences, as if the conversation was a verbal telegram to be paid for by the word. "Can't cry over spilt milk."

"That's not so, Captain—you can cry over spilt milk," Joyce said ardently. "You've *got to* cry over spilt milk."

Jones shook his head. "Never. In my book even a lump in the throat is a luxury."

"My God," said the Poet emotionally.

"Perhaps," said Jones as if it fitted into the conversation. He picked up the flashlight on his desk and absentmindedly toyed with it, trying to touch things across the room with the beam. But it was blotted out by the daylight pouring through the porthole.

"Batteries run down," Jones added thoughtfully, and he fought back the small lump that rose to his throat.

The Poet Gets an Apology

"You mean you sent it!"

"Sure I sent it—it was that or a general court-martial for every one of us."

"Not for me it wasn't. Jesus, all I know is I turned around and saw someone laying into you, so I laid into him. That happens to be the truth. They can't convict you for defending an officer."

"Now who's innocent," the Poet said. "You're dreaming if you think that'll stand up in court. My God, when they're finished with you it'll look as if you organized the whole thing." Joyce turned to an imaginary court-martial. "With your permission, Mister President, the prosecution would like to offer in evidence a newspaper clipping marked 'Exhibit A,' which shows the defendant"—the Poet leveled an accusing finger at Boeth—"being dragged away from an anti-war demonstration after kicking an officer of the law in the balls."

"It was the groin."

"Groin then. Kicking an officer of the law in the groin."

Sitting on the deck, his back against another bank of computers, Boeth laughed nervously. "Well, the fact is I didn't have the vaguest idea what was going on. How was I to know you'd pull a stunt like that?" Boeth shrugged his heavy shoulders. "Maybe you're right. This way we're off the hook and so is he. If they ever investigated a mutiny, they'd find out all about the junk we sank and the plane we cut in half and how he thought we'd been hit by shore fire when the Plexiglas shattered on the bridge."

Boeth looked quizzically at Joyce. "To tell you the honest to God truth, Poet, I didn't think you had it in you."

Joyce smiled self-consciously. "If it's any consolation to you, neither did I."

The bo's'n's whistle shrilled over the ship's loudspeaker system, piping down the midday meal.

Boeth nodded and then shrugged. Joyce shrugged back at him and the two smiled at each other.

Boeth asked, "Does he still jerk off his phallus-flashlight?"

"He still plays with it," the Poet said, "but he's a lot more complicated than we thought."

"And Sweet Reason," Boeth asked, "what do you think of him now that he's pulled off a mutiny?"

"From what I can see," the Poet said, "Sweet Reason didn't have all that much to do with it."

The XO Makes a Discovery

The Executive Officer made his way through the chow line that snaked aft along the inboard passageway. The white sailors who blocked his path he pushed aside with the back of his hand; the black sailors he said "Excuse me" to and then pushed. They gave ground, or so it seemed to the XO, with a slowness bordering on insolence.

As he moved aft, the XO caught snatches of conversation.

". . . with this midget, see, it was like getting laid to a . . ."

". . . pull in eighty dollars a day in tips plus room and board. Shit, man, I know a guy soaked away . . ."

". . . this cop gets sick, right, he asks me to collect for him, right, so I pick up fifty cents here, a buck there, you get it, so when the cop kicks the bucket I don't tell no one he kicked the bucket, I just keep on collecting . . ."

The XO was almost at the midship's passageway when he sensed the change in atmosphere. Men were milling in front of the Doc's office, gesturing, craning, arguing; everyone seemed to be talking at once.

"Who the fuck he think he is, putting one of those things up just when chow is going down?"

"Lemme see, lemme see."

"Forget the mother and let's eat."

"He's sure got guts, he has."

"He's got his nerve, that's what he has."

"Read it a-loud, will you?"

A sailor who felt the XO pushing on the flat of his back turned on him belligerently. "Watch who the fuck you're—" When he saw who it was, the sailor backed off. "No offense intended, sir."

"What's going on here?" the XO demanded. The talking subsided into a sullen silence. Finally Angry Pettis Foreman, a toothpick jutting from his lips, nodded toward the laminated mouth-to-mouth resuscitation chart screwed to the door.

"What the—" exclaimed the XO, and he peeled off the piece of paper taped to the chart the way someone rips off a bandage, in one rapid motion so there will be as little pain as possible.

"I found it taped to the mouth-to-mouth resuscitation chart forward of the midship's passageway," the XO told the Captain a few minutes later. "I think I got it before too many of them saw it."

Jones sat in front of his desk, his shoulders hunched, toying with the food in his tray. The XO offered him the leaflet and when the Captain made no move to take it, the XO asked, "Do you want me to read it?"

Jones nodded grimly.

The XO coughed nervously. "It starts with this darned 'comrades in arms' business again," he said. He expected the Captain to say something and when he didn't the XO said, "Bleeding heart Bolshevik expression if I ever heard one." Still no response from the Captain.

Without looking up between sentences, the Executive Officer began to read the leaflet.

> "Today we have demonstrated what men of conscience can accomplish when they listen to reason. The officers and men of the *Eugene Ebersole* refused to obey the racist pig captain when he ordered them to pull the ~~trigger~~ trigger. This morning, the most elerquent sound in the entire world was the silence of men who refused to kill. It is this silence that will ~~drown~~ drown out the generals and admirals of the Pentagon.
> *The Voice of Sweet Reason*"

For a long time after the XO finished reading Jones didn't say a word. Finally he spoke in a dead voice. "It's him—" He brought a palm up to his jaw to stop the quivering. "It's him or me," he said. "Do you read me, XO? It's him or me. The navy's not big enough for both of us."

"You told me Proper still had something up his

sleeve, Captain—something about some spaces he didn't search yet. Should I get him up here?"

"No," Jones said. "Just give him Quinn's keys. He knows what they're for. Don't want to see him again until he's found this—" Again the Captain racked his brain for an expression he could freight with the contempt he felt for Sweet Reason. "This—" Again he failed to come up with one.

"About the leaflet," the XO said, holding it toward the Captain. "What do you want me to do with it?"

But Jones had turned back to pick at the cold food in the compartmented tin tray on his desk.

Jones Catches Sight of Another Everyday Occurrence

"Now the Captain is on the bridge," Ohm growled into the loudspeaker system, but the sound seemed to melt away in the wind whistling past the ship.

Squinting into the sunlight, which was hard and hurt his eyes, Captain Jones shuffled onto the open bridge. He usually wore sunglasses topside but he had forgotten them this time, and there were large white circles under his eyes where the sun hadn't tanned the skin. He had abandoned his Adlers for green felt bedroom slippers, and the change left him several inches shorter. His khaki trousers were creased in all the wrong places and bagged at the knees. He wore a nonregulation gray sweater with brown leather elbow patches knit by an older sister who lived in Wichita. His eyes seemed to have difficulty focusing, his features still had the blurred quality of melted wax. As he bent over the starboard pelorus peering through the telescopic alidade at the carrier racing into the wind, he looked like an old man fumbling with a key in a lock.

"Congratulations, Captain," de Bovenkamp called, saluting smartly with one hand and pressing his hat to his head with the other to keep it on in the wind. He had been waiting an hour for the Captain to come up on the bridge. "This is one heck of a red-letter day for you."

His hair flying, Jones hissed at de Bovenkamp: "Must you chew that goddamn gum all the time?" Without waiting for an answer he shouted: "We're four degrees off station. Supposed to be broad on the port beam of the carrier for flight operations. Who's the Officer of the Deck?"

The faint whoosh-thump of the steam catapults echoed across the thousand yards of ocean that separated the giant aircraft carrier from the *Ebersole*, and four F-4 Phantom jets leapt into the sky for a strike against the mainland.

"I am, Captain," Lustig yelled.

"You're four degrees off station, Mister Lustig."

"Aye aye, Captain," Lustig said. He ducked into the pilot house to adjust the revolutions per minute so that the *Ebersole* would drift back on station.

Whoosh-thump, whoosh-thump, whoosh-thump, whoosh-thump—four more Phantoms leapt into the bright sky, wheeled into formation and banked through a wisp of a cloud toward the mainland.

A supremely calm, dulcet-toned voice came over the primary tactical radio circuit from the carrier. "Elbow Room, this is Isolated Camera, immediate execute, nine turn, I say again, immediate execute, nine turn, stand by, execute, over."

Lustig picked up the radio-telephone and said,

"This is Elbow Room, roger, out." Then he called to Carr, who was the helmsman: "Left standard rudder."

Lustig's order was carried off in the wind, and Carr turned to de Bovenkamp, who was sulking next to the radar repeater. "Mister Lustig said left, didn't he?"

Preoccupied with trying to catch the Captain's eye, de Bovenkamp nodded, and Carr spun the rudder over and brought the *Ebersole* round ninety degrees to the left, a maneuver that put the destroyer a thousand yards ahead of the carrier. The wind immediately died down.

"Why'd the carrier change course?" the Captain asked.

"Her Foxtrot flag's dipped, Captain," Lustig explained. "She's still got a flight of Phantoms to recover but they're not due in for another few minutes. She'll turn back into the wind when they show up."

Jones sat back in the captain's chair on the starboard wing of the bridge and beckoned to the Executive Officer, who had just come topside. "All right, XO, now fill me in on what Filmore's up to, eh?"

"Well, it seems as if your silver star's come through, Captain—the one we recommended you for after we sank the patrol boat the other morning. Filmore's going to have Congressman Partain personally pin it on you right smack in the middle of the carrier's flight deck. I guess he thinks the ceremony will produce some pretty good footage to sort of wind up the Congressman's visit. They want us alongside to highline you over as soon as they recover the next flight of Phantoms."

"Goddamn, that is news," Jones brightened. Some of the color had seeped back into his face and it made his features more distinct. With mounting enthusiasm he began to go over the details.

"Let's see, I'll have to get rid of this sweater and put on a tie, eh? And get True Love up here with my campaign ribbons and my shoes, will you, XO? Oh, and my blue baseball cap. They film these things in color, don't they? Yes, don't forget my blue baseball cap with the 'Swift and Sure' emblem on it." Jones pivoted in his chair and looked back at the carrier, riding like the Rock of Gilbraltar in the swells of Yankee Station. "She'll probably come around to this course again when flight ops are over, which will put us dead ahead of her. Hmmmm. I guess the best bet would be to come right and make a full circle and come up from her starboard quarter for the highline transfer, wouldn't you say so, XO?" Jones squinted at the sea, trying to judge how the wind and waves would affect the approach to the carrier.

"Coming right sounds as if it should do the trick, Skipper," the XO said. Both men were feeling pretty good now. "I'll get True Love up here in a jiffy."

The Captain had already put Band-Aids over his bleeding cuticles and was lacing up his Adlers when the dulcet voice came over the primary tactical circuit again. "Elbow Room, this is Isolated Camera, immediate execute, turn nine, I repeat, immediate execute, turn nine, stand by, execute, over." Lustig acknowledged the order and brought the *Ebersole* back into the wind, putting it once again on the port beam of the carrier.

"Her Foxtrot's two blocked," Lustig said by way of explanation.

A flight of sixteen Phantoms peeled off into a racetrack pattern that took them low over the *Ebersole* and around the far end of the track toward the carrier, where one by one they settled like ducks onto the flight deck. The seventh jet in line had had its landing gear shot away and belly-whopped down, skidding to a stop a few feet from the edge of the flight deck. Instantly dozens of men in brightly colored jerseys swarmed over the wounded airplane. Through binoculars Jones could see them lift the pilot out of the cockpit by his armpits, lay him on a stretcher and dogtrot off toward the island that jutted from the flight deck. A yellow tractor pulled the Phantom clear and the rest of the jets, still circling overhead in the racetrack pattern, came on it.

"Her Foxtrot flag's down, Captain," Lustig yelled into the wind. "She's finished flight operations. Ah, there it goes, there goes the Romeo flag—she's getting ready to receive us alongside."

"Very well, Mister Lustig," Jones called, standing near the pilot house door. "I'll take the conn."

"The Captain has the conn," Lustig yelled to Carr on the helm.

"Aye aye, the Captain has the conn," Carr repeated.

The primary tactical circuit came to life again. "Elbow Room, this is Isolated Camera, immediate execute, nine turn, I say again, immediate execute, nine turn, stand by, execute, over." Lustig picked up the radio-telephone and acknowledged the order.

"Did you get that, Captain?" he yelled.

Jones nodded, then turned toward the pilot house and called into the wind: "Left standard rudder."

Inside the pilot house Carr looked at de Bovenkamp, who was leaning dejectedly against the radar repeater. "The Captain said left, didn't he, Mister de Bovenkamp?"

"Right," de Bovenkamp said, nodding rhythmically and unwrapping another stick of gum.

Carr hesitated for an instant, then shrugged imperceptibly and spun the rudder over right.

Just as the *Ebersole* began to respond to the helm there was a commotion at the top of the inboard ladder leading to the pilot house, and Proper burst through the pilot house onto the open bridge clutching a typewriter to his chest. A huge ring of keys hanging from a lanyard around his neck jingled as he ran. "I found it," he shrieked, thrusting the typewriter into the Captain's hands. "I found the mother, I found it, I told you I'd find it and I found it. *And I know who Sweet Reason is!*"

Every eye was riveted on Proper.

"You know who Sweet Reason is?"

Proper nodded excitedly. The Captain looked dumbly at Proper, unable to believe his luck, to believe the whole Sweet Reason business was over, then he glanced down at the typewriter in his hands, then back at Proper, then at de Bovenkamp, who was sliding a stick of gum into his mouth, then at the Executive Officer, but the Executive Officer wasn't looking at the Captain or Proper or the typewriter, the Executive Officer was staring out past the Captain, out to sea with a look of depthless horror in his eyes, then Proper was staring in the same direction as the Executive Officer with the same look in *his* eyes, and the Captain followed their gaze, knowing all the time what was there, followed it out to sea and saw the aircraft carrier turning into the *Ebersole*, looming over the *Ebersole*. From somewhere behind him came a moan of terror. Pressing the typewriter to his campaign ribbons, nodding as if what he saw merely confirmed what he knew, Captain J. P. Horatio Jones tilted his twitching head and watched the carrier come on the way he had watched, on more occasions than he liked to remember, the sun come up over the horizon.

Richardson Gets a Little Something for His Troubles

Two decks below the bridge, in the supply office, Richardson finished counting the last stack of bills, checked his total against his ledger, found he was ten dollars over and smilingly slipped the extra bill into his wallet.

Tevepaugh Strikes Up the Single Solitary One-man Band

Facing aft on the torpedo deck in his folding canvas captain's chair, Tevepaugh felt the *Ebersole* heel over and assumed that they were going alongside for the highline transfer. Cradling his red electric guitar in his arms, he reached down, plugged in the amplifier, and tried a few tentative chords. There was a howling feedback from Tevepaugh's guitar—an unbearable shriek of fear from the ship itself! Then the 70,000-ton carrier, four city blocks long, plowed into the 2200-ton destroyer, climbed up and over the smaller ship, hammered down on the smaller ship, shattering it on the anvil of the sea.

Commander Filmore Composes the Epilogue

At sunset Commander Whitman Filmore dispatched his lackey Haverhill to shore by helicopter. Haverhill carried with him a satchel containing the film clips of Congressman Partain's visit to Yankee Station and a news release describing the tragic collision at sea, during flight operations, between one of the greyhounds of the fleet and an aircraft carrier. The destroyer, which sank within minutes of the collision, had unaccountably turned in the wrong direction, putting itself directly in the path of the onrushing carrier. One hundred and fifty-three of the destroyer's crewmen survived the sinking. Among the 102 dead or missing were Captain J. P. Horatio Jones, the XO, Chaplain Rodgers, Richardson, Lustig, Moore, de Bovenkamp, Boeth, McTigue, Tevepaugh the guitarist, Ohm, Carr, Doc Shapley, Saler the cook, Proper, Czerniakovski-Drpzdzynski, De-Frank, Duffy, Angry Pettis Foreman, Jefferson Waterman, Keys Quinn, the Poet, the Shrink, True Love and Sweet Reason.

Endit.

Enjoy this tantalizing excerpt from

THE SISTERS

the new blockbuster novel by Robert Littell,
acclaimed author of THE DEFECTION OF
A. J. LEWINTER and THE AMATEUR.

THE SISTERS is "A sinister, *twisting* rollercoaster
ride, the fastest since DAY OF THE JACKAL."

—Joseph Wambaugh,
author of THE DELTA STAR and
THE GLITTER DOME

"What Elmore Leonard is to mysteries, what Isaac
Asimov is to science fiction, and what Stephen King
is to horror—well, that's what Robert Littell is to
the novel of intrigue. He's a first-rate writer."

—Susan Isaacs,
author of ALMOST PARADISE

Experience the virtuosity of Robert Littell's
THE SISTERS.
On sale February 1, 1986, at your local bookseller.

1

"I'm just thinking out loud," Francis was saying. An angelic smile manned the usual fortifications of his face. "What if . . ." His voice trailed off uncertainly.

"What if *what*?" Carroll prompted. A muscle twitched impatiently in his cheek.

"What if—"

They were, by any standards, the Company's odd couple. Office scuttlebutt held that when one itched the other scratched, but that wasn't it; that wasn't it at all. It was more a matter of symbiosis; of constituting two sides of the same coin. Looking at any given skyline, Francis would see forest, Carroll trees; Francis wrote music, Carroll lyrics; Francis would leap with almost feminine intuition in the general direction of unlikely ends while Carroll, a pedestrian at heart, would trail after him lingering over means.

"What if," Francis was saying, "we were to put our man Friday onto someone with Mafia connections?"

"Mafia connections?"

Francis pulled thoughtfully at an earlobe that looked as if it had been pulled at before. "Exactly."

Francis wore an outrageous silk bow tie that he had picked up for a song at a rummage sale. His sixth-floor neighbors thought it was out of character, which only showed that they didn't really understand his character. It was the unexpected splash of color, the tiny touch of defiance, the unconventional link in an otherwise perfectly conformist chain that set him apart from everyone else.

Carroll, on the other hand, liked to look as if he *belonged*. He favored conventional three-piece suits and starched collars that left crimson welts clinging like leeches to his thin, pale neck. Laughing behind his back, the neighbors spoke about his penchant for hair shirts worn, so they assumed, to atone for unspecified sins.

They were half right. There *were* sins, though Carroll never felt the slightest urge to atone for them.

"The Mafia is out of the question," Carroll announced flatly, a crooked forefinger patrolling between his collar and his neck. He looked past Francis the way he stared over the shoulder of anyone he deigned to talk to. "They will want to be paid in the end. And not necessarily in money. Besides, there's no compartmentalization. If this thing is going to succeed, it has to be tightly compartmentalized. Like a submarine."

"Quite right," Francis remarked, blushing apologetically. "I can't imagine what I could have been thinking of." His face screwed up, his eyes narrowed into slits, a sure sign that his mind was leaping toward another unlikely end.

Francis and Carroll were minor legends in the Company. Somewhere along the line one of the CIA's army of PhD's who majored in African dialects and minored in Whitman had dubbed them "The sisters Death and Night." The name stuck. If you mentioned the Sisters in an intraoffice memo, and capitalized the S, almost everyone tucked away in the Company's cradle-to-grave complex knew whom you were talking about. But only the handful with "eyes-only" authorizations in their dossiers had an inkling of what they actually did for a living.

What they did was plot.

And what they were plotting on that perfect August day was a perfect crime.

"What we will need," Francis thought out loud, defining the problem, "is someone who can carry out an assignment without knowing it came from us."

"Someone who thinks he is being employed by others," Carroll ventured, lingering over means.

"Exactly," Francis agreed enthusiastically.

In an organization where people knew secrets, or made it their business to look as if they did, Francis stood out with his aura of absolute innocence. He invariably wore an expression that fell midway between curious and reluctant, and a Cheshire cat's pained smile that hinted at nothing more morally compromising than the death of an occasional rodent. It was common knowledge around the shop that he regularly lied about his name during the annual lie-detector tests—and always managed to fool the black box.

Compared to Francis, Carroll was an open book. When he felt frustrated, it appeared on his face like a flag. He had started out in the business with "Wild Bill" Donovan's Office of Strategic Services during the "Wrong War" (as he liked to call it; he felt that America had defeated the *wrong* enemy), and quickly made a name for himself by scribbling in the margin of one report: "The matter is of the highest possible importance and should accordingly be handled on the lowest possible level." What he meant, of course, was that *he* should handle it; at the tender age of twenty-nine, he had already been convinced of everyone's incompetence but his own. (Perhaps stunned by his audacity, his superiors gave him the brief. In due course Carroll engineered the defection of a German diplomat carrying a valise full of secret documents, and the betrayal to the Gestapo of the Soviet agent who had acted as their go-between. By 1945 Carroll was already focusing on the *right* enemy.)

Nowadays some of their Company colleagues whispered that the Sisters were past their prime, washed up, over the hill; old farts who amused the technocrats calling the tune; has-beens who gave the men in the Athenaeum (as the Sisters, classicists to the core, called the front office) something to talk about at in-house pours. ("The Sisters proposed that we . . ." "They weren't *serious*?" "I'm afraid they were." "What did you tell them?" "I told them they were *mad*!") There were even a few with regular access to the Sisters' product who recommended giving them medical discharges—and there was no suggestion that the problem was physical. They'd been around too long, it was said, they'd seen too much—as if being around too long and seeing too much inevitably led to deeper disorders. Still, several people in high places took them seriously enough to justify giving them space (which, with its Soviet magazines scattered around a shabby Formica coffee table, looked suspiciously like a dentist's office in Tashkent), a man Friday (whose real name, believe it or not, was Thursday) and a gorgeous secretary with an incredibly short skirt and incredibly long legs and a way of clutching files to her breasts that left the rare visitor noticeably short of breath. After all, it was said, the Sisters had had their share of triumphs. Not that long ago, with an almost Machiavellian leap of imagination, they had ferreted out a Russian sleeper in the CIA's ranks. While everyone else frantically searched the files for someone with a record of failed operations against the Russians, Francis thought the problem through from the Soviet point of view and decided that the merchants who ran the mole would have boosted his career with an occasional *success*. Working on that assumption, the Sisters combed the files looking for someone with one or two conspicuous successes and a string of failures. The suspect they uncovered was delivered to the tender mercies of the Company's most experienced interrogator, one G. Sprowls. After an intense interrogation that lasted seven months, G. Sprowls came up with the right questions and the suspect came up with the wrong answers. There was no trial. The suspect simply disappeared from the face of the earth, at which point the CIA awarded a medal and a pension to his widow rather than acknowledge that it had been infiltrated.

"Someone who thinks he is being employed by others," Carroll was saying thoughtfully—he appeared to be talking to the poster tacked to the back of the door that read "Fuck Communism!"—"can't very well point a finger at us if he is caught, can he?"

There was a single soft knock at the door. Without waiting for permission, the gorgeous secretary, who drew pay and broke hearts under her married name, Mrs. Cresswell, sailed into the dentist's office, wordlessly deposited a box of candies on the coffee table, and then, like a spider ducking soundlessly back into its hole, disappeared. Carroll tore off the lid and studied the contents. He detested nuts and cherries—one gave him hives, the other diarrhea—but could never for the life of him remember which ones didn't have them.

"Look at the code on the back of the lid," Francis said with an air of someone indulging his partner's idiosyncrasy.

"I don't understand codes," Carroll muttered. He snatched a candy at random, peeled off the tinfoil and, baring decaying yellowish teeth, gingerly bit into it. "Caramel," he announced with satisfaction, and he popped the rest of the candy into his mouth. He was working on his third caramel when he suddenly snapped his fingers. "I've got it!" he cried, though the caramel sticking to his teeth made his words difficult to understand. "What we need," he explained when he could finally articulate, "is someone who is highly skilled, intelligent, trained in fieldwork and willing to follow orders without inquiring into their source as long as they arrive in the correct form."

Francis said, "I don't quite follow—"

Carroll rocked back onto the rear legs of his chair. "What we need—" His lips twisted into an expression of grim satisfaction; another flag snapping on the halyard of his face.

"What we need," Francis repeated, his eyes watering in anticipation. Having come up with a perfect crime, he considered it in the nature of things that Carroll should come up with a perfect criminal.

"What we need—" Carroll whined, and because in his experience walls more often than not concealed *ears*, he plucked a pencil from a coffee table and finished the sentence on a sheet of scrap paper.

"—is a sleeper!"

"A sleeper, of course!" Francis wrote in turn.

Carroll retrieved the pencil. "But how on earth will we find one?" he wrote.

Francis grabbed the pencil out of Carroll's fingers. "We might get the Potter to give us the use of one," he wrote.

The Sisters melted back into their chairs, drained. Whistling softly through his teeth, Francis collected the scraps of paper they had written on; they had divided up office chores, and it was his job to shred all secret documents.

Carroll's cheek muscle twitched uncontrollably. "He might just do it," he said in a hollow voice, and in a gesture that had nothing, and everything, to do with ends and means, he waved vaguely, weakly toward the dirty window; toward the dirty city; toward the dirty world out there waiting to be *manipulated*.

2

✤

They made their way in lock step down a freshly painted corridor of power toward the Athenaeum. "You'd think our masters would get tired of battleship gray," Francis commented. His nose wrinkled up in disgust. "Imagine how different this place would look in pale green, or off-white even."

Carroll was too absorbed in his own schemes to worry about color schemes. "He's going to agree," he concluded, as if wishing could make it so. "I know him from the days when he ran errands for Dulles in Switzerland. He likes to keep several irons in several fires."

"Then we must make this seem like just another iron," Francis said under his breath, and flashing an ingratiating smile at one of the Pillars of Hercules, as the Deputy Director's two secretaries were known (one handled people, the other paper), he announced in a voice ideally suited to pulpits, "We are responding, like good dogs, to our master's whistle."

"Where *do* you get your ties?" the Pillar who handled people asked, waving them toward the appropriate door. She reached under her desk and dispatched a surge of electricity toward the appropriate lock. The door clicked open just as Francis reached it.

"What do you think of our halls?" demanded the Deputy Director, swiveling away from *his* man Friday to confront the Sisters.

"I would have made a case for pale green or off-white if someone had consulted me," Francis replied sulkily.

"Oh," said the Deputy Director, obviously disappointed. "I more or less liked the battleship atmosphere conveyed by the gray. Keep us all on our toes, don't you think, Harry?"

The Deputy Director's man Friday nodded in brisk agreement. He was immaculately dressed except for a discreet sprinkle of dandruff on his sloping Brooks Brothers shoulders.

"Yes, well," the Deputy Director said enthusiastically.

He pasted back a stray strand of battleship-gray hair with several fingertips. "If you don't mind, I'd like to make this a quickie," he announced. "I'm supposed to be up on the Hill in forty-five minutes. There will be photographers. I still have to have my hair trimmed." He swiveled back toward his Harry in panic. "You're absolutely sure I'm scheduled for Matthew? That new man who handled me last week butchered my sideburns."

"I checked on it myself this morning," Harry said impassively. "Matthew has cleared his book for you."

Relieved of another nightmare, the Deputy Director returned to the Sisters. "About this Op Proposal of yours"—he pulled a lemon-colored file card from a lemon-colored folder and tapped it with the back of a manicured fingernail—"you really think he may be ripe?"

Carroll arched his neck to relieve the pressure of his collar. "He's lost three sleepers in six months," he explained to a point on the wall over the Deputy Director's head. "His name is mud."

"He's been put out to pasture," Francis added hopefully. "He is bound to be nursing bruises. And then there is the matter of that wife of his . . ."

"*I* didn't know he'd been put out to pasture," the Deputy Director whined in irritation. "How did *you* know?"

"We learned about it from the Germans," Carroll said reluctantly; he had a journalist's instinct for sources.

"*Our* Germans or *their* Germans?" the Deputy Director wanted to know.

"Ours. It was buried in one of their Y summaries about a month ago," Francis added. "I suspect no one picked up on it because they identified him by his real name, Feliks Arkantevich Turov, as opposed to his working name, and not too many people put the two together."

"But you put the two together," the Deputy Director's man commented dryly. He was one of those who favored terminating the Sisters with medical discharges.

"That's correct," Carroll shot back without looking at him. "We have a head for names."

Francis added, "And faces. And places." And he beamed a smile of pained innocence in Harry's general direction.

The Deputy Director closed the lemon-colored folder with an irritated snap—he didn't mind dissension as long as it took place behind his back—and slipped it into a file drawer labeled "Current." "How do you propose to get at him?" he asked.

Carroll treated himself to a deep breath; they were almost home. "We'll use the Germans as cutouts," he said. "They'll farm the contract out to some free-lancers. If he's not buying, he's not buying from the free-lancers."

"If he buys," Francis chimed in, "we will plant our man Friday on the receiving line when he comes over. He will skim off the cream while it is still fresh and leave the milk for the farmers to market."

"You'll have to give the Germans something for their trouble," the Deputy Director commented unhappily.

"Maybe money," suggested Carroll. "Maybe access to the cream."

"Maybe only brownie points," offered Francis. "They wag their tails every time we toss them a bone."

The Deputy Director glanced quickly at his wristwatch. "Work linear," he advised. "Limit this to you two. Me. My man Friday. Your man Friday. We can circulate the product later to our clients without saying where it came from."

"We always compartmentalize," Carroll said matter-of-factly. "It is our trademark."

The Deputy Director cleared his throat nervously. "Just so long as you don't compartmentalize *me* out of the picture."

Everyone smiled at the utter absurdity of the idea.

Carroll had one hand on the doorknob when the Deputy Director called after them. "By the way, what is it you expect to get from him if he buys?"

The Sisters exchanged looks. "Odds and ends," Francis said, smiling innocently.

"Ends and odds," Carroll agreed, and he brought a palm up to his cheek to still his wildly twitching muscle.

Under the angled beams of his attic workshop, in a cone of
pale light cast by a naked bulb dangling overhead, the Potter,
Feliks Arkantevich Turov, rinsed his small, powerful hands
in a pan of lukewarm water, then kicked the wheel and
leaned over the turntable. The fingers of his right hand curled
around the outside of the damp clay. His left hand dipped
delicately into the cylinder, the thumb hooked back over the lip
so that it rested lightly on his right hand. The act of touching
transformed the two hands into one perfectly coordinated pincer-
like instrument. Wedging the clay cylinder between the tip of
one finger and the joint of another, he brought up the wall.

The Potter had learned the art at the feet of a Japanese
master who claimed that throwing a beautiful pot was as
difficult as printing your shadow on the sidewalk. In the end,
potting represented a classic case of mind over matter. Some
days were better than others, but when the Potter was very
good, he could overcome the natural tendency of the clay to
become what *it* wanted to become; he could tame it, channel
its power, control its pulse; he could force it to flower under
his fingers into a form that already existed in his head.

If only he could control his life the way he controlled
the clay! At fifty-six, the Potter already felt as if he were
"tied up to the pier of old age" (Turgenev's phrase, first
quoted to him by Piotr Borisovich, his last, his best sleeper).
Turov's face resembled nothing so much as wax about to
melt, giving him a distinctly blurred look; people who didn't
know him well often had difficulty bringing him into focus.
He was short to begin with—five feet, four inches. Since his
obligatory retirement earlier in the year, his shoulders had
gradually sagged, as if laboring under a great weight; his
body had taken on a dwarfish appearance, underscoring its
essential awkwardness. Only his forearms and his hands,
conditioned by hundreds of hours of kneading clay, retained
anything resembling youthfulness. To his own eye, he looked
like one of those worn-out government functionaries visible

in the streets at the start of any workday; they never seemed to hurry, eloquent evidence that they had precious little enthusiasm for getting where they were going. Like the bureaucrats, the Potter seemed to be living off emotional capital instead of income, the way a starving man lives off the protein already stored in his body.

The Potter fixed the lip of the cylinder, braked the wheel to a stop with a scuffed boot, then reached for the length of piano wire Piotr Borisovich had once fashioned for him and cut the vase off the wheel. He turned it upside down and tapped on the base, then set the vase on a shelf next to his electric kiln. When the spirit moved him, he would glaze it and fire it and offer it to some neighbors who always brought him a handful of mushrooms when they came back from their country *dacha*. Either that or he would smash it into a thousand pieces during another tantrum.

Outside, gusts of soot brushed past the grimy attic window. The Potter glanced at the sliver of Moscow River he could see off in the distance between two buildings. In the old days, when things were going well, when he had been the *novator*— the man in charge—of the sleeper school, he and Svetochka had occupied an apartment *overlooking* the river. There had been a bedroom, a living room, a study, a heated workroom for his potter's wheel, a kitchen, even a bathroom— an almost unheard-of eighty-eight square meters—and they had it all to themselves. Then, when Svetochka called him "my Jew," there had been affection in her voice. Nowadays they lived in a building with paper-thin walls and shared forty-five square meters with another family. And there was anger in her voice no matter what she called him. Or ever worse, boredom. On more than one occasion he had caught her suppressing a yawn when they made love. If he didn't notice her suppressing yawns anymore, it was because he looked up less. With his head buried between her legs, he still managed to forget the unlaundered years (Piotr Borisovich's phrase; from the moment they met, the Potter had been struck by his way with words): the rats scurrying around the labyrinth in the late thirties, when he first joined what was then called the NKVD; the seventeen months spent behind German lines in the early forties; "sanitation" expeditions in the wake of the advancing Red Army in the middle forties then the endless death watch of the late forties and early fifties as everyone wordlessly waited for the old buzzard in the Kremlin to give up the ghost.

The Potter could hear the telephone ringing under his feet. He could make out the sound of Svetochka's stiletto heels as she raced to answer it before the people who shared the flat could. In ten minutes the woman whom everyone invariably mistook for his daughter would slip into her imitation fur "soul warmer" and leave. Another rendezvous with another hairdresser, she would say. Another store selling imitation leather gloves that you can't tell from the real thing, she would say. Only when she came back later—much later—her hair wouldn't look any different, and there would be no imitation leather gloves in her pockets. They had run out just before her turn came, she would say.

It occurred to the Potter, not for the first time, that illusions don't die, they rot like fish in the sun. They torture you with *ifs:* what might have been if one of his sleepers hadn't refused to obey his "awakening" signal and disappeared; if a second, happier in America than in Russia, hadn't gone over to the other side; if a third, inside the CIA, hadn't been ferreted out by someone with an astonishing capacity to think the problem through from the Russian point of view. All within a six-month period. The Potter had trained the sleepers in question. He was accordingly rated on how well they performed. When the ax finally fell, there had been talk of exile in Central Asia, talk even of a prison sentence. But his record had been impeccable up to then. So they had put him out to what they thought of, all things considered, as generous pasture: a smaller apartment, a monthly stipend large enough to keep him in clay and vodka, even a self-winding Czechoslovak wristwatch delivered, without ceremony—with a certain amount of embarrassment—on his last day in harness. "For Feliks Arkantevich," the inscription read, "for twenty-seven years of service to the state." Service to the state! He might have been a street cleaner for all anyone could tell from the inscription.

Surprisingly, Svetochka had taken his fall in stride. Not to worry, she had said, Svetochka likes her Feliks even without access to the school's warehouse; Svetochka will always be Feliks' little girl. Eventually her last pair of American stockings had gone into the garbage, and her tone had begun to change. The Potter took to waiting on a side street near the warehouse; friends slipped him an occasional American lipstick or eyebrow pencil, and Svetochka would throw her arms around his thick neck and make love to him that night the way she had when he had been the *novator*. But neither the lipsticks nor her ardent moods lasted very long.

"Feliks!" Svetochka's high-pitched voice drifted up through the floorboards. "Can you hear me, Feliks? There's a phone call. Someone's asking for you. Feliks?"

"He's coming," Svetochka assured the caller, afraid that he was one of Feliks' friends from the warehouse and might get impatient and hang up. "Only a moment."

"So: I will wait," the voice said quietly.

"*Slouchouyou*," the Potter mumbled into the receiver. He had an instinctive distrust of telephones common to people who came to them relatively late in life. "What do you want?"

A voice with an accent the Potter couldn't quite place replied, "So: if you please, note the number I will give you, yes? If you need a private taxi, dial it and one will come to your corner."

The Potter's hand, suddenly damp with perspiration, gripped the phone. "I don't take taxis. They are too expensive. When I go somewhere, I use the metro or walk."

"Who is it?" Svetochka whispered.

"Please note the number," the voice on the other end of the line insisted. "You never know when you will need it. So: B, one-forty-one, twenty-one."

"What does he want?" Svetochka whispered.

"You have the number, yes?" the voice asked. "B, one-forty-one, twenty-one."

"I tell you that I do not use taxis," the Potter blurted out, suddenly frightened. "Go to hell with your number." And he slammed down the receiver.

"Who was that?"

"Nobody."

"How can you say it was nobody? Somebody phones you up and according to you it's nobody." Tears of frustration formed under Svetochka's heavily made-up lids. "Somebody is not nobody!" she cried in that tightly controlled voice that angry Muskovites use in communal apartments.

The Potter had a good idea of what the call was all about. He had made more than one like it during his four-year stint as KGB *rezident* in New York. It was a contact, an approach, an invitation to what the Merchants at Moscow Center called a *treff*—a secret meeting. Only it wasn't the Moscow Merchants who had initiated it; on that he would have wagered a great deal.

Svetochka began struggling into her soul warmer. "Where are you going now?" the Potter demanded.

"Nowhere," she sneered. "Nobody is who called. And nowhere is where I'm going."

The Potter sprang across the room and gripping the lapels of her coat in one fist, lifted her off the ground.

"You are hurting Svetochka, Feliks," she whispered. Seeing the look on his face, she pleaded, "Feliks is hurting his Svetochka."

The Potter set her down, slipped a hand inside her coat and clumsily tried to embrace her. "I only wanted to know where you were going," he remarked, as if it could account for the outburst, the months of tension that preceded it, the conversationless meals, the slow seeping away of intimacy.

"All you had to do was ask," Svetochka snapped, conveniently forgetting that he had. She fended him off deftly. "Svetochka is going to baby-sit for a girlfriend so she can go birthday shopping for her husband."

"Children are in school at this hour," the Potter said.

"Her child is too young for school."

"There are neighborhood nurseries for babies."

"This baby has a fever," Svetochka explained quickly. "He can't go out." With her teeth clenched, she spit out, "Svetochka doesn't ask you where you are going every time you put on your coat."

"You are lying," the Potter said simply, tiredly. "There was no hairdresser. There were no imitation leather gloves. There is no sick baby."

"You have a nerve . . ." Svetochka was screaming now. Down the corridor, the people who shared the apartment discreetly closed the door to their bedroom. "You didn't never use to . . ." Her phrases came in gasps; they no longer seemed to be glued together by grammar or sense. ". . . not going to only always take this . . ."

"Enough," the Potter muttered under his breath.

". . . think maybe you are doing to Svetochka favors . . ."

"Enough, if you please."

"Well, it don't even work like you maybe think . . ."

The Potter's arm swept out in anger, brushing a glazed bowl, one of the best he had ever made, off a table. It struck the floor, shattering at Svetochka's feet.

"Enough!" shouted the Potter.

Svetochka, who fancied herself something of an actress, could change moods in a flash. Now she screwed up her face to indicate that she had been mortally offended. "It is not

Svetochka who will clean this up," she observed icily. Pivoting on a spiked heel, leaving the door to the corridor gaping open behind her, she stalked from the apartment.

The Potter poured himself a stiff vodka. When he had been *novator*, he had drunk nothing but eighty-proof Polish Bison vodka. Now he had to make do with cheap Russian vodka, to which he added the skin in the interior of walnuts to give it color and taste. Svetochka would come back later than usual to punish him for his outburst. He would mumble vague apologies. They would both act as if everything had been his fault. The Potter would shave for the first time in days, hoping she would notice and take it as a sign that he wanted to make love. He would watch her undress and make a clumsy effort to fondle her breasts. She would put on plastic hair curlers and turn away in bed, complaining about a headache. He would make an awkward declaration of love. Because the Russian language was devoid of articles, it would have the staccato quality of a telegram.

It was Piotr Borisovich who, during one of his English-polishing sessions with the Potter, had commented on the difference between English and Russian. Where English dallied, meandered, embellished, Russian took the shortest path between two points; Russian political thinking could trace its roots to the Russian language, Piotr Borisovich had said. In what sense? the Potter had asked. In the sense that Communism was essentially a shortcut. Are you against shortcuts? the Potter had asked; it had been early in their relationship and he was on the alert for ideological faults. I am all for them, Piotr Borisovich had replied, his head cocked, his eyes smiling, on the condition that they get you there sooner.

Curious he should think of Piotr Borisovich now. Or shortcuts.

The Potter shrugged. In his heart of hearts, he understood they were all connected: the phone call, Svetochka, Piotr Borisovich, shortcuts. For the next two days he tried to put it out of his mind. And thought he had succeeded. Then, without premeditation—he wasn't sure whom he was calling until he dialed—he picked up the phone and composed the number. He heard the phone ring once. Then the voice with the accent he couldn't quite place said, "B, one-forty-one, twenty-one?" as if it were a question.

Almost as if he were following a script, the Potter supplied the answer.

ABOUT THE AUTHOR

ROBERT LITTELL is a former *Newsweek* journalist and the author of six other world-renowned novels, among them *The Debriefing*, *The Amateur*, and his most recent, *The Sisters*. Born in New York, he now makes his home in France.

Special Offer
Buy a Bantam Book
for only 50¢.

Now you can have an up-to-date listing of Bantam's hundreds of titles plus take advantage of our unique and exciting bonus book offer. A special offer which gives you the opportunity to purchase a Bantam book for only 50¢. Here's how!

By ordering any five books at the regular price per order, you can also choose any other single book listed (up to a $4.95 value) for just 50¢. Some restrictions do apply, but for further details why not send for Bantam's listing of titles today!

Just send us your name and address and we will send you a catalog!